Imaginative Qualities
of Actual Things

*I*maginative Qualities *OF ACTUAL THINGS*

by Gilbert Sorrentino

PANTHEON BOOKS

A DIVISION OF RANDOM HOUSE, NEW YORK

10/1972
Genl.

PS
3569
07
I4

ISBN: 0–394–47108–3

Library of Congress Catalog Card Number: 72–155772

Design by Kenneth Miyamoto

Manufactured in the United States of America
by Haddon Craftsmen, Scranton, Pennsylvania

FIRST EDITION

To Morton Lucks and Dan Rice

Contents

In the mind there is a continual play of obscure images which coming between the eyes and their prey seem pictures on the screen at the movies. Somewhere there appears to be a mal-adjustment. The wish would be to see not floating visions of unknown purport but the imaginative qualities of the actual things being perceived accompany their gross vision in a slow dance, interpreting as they go. But inasmuch as this will not always be the case one must dance nevertheless as he can.

—WILLIAM CARLOS WILLIAMS

1
Lady The Brach

WHAT IF THIS young woman, who writes such bad poems, in competition with her husband, whose poems are equally bad, should stretch her remarkably long and well-made legs out before you, so that her skirt slips up to the tops of her stockings? It is an old story. Then she asks you what you think of the trash you have just read —her latest effort. She is not unintelligent and she is— attractive. A use of the arts perhaps more common than any other in this time. Aphrodisia. Powerful as Spanish fly or the scent of jasmine. The most delicate equivocation about the poem, the most subtle relaxation of critical acumen, will hasten you to bed with her. The poem is about a dream she had. In it she is a little girl. Again. Most of her poems are about dreams. In them she drowns in costume, or finds herself flying naked. At the end of the dream she is trapped. Well, critic, tell her the poem has the clear and unmistakable stink of decay to it. Tell her. Is seeing, finally, the hair glossy between her thighs so important that you will lie? About art? You shift your body and hold the poem out—judiciously—before you, one eye half-closed. Reach for a cigarette. Well, you say. Well—this poem . . . Her eyes are shining, they are beautifully sculptured, and dark. She uncrosses her legs, the nylon whispering, and recrosses them. The nylon whispering. Bends forward to accept a light, looking at you, seriously, intently, waiting for your judgment. I have nothing to say, the poem is unknown to me. Others, that I have read, are watery and vulgar, but perhaps her craft has somewhat improved. She's been reading Lawrence— a bad sign, but . . . she understands him. As who does not? Well, you say, again. Penis a bar of steel. We can have a large third-rate abstract expressionist or hard-edge oil behind this scene, or a window with a view of a Gristede's. If in the country, a small grassy hill falls gently away from the picture window behind which the two figures are arranged, gently away to a lawn on which a group of young drunks is playing touch football in the darkening November afternoon.

Sept. 25, 1964

Dear Mama,

I just wanted to drop you a line to tell you that Lou and I are back here now in Berkeley, the honeymoon is over,* and I've settled down to becoming a pretty good housewife. Our honeymoon was really great and Laguna is too beautiful for words. Lou and I tried to learn how to surf there, and you would have laughed to see the spills we took. After a while, though, I must say, we got pretty profisient at it, especially me. You know I've never been modest!

The apartment we have here is a studio type with blonde furniture, matching drapes and rugs, everything is color-keyed. Looks like a Hollywood apartment—or should I say "flat"? Lou is going to school, and doing pretty well there, considering the fact that most of his instructors stopped thinking about ten years ago. I'm learning to cook and even bake, and Lou's not dead yet, so I suppose I'm not doing too badly. Lou has this job that I told you about in my last letter, driving a truck for the Examiner, so he has to leave the house about one every morning. But he's back at six, sleeps a few hours, then has breakfast and goes to school. It's hard on him with school, the job, and his writing, but we're very happy. I spend my free time reading, so that I can talk to Lou and his friends without being too hopeless. Berkeley is a lovely town, lots of trees,

*This phrase is used without irony.

quiet, very collegiate. Our next-door neighbors are two
grad students, a husband and wife, both anthropologists,
and we've been over to see them twice since we got back,
for drinks.

Well, I just wanted to let you know that we're safe and
sound, and that married life agrees with me. I'm really
sorry that you and Daddy couldn't come to our wedding,
but I'm glad that you're happy for us. And Lou and I are
delighted that you and Daddy have met Lou's mother and
that you hit it off. I've got to go now and meet Lou. We're
having our "traditional" Monday night Chinese dinner.

All love to you and Daddy, and xxxx
Sheila

December 27, 1963

Dear Fred,

I'm writing because I'm embarrassed to speak to you.
Actually, I'm also embarrassed to write.

I won't be able to see you. I'll explain. Due to my "clear-
eyedness" and not to my clear thinking, I've hurt someone
very much. Next, you were going to be hurt.

Last night, my future husband made visible his jealousy
and disproportionate dislike for you. I was unable to assure him of the innocence of our future meeting. Prehaps
I wasn't convinced myself. You see, I find it difficult to
understand why anyone would accept "one-time-only"
circumstances without having some "designs." The more
I tried to explain, last night, the weaker, I felt, my convic-
tions were beccoming. No, I don't understand at all.

I think you'll not be too angry with me, though. You may
or may not know what it is to love someone and be hurt
because you've hurt them.

Sheila

From intelligence to art. So Sheila Henry's progression.
A learning of trigonometry, locked into a milieu which
has as its mentors and guides the mediocre. This is not
odd, nor out of the ordinary. On the contrary, the talented
amateur is everywhere apparent. "If I could climb mountains or sky-dive, I wouldn't write poems." So Freud is
"proved." In the case of Mrs. Henry, sex also operates as
a factor. Her energies directed toward the poem, since to
the uninformed, it takes little energy, and less time.
Hacking out a novel, on the other hand, is sheer labor, no

matter the ineptitude. We deal here with a specific young woman, one whose childhood is not germane to our desires. Art as mathematics. Good students and bad. It is a matter of how one's intelligence is fitted to the social possibilities of the environment, no? That is, the bright star of the cultural clique in Indianapolis, at his brightest, is less "interesting" than his brother star in San Francisco. That is why New York is filled with glittering people who play with vomit. To propose a clear situation: Sheila Henry is the wife of Louis Henry, a bad poet. Through him she meets other poets. She begins to write too. The only difference between her poems and his is the degree of surface ability achieved, i.e., his bag of tricks is fuller. You see, she wants to be some one. A laudable goal. The Dean's list, the whole name, in type, the precise letters of the true name. Out of the swamp of half-drunk wives of young executives and university instructors who discuss the Beatles and Stones and call policemen pigs. Revolutionaries of the elegant lofts. Supporters of the NLF in Great Neck. Sheila wants to be some one. The clear letters on the list, her name. Sweet erections a bonus. You will understand that they are not necessary, but a bonus. Is there a creative figure who has not had a desperately confused sex life? Perhaps even Lou is somewhat pleased by the confusion. Laboring over his formulated verse, proffering criticism to Sheila. She wants him to care. Who else on Ocean Parkway had read *Paterson*?

FANTASY
>   *for D.*

you said
they were holy elements
that comprised the earth
>   and i believed you
>   i believed you
meant it.

and is love a holy element? i asked
in your love-
lit eyes i see
the smart of lust

—Sheila Henry

These men—who did such marvelous things—*wanted* her. So what should she do but avail herself to them? What marvelous things? Well, they thought about things, they talked about things, some of them were doctors in residence at the most fashionably grim urban hospitals. There was experience etched into their faces, their young faces. One owned a share in a terrific bar to which the most brilliant young people crowded. Another pleasantly shocked her by knowing his Yeats as well as Lou did. And he wasn't, well, he wasn't *Lou*. He had a Corvette, smoked elegant, thin cigars. His teeth shone when he cracked an easy smile at her. They thought about things. They marched in the peace parades. The one with the interns from Bellevue. So moving, the wind snapping the American flag above the dazzling brightness of their whites.

She and Lou were drunk, the party had been a bore. Somewhere uptown, vaguely in Washington Heights. The girls had been single for the most part, and young, but Lou had danced only with her, excited. He had had only one extended conversation with an older man, about the verse of Samuel Greenberg. They weren't that drunk that they couldn't get home on the subway. Along the dark streets bordering Prospect Park he kissed her repeatedly, letting his hand move gently over her thighs and up between her buttocks. She remotely wanted him. She may have thought of her current lover, as perhaps Lou did, who knew him, and rather liked him. He was a lawyer with a special interest in the eighteenth-century novel. In the apartment, she pulled off her dress and sat on the couch while Lou went to mix them a nightcap.

It is pertinent that I say that Sheila was not a particularly lascivious woman. What she wanted was thorough
and repeated orgasms. How they were achieved was of
little moment to her, so that, while she was, in effect, a
particular kind of modern-day whore, there was none of
the whore's finesse about her; she had little sexual style.
At this moment she relaxed on the couch, still open to the
pleasure that she knew Lou would give her if she allowed
it. Perhaps a sweet tinge of guilt at being unfaithful to
her lover.

Lou came in to the living room with two Scotches. He
was naked, his penis swollen and half-erected. On his
face he had painted, with her mascara, a mustache and
goatee.

There is no point in writing pornography here. To be
clear, this: instead of mounting Sheila, he masturbated
himself and her, while he worked a candle in and out of
her anus with great skill, so that Sheila came almost at
the moment that she became aware of what he was doing. A minute later she wanted this. She had always
wanted this. It was part of the mental paraphernalia of
the erotic that she had taken with her on their honeymoon. Not this specific act, but something weird, something thrilling. Lou was a decisively uninteresting man,
most times preferred to make love in the dark. He would
say, "O baby, O my dear baby" in orgasm. There were
times when she ached to ask him for certain gratifica-
tions. Just to try them out. What was the use?

But here he was, with this painted face, the candle, he
said nothing, but worked for her, she was aware of how
she must look to him, her hips moving, straining to meet
his silent lust. He was her lover. Not even—real, but a
man from a dirty book, a blue-movie man, the salesman,
the cop, the priest, the man with shoes and black socks
on. She thought of him with these things on. No. Rather,
she thought of Lou as her lover with these things on. She
thought of Lou as Che Guevara with black socks and
patent leather shoes, and Che was her lover. He was—
let's call him Milt. His name doesn't matter, I don't recall

her lover's name, but Milt will do. So she said, "Milt, O Milt, fuck me." She whispered then, "Fuck my asshole, Milt, fuck my asshole."

What she wanted was a mirror so that she could look swiftly and see what she knew was her face serene in her pleasure, its idiotic half-smile. "The lineaments of gratified desire," she said. "Fuck my ass." Lou reached his orgasm—this is heavily literary, but nonetheless true—precisely at the moment she quoted Blake.

When she next met her lover, who had, let's assume, a real mustache and goatee, she wanted him to do what Lou had done, but of course, he didn't, and of course, she couldn't ask him to. All they went through was the usual cunnilingus, fellatio, and fornication. That sentence sounds like a fragment of a dirty joke. She was cold and aloof, and he was troubled. Women! he thought, and knew that their affair was about over. She was disappointed in him, because she wanted him to be Lou, who was not Lou, but her lover. So she sought, and found, a new lover soon after.

It is clear that Sheila's husband can only satisfy or at the least intrigue her by being someone else. If this is a common experience—which it may well be—among the married, shall we then select the "perverse" for our observation? We will select then, it would seem, much of our world. The most incredible fantasies hover behind the simplest kiss at a party. Sheila desires what only the man she lives with can give to her. But he cannot give this to her as the man he is. So does he seek his balm in art, thinking that it can establish his ego. Suicide is committed out of despair much less grievous than this. I cannot define the final configuration of their lives, except to guess that divorce will not remedy it.

But this story is invention only. Put yourself into it. Perhaps you are already in it, or something like it. Suppose that a lover had moved Sheila to Lou in this way? That the entire situation had swung in the opposite direction? In that case, this couple could have found perhaps, in their marriage—all the pleasure inherent in all the flesh of the world.

May 12, 1966

Dear Dick,

I think it's clear, after the other night, that we ought to stay away from each other. I don't want to hurt Lou any more than I've already hurt him.* He's put up with my "indiscretions" on more than, I'm afraid, one occasion, and I really am sure that his esteem and friendship for you would really affect him terribly, no matter how ephemaral an "affair" we might have. I'm also thinking of April, whom I have always had a really warm and marvelous relationship with. It would be almost nauseating, physically, to go to your apartment while she is at work.** I may be attracted to you, I think that it may even be a mutual attraction, but we have to consider Lou and April.

I've written half a dozen poems trying to crystalize what I feel after the other night, but I've thrown them all away, except for one. I'd like to show it to you—if you want to see it. But it's best if I mail it to you. Another meeting seems out of the question, at least until we've both got hold of ourselves and realized that we have a responsibility to other people who love us and whom we love.†

So, Dick, let's be good friends, as we have been, and try to forget the other night. It was just a kind of magic anyway, black magic. Something like poetry?††

With devotion, and care,
Sheila

Some Things Sheila Henry Grew to Care for: 1966–1967.
Larry Poons' work: Bart Kahane pointed out his excellence.
Larry Rivers: She met him at a party.
Pantyhose: SMOOTH UNBROKEN LEG LINE.
Madame Bovary: She understood her anguish.
Guy Lewis: Who even drunk yet hath his mind entire.

---

*This sentence is an example of automatic writing.

**This may be taken to mean: Is there any chance she might return before six o'clock?

†"and whom we love" is an afterthought.

††The question mark is intended to make the remark profound. An error of youth.

Bunny Lewis: Her gentle guidance of Guy's life and writing.

Samuel Greenberg: Probably the most underrated poet of his time.

Emanuel Carnevali: Probably the most underrated prose-writer of his time

Barbary Shore: It has Mailer's most brilliant flashes of pure prose.

Harry Langdon: Really the best of the Great Clowns.

Ricard: More subtle and somehow more—*exact*—than Pernod.

Murray Mednick: Had claim to the top rung of the American theater.

Frank O'Hara: He died.

Jack Spicer: He died.

Leo Kaufman: He was a sweet guy.

Che Guevara: He was a *man.*

Ho Chi Minh: He was a *great* old *man.*

Anal intercourse: She almost fainted with the pleasure.

Algernon Blackwood: As good as Poe in his way.

Lou: He loved her.

We discover the young woman on the beach at Laguna back in 1964. It is dawn, actually just after. Glittering sea, etc. Sun, the powdery sand, etc. Whatever Laguna is like, another California beach. Sheila is dressed in a black one-piece swimsuit, a flowered blouse to keep the dawn's chill off. Ship 'n' Shore, part of her trousseau. A half-mile back at the beach hotel, Lou is asleep, unaware that Sheila has left the marriage bed. He went to sleep thinking of their "first breakfast together." Now, it seems clear that their first breakfast will be somewhat strained, unless Sheila can get back to the room and into bed again before Lou wakes. Let's say that she won't be able to make it. Why is she walking on the beach, alone, on this first morning of her wedded life? Now, we shall bring the powers of the novelist to bear.*

---

*This is not a novel. More a collection of "bits and pieces."

Sheila, tense and nervous after the disappointment of
... Sheila, disappointed after the nervous consummation
of ... Sheila Henry, Lou's wife (I am Lou's wife, she
thought) ... When she woke that morning she gazed at
her husband's quietly sleeping face with enormous ten-
derness ... Now she was a woman, she thought, a true,
complete woman ... (Slight, fleeting leer) ... and so big
it was, so big and hard ...

Now we have the idea. Television and the film are by
some thought to be more subtle and sophisticated than
prose because they can register this cliché in one swift
image, that is, the cliché is somehow ameliorated because it passes swiftly. One bad still worth a bad short
story.

Sheila wasn't disappointed, she was slightly stunned at
Lou's lack of imagination. He was a remarkably virile
man and had achieved (a good word) five orgasms by two
in the morning. She had come herself "countless" times.
(Years later, she was first to say, and then believe, that
their wedding night had been a total disaster. That's because she retained of it this single cinematic image of
herself walking on the beach in the early morning, alone,
somehow forlorn, while her insensitive husband slept
numbly on, oblivious to her needs.)

You have to understand that she and Lou had been
lovers for a year before their marriage. They had made
love in cars, in parks, at parties, in hotel rooms, on
beaches, in hallways, on the street, on a roof, etc. That
was perfectly fine with Sheila. But she had an idea that
marriage would engender a spicy perversity, an elabora-
tion of method, that would signal to her the fact that she
was, indeed, married. She had come out of the bathroom
the previous night wearing a short, transparent black
negligee, under it matching bikini panties. Lou had said,
Wow, and removed them, the way he had many times
removed her panty girdle. Hands on, garment off. She
had no idea what she wanted him to do, but it was off so
fast, so—decisively. A dollop of honey on her vulva?

Strawberry jam on her nipples? Trading food back and forth between their (eager, searching, straining) mouths. That was in Joyce somewhere.

Her problem was that she had married Lou. If she had married another young man, this would have been expected. But Sheila had never met a man who was going to be a poet. Who was a poet. That Lou was a rotten poet was beside the point. She didn't know he was a rotten poet. When she finally came to realize he was a rotten poet, she was a rotten poet too. Rotten poets who think of furthering their careers come to think of themselves as: (1) ahead of their time; (2) important minor figures; (3) part and parcel of the "exciting" art world. But in Sheila's mind at this time of her marriage, a poet was not a man who would remove one's Bonwit Teller negligee and panties as if they were weekday foundation garments. She didn't know, as noted, what a poet should do with them, but not that. So she was disappointed. Lou missed. Though she purred, in postcoital splendor, as he read to her from *Personae,* that was later on in the honeymoon. The wedding night had been lacking in brilliance for her. And because certain films had taught her to do this (certain books too), she put her Whispery Blush of Allure Bonwit ensemble away, never to wear it for Lou again. She wore it for other men, who also removed it peremptorily, but that was different.

Is it thoroughly foolish to think that if he had paid homage to her resplendently seductive figure in its carefully selected deshabille—and yet had been fumbling, perhaps even barely potent, in the act of love—she would have felt thoroughly tender toward him? I think it *is* foolish to think that. She may even have hated him. In that event, he might never have encouraged her literary efforts, and her remarkable future infidelities would have had to be unilaterally achieved.

Sheila missed Brooklyn. This may be thought to be a facetious remark, though I once said, in a poem, "there is absolutely nothing funny about Brooklyn." But it wasn't Brooklyn that she missed, it was proximity to the familiar. She wanted to play Lou off against the known. She was thoroughly tired of him by now, and thought there must be something wrong with her, since they had been married only six months. She didn't need Brooklyn, or any other place; what she needed was a divorce, or separation. But even those swinging, hip, groovy, rich, and intense people in Hollywood made marriages that lasted longer than six months. What could she tell her mother? She had married Lou against her advice. Her mother had been against it, because her mother had a picture of Sheila in her head: gangly limbs, hairless genitals, tiny breasts that needed no brassiere. Lou, on the other hand—whom she had spoken to twice—hairy hands, big feet, a five o'clock shadow, etc. It wasn't quite "my little daughter." Mrs. Ravish* knew better than that. But the image of this hairy student covering her daughter set her against the marriage. Mr. Ravish, on the other hand, liked Lou because Lou liked football, and liked it the way Mr. Ravish did. It wasn't just a game to them. It was a calling, a combat, the Whole World Made Game. Nobility of Battle. They brought to football the mentality of the "intelligent columnist," i.e., the world is what you make it. When they weren't discussing the game, they watched it or played a table model that Y. A. Tittle himself thought was great. (Y. A. wouldn't say that if he didn't believe it.) The hulking linemen, the fleet backs, the serene quarterback, head filled with arcane codes. At all events, they liked each other, so Mr. Ravish was in favor of the marriage.

Her mother would say, "See?" Her father, "Why?" So Brooklyn and its familiar streets would substitute for separation. But how would she persuade Lou to go back? He had another year at Berkeley before his Masters. (Ameri-

*Not a bad maiden name for Sheila.

can Literature, thesis on "The Geography of *Paterson.*")
He wanted to finish there.

To get her back after a long talk with Lou would be
boring to read as well as write. You have all this conversation. Editors can say, "He certainly has a fine ear," or
"He certainly can write." We've had enough conversation
to last us a thousand years. They imagine that dialogue
is hard to compose. Confusion of mime with selection. I'll
bet you five dollars that all novels written by editors (let's
not forget journalists) are filled with pages of Incisive
Dialogue. These are the wits who make fun of Henry
James.* You know the type, they say: "Did you ever read
James' dialogue?" (They just finished novels with catchy
titles: *Rumble in Heaven. Pudding Junction. A See of
Delight. New Haven for Lovers.*) Action! We need action!
End of digression. I think we'll put her head in the oven
one calm Sunday morning.

She did it when Lou went out for the Sunday papers
and coffee cake. It was an act, and Lou, smelling gas
when he got home, found her on the floor, the oven door
open, the windows closed. She was groggy and tears
rolled down her face as Lou kissed her in front of the
door, open to their back yard. He knew that she had
rigged this, but he also knew that if she were desperate
enough to rig this, something was wrong. She wanted to
go home, she said. Something was happening to them, to
their marriage, out here. They went home to Brooklyn.

This is better than a long talk, right? Think of them as
Steve McQueen and Jean Seberg. Coffee cake all over the
floor. Then a few seconds of a Boeing 707.

*Some Things Sheila Henry Liked about Lou Henry, 1963–
1967.*
Ears.
Desert boots.

*They read *Daisy Miller* and *Washington Square.*

He sniffled when he read *Nineteen Hundred and Nineteen.*
The way he tossed salad.
The way he wore his hat.
His poems.
Calling William Carlos Williams, "Doc" Williams.
His admiration for Dick Detective.*
His knowledge of football.
The way he held his knife.
His buttocks.
His understanding of D. H. Lawrence.
A crown of Petrarchan sonnets he wrote for her twentieth birthday.
The way he alternately washed and sucked her breasts when they showered together.
Old suede jacket.
The look of his genitals in jockey shorts.
His contempt for his instructors.
His acceptance of Milt, her first real lover.
The way he sang off-key.

Sheila's lovers were all unsatisfactory. Not true. What was true is the fact that Sheila's taking of lovers was unsatisfactory. She retained a strong affection for Lou. She loved him, even, and the love surfaced at times with fierce strength. This is a common occurrence. The mind will not let us rest. The most disastrous affair or marriage has moments of great serenity that assert themselves long after the couples have parted. We deny their truth to our grievous cost. The problem is . . . the problem is to comprehend the feeling of loss in the fall. I won't stand still for an instant about the death of the earth, coming of winter. Spring is more bitter than any smoky October. Take the fall, in relation to yourself. The blood stills. The problem is . . . to love, to love, but at the same time understand that we all ache for each other. The young wife

*Who may figure large in our story.

whose thighs set your mouth tense with desire: her husband lusts to caress your own wife's breasts. Then why can't happiness spring clear from the adulterous affair? Why doesn't Don Juan grow strong in his rutting? The problem is . . . to realize that assuaged desire does not sate, or still, the mind's hilarious complexities. Those who do not understand this are at a loss to comprehend the true anguish of the flesh—that in imagination we die, and die, and die again. The careless and perennial adulterer is understandable only outside any moral framework: he is a man who lacks imagination. In his orgasms is centered the energy that can generate the subtle differences that drive the poet to his obsession. Out of this sort of spastic adultery come remarks like "they're all the same upside down," "they're all the same in the dark." If those things were true we might all be able to let rest our painful intercourse. The Devil walking to and fro upon the earth. For what? Cannot the Devil take any shape and possess any flesh he so desires? Incubus or succubus, animal or silent zephyr—they are his province and possession. But in his imagination he constructs the lambent chastity of paradise: which he has lost. Love is no comforter, the poet said. Rather a nail in the skull. However read, that sits true. It *is* a nail in the skull. Or: rather to *have* a nail in the skull. What anodyne to ease that agony? While the body heaves and shudders the imagination staggers through the sweet wind off the ocean, straining to recall the precise contours of the youthful face its earlier acrobatics played over.

In old New York, in old New York, etc., etc. Old Brooklyn. It was here that Sheila came to think of Lou as an unvarnished schmuck. Since she was Jewish, the word came naturally to her. She was once awed by him. Who else on Ocean Parkway had read *Paterson?* But she had begun to write poems herself. Why not? "I could write a book" is a timeworn phrase of the educated. To which there is no reply. Or a buck and wing, a fast smile, slow shuffle of the feet. Don't get me wrong—I like Sheila. She might as well write poems as Norman Mailer. Or Alan Dugan. (What of Hyam Plutzik? I hear you say.) Hyam Plutzik as well. But Sheila did not think of Lou as a schmuck *because* she had begun to write poems. It was because he helped her in her writing, became her reader, critic, and mentor. She was "influenced"* by him. If there is one thing that had become immutable in Sheila's beliefs, it was that the poet, the real poet, did not help his wife to become a poet too. The real poet was obsessed with his poems, his life, an egoist, selfish, boorish, rude, crazy. A great, romantic thing, into the breach, kill me tomorrow let me live tonight! and so on. Long hair and flowing lips, falling on the thorns of life, tortured to death in stifling university jobs, the Great Soul Writhing Underneath.** Swift, intense, and destructive affairs with female undergraduates, too many vodka martinis, Fuck the Dean! Fuck the Chairman! Casual quotations from Mao dropped into a discussion of Camus (bourgeois colonialist mentality). Anything. Everything. But not teaching one's wife to write poems. Let her cook food. (Ah, food! Chomp, slurp, good!) Arrange a single daisy in the slender and exquisite vase some literary friend brought from Japan. So that the poet might compose a verse or two about this daisy and his love: an occasional verse, a fragile thing that may grace the first page of the new campus mimeo magazine, *Mu'fugga,* of which he is faculty advisor. "Well, we can't really call it *Motherfucker,* boys," he laughs, the motherfucker, "but there *are* ways around that!"

But not to teach her to write poems. In old New York, in old New York, they lived in Lou's old house, with Lou's mother, who acted as if they had just been married the day before, sex jokes in the morning, grins, laughter. Ah well, she was doing her best too. An old and dear friend of mine stopped going to his analyst because he got tired of the analyst telling him about the disastrous effect his

*"Influenced" is a mouthful, no?
**A snide reference to Theodore Roethke may be intended here.

parents had had on him: whereas he knew that he had been the major reason for the destruction of his parents' marriage. As Dr. Williams says: "But through art the psychologically maimed may become the most distinguished man of his age. Take Freud for instance."

We can then realize her misery and sadness when it became apparent to her that her poems were becoming as good as, if not better, than Lou's. So that she begins to criticize his work, self-effacing and diffident, but: "Well, Lou, don't you think you've already *said* this . . . ? I mean this stanza is really all taken care of here at the beginning of the poem? I've found, in my own work—" With the phrase, "in my own work," she asserts her serious ambitions.

AN OLD PROVERB*

and in the dream lou
and i were going to skin a cat. our
cat.
    that's an old pro-
    verb
i thought i said. i said i
don't want to, lou.
but he was smi-
ling at my
      terror holding the raw blood-
      y carcass in red hands

Feb. 14, 1967 (Valentine's Day)
My dearest Lou,
Everything is lovely here, but now that I've been here 3 days, more and more, I wish you had come. I'm grateful to you for letting me get off by myself like this, and I'm sure we both needed it to think things out, but I miss you terribly, and think of you all day long. I hope you're working on that long poem that's been giving you so much trouble. Although I've got my notebook here I haven't written anything—all I do is read (when I'm not skiing and gossiping with all the single girls). How old and wise and married I feel! I've read A Clockwork Orange, In Cold Blood, and

---

*The first poem Sheila wished to preserve.

am about into The Lady in the Lake, which is really a teriffic book! Why didn't you insist earlier that I read Chandler? He's so much more than just another detective story writer.*

Lou, my dear, I'm sure now that everything will be better when I get back home—it's just the effect of having lived with your mother for so long. It upset me terribly. I felt as if I was competing with her for your affection. But I miss you terribly and I've thought so much about all the ways I've hurt you and, I suppose, about all the ways we've hurt each other, that I think we have possibly been foolish.** I've been cruel to you Lou, but I *do* love you, and always shall.

I'm going to go and have a bite of lunch now with a *very* chic girl who works for a Mad Av ad agency as some sort of super girl Friday. She's quite shallow, but really very groovy, and sweet. A lot of fun. I think we'll go skating this afternoon and see a movie tonight. Help and Hard Day's Night are in town and you know how mad I am about the Beatles.

Thinking of you, always, my dear. And love and love and love on Valentine's Day—

Sheila

Some Things Sheila Henry Disliked about Lou Henry, 1963–1967.
Baggy pants.
His passion for football.†
The wispy mustache he tried growing on and off.
Ketchup on pork chops.
The way he sipped his tea.
Dislike of cats.
His lack of interest in her dreams.
His dislike of Guy Lewis.
Unshined shoes.
That he hated straight whiskey yet drank it consistently.
The way he undressed her.
Was absolutely lost on the IND and never admitted it.
Penchant for kasha knishes.

*A commonly held opinion.
**The meaning of this sentence is obscure.
†She suspected it was a false passion.

Psychological Background to Assist the Reader in Understanding Sheila's Character Development and Motivations.

When Sheila was ten she masturbated in her father's car outside Nathan's Famous in Coney Island. Rhythmically squeezing together and relaxing her thighs, she ate a hot dog the while.

When Sheila was an innocent ten, she masturbated in her father's sinister car outside Nathan's Famous in sordid Coney Island. Rhythmically squeezing together and relaxing her nervous thighs, she stealthily ate a hot dog the while.

The "hot dog" is a bona fide phallic symbol. Any book dealing with Erotica worth its salt will have a picture or two of some starlet (say Diana Dors or Mamie Van Doren), lips wetly gleaming,* about to surround with eager mouth the pedestrian wiener. These pictures are under the section headed "Fellatio." The reader's response should run: "Looka that, looks like she's suckin' a cock!" This is a subtle business.

A future of college towns, trees, frost on the lawns, alert faces of Lou's adoring female students. Stretched before her. (No matter that Lou had left his job. She knew it was a temporary perversity.) Literary parties, weekends and holidays in New York. Intelligent people, terrific lovers with good manners and unflagging virility, muscular thighs and white teeth. Ah, God, what a bore. Ennui. She would become Madame Bovary. She thought. Lou's academic career solidly progressing, teaching courses in Contemporary American Literature, his work being published more and more widely, his criticism, and translations of Lorca (by "a poet in his own right"). She was twenty-five and this would take up perhaps forty-five more years. She could have staggered and fallen with the realization of it. Instead she slept. She seemed always to

*He turns a nice phrase.

be asleep, and Lou wrote a series of poems (a cycle, he called it) entitled *Sheila Sleeping*. They were published here and there, and finally came out in a small portfolio, limited edition, on rag paper, with linoleum cuts by Guy Lewis. A collector's item. Sheila slept on.

Give me something, she said. Make me happy. She was waiting for life to give her something, this was intolerable. Take me to the zoo. Fly me to the moon. A new blender to make a pineapple-spinach frappé. No cavities. An orgy at the home of John Lennon. She slept, lovely girl. There would be art, she would take new lovers and write more bad poems. New things. Maybe children. *The Collected Poems of W. B. Yeats.* A new restaurant. A new bar where Norman Mailer hangs out (with his boxer's walk, dear Jesus).

She will not allow her imagination to yield up the clear image that death is the reward and life no preparation for it. It's a pleasure to lose—like Frank Sinatra. She slept, she slept, through days and nights, laid Dick Detective with a kind of spectacular carelessness, which pleased her because it frightened him. I mean, she was game for anything. Standing at a bar one night she masturbated him without opening his pants. Lou, "a poet in his own right," "also a poet, who has been widely published," at home (wherever that would be) battering Lorca's delicate measures to death. I would end this all tragically, but there is no tragedy here.

The roach is millions of years old. Tell the roach. Tell the exquisite ephemeroptera, that has no mouth parts. Tell the female mantis as she devours her mate. With perfect calm he continues fucking as she eats him.* Tell your mother and father. Tell a marriage counselor. Tell Lou. No need to tell Lou, he knows you want something. He'll take you to the country for a weekend. "A change of scene," he says, his heart dying in him. Tell George Plimpton, he'll turn into Lou for a month and write a

---

*The genitals are left till last.

book that will explain it to you. (Explain it to me! Sheila says. Explain it, Dick! She says to the Detective, sucking his anus. He groans in pleasure and later, over a nightcap, tells her how much he loves April.)

There was a boy of fifteen sent to a hospital for the criminally insane for a misdemeanor. Through a mixup of records, he was kept there for fifty years. Imagine his gentle, stunned face, his body flinching in the noise from the jukebox in her bar. He has never had a woman, nor man either. He has never heard a word of love. Sheila can tell him. He's standing by himself at the end of the bar. Somebody says he thinks he's an old surrealist painter who's lived in Paris since the twenties.

2
Brooklyn-Paterson Local

A T CERTAIN MOMENTS, the most unfortunate ones for his peace of mind, that is, moments that were imbued with the best of his marital pleasures, Lou recalled an hour of blissful sleep that he had enjoyed, years before, with a whore in a hotel room. I say, "years before," but it had been just a year before his marriage to Sheila, in a time of despair over the fact that he thought he had lost her. The reader may consider that it would have been better had he lost her, better for both of them. That's because he's an outsider who thinks he knows best. These people aren't real. I'm making them up as they go along, any section that threatens to flesh them out, or make them "walk off the page," will be excised. They should, rather, walk into the page, and break up, disappear: the subtlest tone or aroma (no cracks, please) is all that should be left of them. I want you to remember this book the way you remember a drawing. In all events, Lou remembered this sleep, it was a sleep that cleansed and relaxed him, it lasted perhaps twenty minutes, it was a sleep such as he never had before nor since, with lover or wife. It confounded him that it should be so. These are specific emotional sets that life proffers us.

Does this memory mean that Lou should have married the whore? Or does it mean that she was his destined lover? Or does it mean that this sleep was a sign warning him against marriage with Sheila? Not at all? Then what does it mean? Why has he never had such a sleep with his wife? The memory troubles him. He can transport himself to that room and recall the lucid sense of his body as it awoke, the girl next to him, smoking. His eyes unfocused, on the ceiling. This, of course, is the exact incident that he should reveal to his wife, confess, if you will. But how can he tell her that his most perfect realization of peace came about with a girl whose name he did not know? (She had told him, but he had forgotten it five minutes later.) On the wall of the hotel room there was a framed print of Old Glory, unfurled and cracking in the wind. The slightest twist to this story, one way or the other, vulgarizes it and thus makes it palatable. The camera cannot tell this story without destroying its root meaning. From love, to sleep, to a shot of the flag on the wall. The simplest reader of *Avant-Garde* will understand that. The flag. Love. Sordid. America in the sixties, ugghh. While we know that's not the point, the point is the sleep, the flag is there. Let's suppose that it was the flag of Australia so pictured. The camera would show that to no effect whatsoever—none at all. Whereas I can say: "On the wall of the hotel room there was a framed print of the flag of Australia, unfurled and cracking in the wind"—and Lou's sleep remains our focus. If the flag annoys you, take it out of the room. But this story cannot be transmuted into the bawdy or base, no matter what twists are given it.

Lou never saw a picture of Old Glory after this that reminded him of that room, that girl, that sleep. The picture was *there*. I place it on the wall to extract and refine the essence of those two naked bodies, to make them prose. To make them absolute prose. To prose them.

As I say, this is the incident that Lou should have revealed to Sheila. It was no good at all otherwise. Out of it came wonder (which led Lou to write some poems, better left unwritten) or guilt, since he couldn't understand why he should be so suffused with sweetness by this memory. Erotically, it was useless to him, although he had tried to employ it that way, transferring the clarity of the remembrance to his relations with Sheila —she would become the whore, the whore was—at that time in the past—Sheila, and Lou would be young. Younger. What I am getting at is that he would be unmarried. But he could not recall anything of the sexual acts that preceded the sleep. He can invent sex acts, but this not only does not assist him in his relations with Sheila, it sullies the reality of the sleep. He wants this to happen with Sheila. Then he will be able to tell her. Since it does not (perhaps it will, someday, after we have done with them), the episode becomes more and more impeccable, and more and more impossible to unburden himself of. Thus he is cloistered with his banal memory. Out of such simple repression come his lackluster poems.*

How did they meet? How did they meet, my friend? ("Friend" in songs may stand for the stranger at the bar.) Oh, yeah, Oh, yeah! Where the Baby Ruth sky comes down on the Tootsie-Pop tree! Well, how did they meet? My friend? Let's say here and now, and be done with it forever, that they met in Brooklyn College, Boylan Hall, in a class in English Literature—English Non-Dramatic Literature of the Sixteenth Century to be precise. Write a sawng or two about that. I saw you in the sunlight from the window/ Your golden hair was yellower than sun. Choo. Choo-choo ch-choo. All right, Lou and Sheila have

---

*Out of such simple repression come also brilliant poems. But not by Lou.

met. At the moment Lou was on the threshold of *willing* himself into poesie. Sheila was a sometime admirer of the modern classics. Lou was reading *Paterson*. Sheila became deeply interested in the thematic structure of that poem. They went out a few times, poetry readings, concerts, to hear folk artists, rock bands, 100-percent black white men who were into their own thing, man. *Caramba!* One dark night Sheila gave Lou a blow job in Prospect Park. She was pretty good at it, Lou thought. His opinion was based on the pornography he had read, nothing else. Thinking about this, Lou is really a sad case— he fits right in. In any event, Lou thought of this as a manifestation of love. It was. It is perhaps the coarse, blunt phrase that makes the word "love" seem out of place. I can rephrase it. One dark night Sheila and Lou, in the warm breeze of Prospect Park, made love for the first time—sensual, passionate, deep love. Now, if you want to make this "blow job" or "sucked him off" or "performed fellatio," go ahead. How about "Her eager mouth sought out the source of his manhood"? This is your problem, but before you dismiss this whole thing with contempt, remember that Lancelot and Guinevere, Antony and Cleopatra, Hero and Leander— all these star-crossed lovers—were involved in acts such as these. I mean that it is likely that Guinevere "sucked off" Lancelot. The fact that the famous and the celebrated indulge in erotic practices usually treated with circumspection makes for a pretty picture—and an erotic fantasy that informed much of the aesthetics of the pornographic comic books which served as the sex manuals of my youth.

Then they did many more things. Romance in the dark with you. This is all real. They were in love. And love tolerates all songs. The first time I was in love "Orange-Colored Sky" by Doris Day was as beautiful to my ear as Campion's "My sweetest Lesbia . . ." (I see I have finally revealed my essential plebeianism.) After, they did many more things, they graduated and Lou moved to Berkeley so that he could do graduate work, Sheila joined him and they married. O.K. (There's a novel there, if any of you novelists want to write it you're welcome to it.)

LOVE FEAST*
we ate peanut butter and grape
                jelly
• on saltine crackers
             looking at each other
• looking at each other • no point
            to this memory
it amounts to nothing
let us admit
            simply
• that we loved each other
and we love each other.

The percipient reader will note two things, at the very least, about this poem—which was one of those Lou considered a breakthrough in his art. One, that his talents, at this date, were for narrative, and had little to do with the art of verse. And, two, that a tendency that Lou was never to shake shows up in this short verse, that is, the tendency to think that a bad or trite line, if set by itself, space above and below it, somehow transcends its own weary language. Later on, he would become more aware of this and attempt to disguise clichés by litanizing them, i.e., by employing the theory that something that is rotten becomes less so as it is made formally repetitious; and also by polluting the cliché with the addition of out-of-place adjectives. This came from his misunderstanding of Lorca, and Lou was not alone in his ignorance. A National Book Award winner of recent times has achieved his reputation by conscientiously making himself into Lorca with a corncob. But Lou's basic trust in the "floating cliché" was implicit. If he centered the words "I Love

*The occasion for this poem of Lou's will be dealt with later.

You" on the page they took on a mysterious poetic electricity for him. Of such beliefs came his dislike of Wallace Stevens.

Things Lou Henry Would Have Been Better off Being.
An editor at a publishing house anxious to keep up with
  "what's happening."
A Tarot adept.
An unlocker of the mysteries of astrology.
A teacher in a private school for bright children.
A "new-image" book reviewer. ("Mr. Garf, while very
  much at ease in his factual bag, fails to supply, or even
  to guess the reason for Miss Woolf's insistence on a
  Pakistani dildo. Given the rather weird atmosphere of
  Bloomsbury at the time—an atmosphere that perhaps
  only the Marquis de Sade would have been bored by—
  it seems to this certainly unjaded reader . . .")
An admirer of Nabokov.
A Fellow of Reconciliation.
A Jewish liberal.
A copywriter for an ad agency.
A movie star "with ideas."
A composer of folk-rock songs.*
An experimental novelist.
A Communist.
A Communist dupe.
An anarchist.
A revolutionary.
A devotee of Paul O' Dwyer's toughness and incorrupti-
  bility.
A good poet.

We will place Lou at home one night, in Brooklyn. He is
alone, reading a book. *The Deer Park,* perhaps, which he
had never read. Some phrase or particular set of syntax
takes him away from the book and moves his thought to

---

*Lou composed a folk-rock song, a fragment of which will be reproduced in its proper place.

Sheila. She is out, at a poetry reading, or she is with some lover, or she is at the poetry reading with some lover, or later she will meet some lover. Lou knows all this and is helpless against it. He aches to feel how she feels, he wants to understand her completely so that he can cope with her irregularities. He wants to be Sheila, put himself into her head and body. He gets up from the chair, marks his place in the book, and very calmly undresses, goes to Sheila's drawer and takes out a pair of stockings, panties, and a garter belt, and puts them on. He looks at himself in the mirror in the bedroom. Ludicrous. He feels the gossamer of the nylon on his legs, the soft, slippery feel of the underwear against him. How does she feel in these garments? How does she feel when some man takes off her dress and looks at her before him, like this? He wants to be her. He wants Sheila to fuck him. You who read this, imagine your sex changed for a week. I don't speak of homosexuality: that is sexual reformism to rescue one from terror. What I mean is revolution. Or the attempt at it. (Lost from the start.) This transvestism is Lou's commitment to revolution. Hopeless. The impossible desire of the male to be penetrated by his mate. And her imagination, unleashed, as she images herself, heavy with balls and phallus, mounting the familiar body of her husband. To lay these images to rest, the couple may endeavor to explore the sexual possibilities open to them. The realization that they cannot ever become each other strengthens their love or destroys it. If a man should put on his wife's underwear and stockings so that he may more perfectly comprehend her and his love for her—what then do we judge to be his aberration?

I've told you about the morning after the wedding night when Sheila walked on the beach at Laguna. Lou knew this. He woke up and saw the space, rumpled, in the bed, the mussed pillow, etc. Another movie shot. He walked out on the terrace and saw her far off down the beach, wading in the surf, her blouse bright in the sun and float-

ing spume from the waves. Their breakfast was, indeed, "somewhat strained." But Lou wasn't angry, he
was frightened. He said nothing, nor did Sheila. He was
frightened at being married and assumed that she was
too. If he had told her this, perhaps she would have told
him about her disappointment in their wedding night.
Would that have fortified her against her propensities for
infidelity? I doubt it. I can witness all these things, make
up what I don't know, but I can't adjust any of it. In the
smallest of flashes, bits of mica, things may be revealed
to you (and to me). I don't understand the motivations of
these characters I've invented. I could make up a good list
of them. If I were to write a novel they could all have a
childhood, an adolescence. Loss of virginity, etc. First
indication that the world is cruel. Read *Studs Lonigan*,
please. *Look Homeward, Angel. From the Terrace.* Now,
there you have motivation. I can bring you through 350
pages, right up to Harvard, 350 more to Executive with
Unhappy Marriage, Troublesome Mistress, and Drinking
Problem. In other words, tell you what you think you need
to know. But you don't need to know anything—see a
movie. In this book, I'll muddle around, flashes, glints,
are what I want. It's when one is not staring that art
works. In the middle of all the lists and facts, all the lies
and borrowings, there will sometimes be a perfect revelation. These curious essences. The shape and weight of
a sentence that lances you. Babel's famous period, its
exact placement. These perfumes. So you'll bear with
me. Lou was frightened. I like the idea that he was frightened. After breakfast they went back to their room and
made love for the rest of the morning. Everything was
much better that afternoon, they swam, and before dinner, Lou read to her from *The Portable Blake.* They were
both naked, lying on the bed, Sheila's hand toying with
Lou's pubic hair. Blake would have liked that, maybe. At
least the picture of it. If, on the other hand, Lou had been
reading from *Les Fleurs du Mal*—but who would read
(certainly not Lou) Baudelaire on a honeymoon? You can

hear him, looking at those healthy bodies, full of vitamins and brown with the sun: "... *vous irez, sous l'herbe et les floraisons grasses, moisir parmi les ossements.*" Dark man, dark. Fat-bellied Sartre, belching his good wine and food in pungent breath over still another radical petition, calls his life a deliberate failure. So be it, M Sartre: Success.

I have said that Lou willed himself into poetry. How this came about is a long and involved story. Let it stand that he did so. At first, the poems were shown to friends, or kept to himself, but later he began to publish them in little magazines. He was a poet. I would guess that William Carlos Williams was responsible for this in the way that George Herriman might be held responsible for Roy Lichtenstein. These masters cannot be blamed for the aberrant desires of a minority of the populace. It comes down to: "Hell, I can do that too." And you're off. If things fall right, you'll be accepted after a few years, and take your place among that great body of useless grinds who won't for a minute stop expressing themselves. Borrow, borrow, you can get into Williams and get the very names of shrubs and wildflowers into your work—anything but the terror that dominates your own life. Lou's thinking went, perhaps, like this: If I avoid the demons that maraud through my intelligence, I'll write poems that are acceptable. I'll always know that when the time comes I'll confront these demons and out of the confrontation will come great poetry. The next step however is more difficult and can lead to total destruction. That is: the confrontation with the demons does not necessarily lead to the creation of great art (or any art at all). You can writhe in the darkest pit and filth of yourself and come up with some dull fragment of *vers libre,* indistinguishable from that of a hundred contemporaries. Thus pain does not guarantee anything. Art, you see, is not interested in your suffering. It is not a muse. Look at Robert Graves—all that palaver about his Goddess, and all those third-rate poems. What is one to do with that chatter?

But Lou is our man here. What about Lou? Answer: he wants to live a simple life and be a brilliant poet. These things do not go together. (I know I am on the thin ice of romanticism here.) That simple life. I mean, Lou was one of those who thought enviously of men who lived—all of the year, or most of it anyway—in the woods, or the mountains, or at the beach, etc., etc. That was the simple life. There they were, sturdy with boots, pipes, and notebooks, chopping wood for the fire, observing birds, checking out the sunset, the sunrise, the changing seasons. Shrewd and loving observations of their neighbors, who had finally after all this time come to regard them as acceptable, etc., etc. Nauseating stuff. These dolts keep these enormous notebooks in which they tell us city slickers all about nature, and their lives in Maine, or Big Sur, or Colorado, or some other goddamned place, full of trees and the rest of the stuff of poesie. God, what a fucking bore it all is. They lead the simple life, they note all this trash down in those damned notebooks. "Observe the turning of the leaves." "What bird call was that I heard this morning in the icy stillness?" Arrghh. "Today I finally got the old stump out. Celebrated with a half-pint of applejack." And we read this swill. Not one year goes by but some little magazine runs excerpts from one of these "woods journals" by a poet—there is also a small collection of his verse in the same issue. The poems have titles like: "Top of Pink Tit Mt.: Cold Beans." And we sit choking on the polluted air of divers cities, marveling at the freedom that can open the world of such verse to its practitioner. Simplicity! The simple life! It was what Lou wanted—or thought he wanted. Simple life. Brilliant poet. With demons in reserve for his later years, when he could haul them out and write his Great Poems of Maturity. If somehow Sheila could be fitted in, i.e., if she would be a Good Wife, that would be fine too. Lou was one of those men who confused passing happiness or misery with the sources of art. The world is full of them. When one disaster or ecstasy is over, they turn to another. The war in Vietnam has spawned a thousand poets. They think their rage and impotence will make the poem. It is a banal truism that all the occasional poet needs to write a poem is an occasion. There is no lack of them in the world. That picayune poetic charge galvanized by a new friend, another storm, some red barn somewhere, anything.

The world is what you want it to be: thus Lou's belief. This is necessity in a revolutionary, but disaster in an artist. Sheila should have kept going south that morning in Laguna. A simple girl who got stuck with art. No life for an American. Particularly if the art is specious. Should have kept going south to Mexico. Which reminds me of a story.

A friend of mine, years ago, after a first trip to Mexico, was deeply impressed by the Mexican Indians. He had read *The Plumed Serpent* and tripped over it. What most struck him was the image, bright in his mind, of these Indians, squatting by the side of the road, impassive, "their eyes like black stone, onyx, sitting there as if waiting for death." In his speech, "death" came out "Death." Another friend, who *was* a Mexican, said that they were waiting for the bus to come along and didn't feel like standing. So Lawrence and a dozen movies were shaken to their foundations. The first friend was outraged and wouldn't speak to the Mexican friend for two weeks. His Plato was impugned. The world is NOT what I want to make it? He returned to Lawrence in a rage. Those Indians! A bus? A bus!? He was personally attacked, he felt. They were waiting for Death!

The reader will see that what I am driving at is that these words that he is reading—are words.

What did Lou do when Sheila went away to the ski lodge that grim February? It was supposed to have been a trial separation to see if they could work things out for themselves, in their heads. It was nothing of the sort. They were both relieved to be away from each other. Sheila was always pleased to be away from Lou lately—his dense conversation about art, his painful ambitions—and Lou devoted so many nights to long conversations about letters with other budding poets.

Lou was so inured by now to his wife's infidelities that he took it for granted that she was having a brief affair at the resort. The "chic girl" from the ad agency was, for Lou, a euphemism for some young man. Perversely, Sheila was faithful to Lou the whole time she was away. Maybe she thought there was no joy in infidelity if it was so easy to be unfaithful. That's not true. Sheila's faults did not include television ethics. (We all know about television, right? A new, exciting medium, "still in its infancy." With dung all over its fingers, which it makes you smell.) The night after she got back she went to bed with Dick D. In tears. Wondering how she could do this to Lou. Not really wondering, but occupying that locus for the Detective's benefit. Throw a little guilt his way. "I love April, God how I love April," was his talismanic incantation to ward off guilt. He employed it that night.

Some days later, Sheila, disturbed by the fact that Lou has not queried her about her activities at the lodge, tells him that she had a brief, "searing" (her word, I'm sorry) affair with the hip girl—her first lesbian experience. This is a total lie, absolute invention. She is impatient to destroy Lou, and unconsciously concludes that even his devotion to letters will not strengthen him against this. But what happens is that Lou gets hot and rapes her, with all her clothes on, on the couch, after dinner.

Sheila was disgusted and shocked. I once knew a man whose wife confessed to him that she had given his best friend a "blow job." (You will remember Guinevere and Lancelot and forgive me.) She was nauseated and deeply hurt when her husband, in his sickness and despair, begged her to give him one, there and then. (They were at the breakfast table.) He even went so far as to expose to her his erected penis. What she had expected was rage, violence, even blows. So that she could be secure in her conception of her honesty in being so ill-treated. What she thought of as her honesty. The last thing she wanted was for her confession to be employed as an aphrodisiac. Henry Miller uses this scene of sexual confession in his books, except that he writes comedies of misogyny. The sexual confession is a love philter and leads to more love. The scenes end with everyone sleeping peacefully. These marvels of romance which pass for life. God bless him. And all his trembling hands that make us squeak.

Sheila was disgusted and shocked. Hurt. Ah, the flashing perversity of the human brain. Lou's mind, the pictures in it. So precisely outlined. Sheila and this svelte girl, the most impeccable white underthings, silk and lace, on floor and chair, their spread thighs, shining heads moving gently between them.

SHEILA SLEEPING: IV

insane and we love death
to destroy or be destroyed
one side of the coin or the other
if our black and white linoleum
is not waxed it will be
                      dirty

lose its gloss
its gloss unable finally to be
anything more than dirty

Sheila is sleeping now
last night she did not sleep at all.

our kitchen floor is dirty
more often than not—it is a great
battle we wage against dirt—it must
be washed and waxed—the floor—
once a week
• the mop turns black. a
long slow battle we neither win nor lose.

we survive. the floor
•   survives—

the dirt is what we
are destroyed by if we talk
of it. it is less complex
to allow Sheila to sleep.

But Lou would punish her anyway. Certainly not consciously. He laid it all on art. What he decided to do was
to stay home and write, and send Sheila out to work. He
quit his assistantship at CCNY, and bought a new typewriter. Sheila went to work for one of those corporations
that publish fifteen or twenty different magazines—most
of them of the adventure variety. I once tried to get a job
at one of these places. At the time my ass was hanging out
of my pants, as the vulgar saying goes. The managing
editor was a writer who, at this writing, has achieved a
certain fame with his novels and plays: they are all of the
Bittersweet-Pain-of-Being-a-Neurotic-Jew genre. I am
happy to report that since his success his work has not
deteriorated in the least. Anyway, I didn't get the job,
which entailed rewriting the fearful prose of the con-
tributors into the fearful prose of *Muscle* or *Fist!* The
writer said that he thought I'd be unhappy in the job, I
was really a . . . little too . . . uh, good, too . . . intelligent
to be happy there. Miserable bastard! Implying that I was
Seeking a Career. I squeezed my token and quarter together in my pocket and walked out onto the streets of
Gay New York. Later on I got a job as a clerk in a typeshop
run by a guy who read Robert Frost and listened to Bartók
so he thought he could tell you things. He had opinions
about things, right? Well, Sheila went to work in a place
like the magazine corporation I speak of—maybe the
very same one. (Our Author is no longer there. He's somewhere in the Hamptons, telling people things. Has drinks
with Artpeople* there.)

So Lou stayed home to write and Sheila went to work.
Keep her off the streets. Straighten her out. Make her eat
shit. Support the artist. It was better than walking out—
admission of weakness. This way he could very subtly
flaunt the fact that his wife thought so much of his work
that she would support them both. There is a particularly
powerful humiliation for a woman in this sort of thing,

---

*Let's not talk about Artpeople just now.

notwithstanding the modern concept of sexual equality. It's more humiliating than insulting a woman in public —those delicate insults, tendered with love, "good-natured." You know the routine. "Come on, you old bitch." "I'm sorry, I didn't hear you, chubby." "Did you say you wanted another drink, you sweet lush?" It's one thing for a woman to support her artist husband if his work is of a quality that commands respect. It's quite another if she knows it's third-rate. The support of third-rate artists should be left to those who can best support them—universities and foundations. It tends to prevent them from prostrating you with boredom as they go into their nobody-has-the-courage-to-listen-to-me act. Everybody gets a piece of the action and art remains a game for the intelligent.

So Lou, who could not keep Sheila's ass, literally, out of strange beds, sent her ass to work.* If she must fuck, he said, in effect, I'll get something out of it. A kind of sweet revenge. If she must be unfaithful, if she must have her endless thrills, she must also face Monday morning. I don't know how Sheila felt about all this, but I suspect that she was delighted to get out of the house all day, and the hell with Monday morning. Then too, she no longer had to listen to Lou telling her about the schmucks in the English Department, etc., etc. What troubled Lou most was that she spent most of her time at home sleeping—out of this fact and the self-pity it aroused, he composed his cycle, *Sheila Sleeping,* as I have already noted.

With the composition of the cycle, *Sheila Sleeping,* Lou may be said to have settled into his mediocrity. Everything bad in his work had become solid, stratified in these poems, so he considered that he had achieved a style. He had. I'm not being funny. There are hundreds of bad writers who do the same thing. When the style has persisted long enough, and found its way into the pages of

*Sending one's ass somewhere is basically an activity of the military. Cf. "haul ass" to denote swift movement from one place to another.

dozens of literary journals, the men begin to offer, as teachers, the virtue of their knowledge of art to an unsuspecting gang of bright students. They "teach." Or write reviews. They expect to be accorded the respect their position demands. Lou had just about reached this point. Some fool wrote a piece about his cycle in a magazine put out by a group of intense students in Tulsa, Oklahoma (recruiting center for the New York School), comparing his work to the lyrics of Donovan. There he was, Lou, straight. Set into his chasm. A New Poet. He had correspondence with dozens of literary figures, men who translated Rilke over and over again, and who ended their letters with things like: ". . . and as I come to the end of this too-long letter, outside my studio window I see the moon, a white clipper, plunging through seas of streaming cloud." That sort of thing. He was doing all right. Not bad. All these people liked him because he was—what? Because he was playing the game as they were.

What I'm saying is that the last thing any of these people cared about was art. The artist's particular devotion is the one thing that cannot be reached or tampered with. He is hated and feared—these emotions disguised as admiration. A case in point: a poet can publish a book of beautiful, clear, and powerful poems, which sets off all sorts of terrors in the community of dabblers. What happens is that somebody will write a review that picks on one poem, or one line of a poem, and tears and worries it. Letters will come, saying that the book is fine, but the line so-and-so seems a little labored, etc. It's the old con of "grudging admiration." Years ago, one used to read jazz reviewers who assaulted recordings by Charlie Parker because on a couple of tunes his reed squeaked. They'd say: "It's really unforgivable that a mature musician, a professional like Bird, sees fit to let a master like this one go through." Then they'd say: "Kenny Clark's drumming on the non-ballad takes, is, as I have pointed out consistently over the past year, too loud. There are certainly other bop drummers available to Parker . . ." And on, and on. How they hated him.

You can bet your life that Lou would get a prize or two within the next five years. This is known as mutual ass-kissing, a vulgar phrase. One kiss, one sweet caress. You Gotta Have Heart. Not for *Sheila Sleeping,* I think. Journeyman work. But maybe for that. You can't tell. People got prizes for saying that Lyndon Johnson was a fool. They bought their typewriters with his money. Revolutionaries.

"None of you bastards / Knows how Charlie Parker died."

I'm going to make up, based on my own experience (plus inventions and lies), an early rendezvous between Lou and Sheila. He's humming "I Think I'm Goin' Out of My Head."* Sheila is waiting for him in the apartment of a girl friend whose parents are away in Florida—friend on a date and wouldn't be home until about three o'clock in the morning. Dream of youth. The place is in Flatbush—Kings Highway or thereabouts. Lou takes a cab. It was a movie or two that Lou had seen, "heart pounding," etc. The lights seemed softer than ever before along the tree-lined streets around Brooklyn College. When he got to the apartment, Sheila came to the door, utterly lovely. As it turned out, she had on a pale-orange dress, a plain gold bracelet. Standing in the doorway, behind her, gentle light from a spacious living room. Books. Old, solid furniture. A baby grand piano. A small bar in a little alcove. (I remember this night perfectly, drunk as I was.) They had some drinks and played records on the phonograph. The Supremes. The Beatles. Ballads by some strange old man, Don Byas.** They kissed and danced and kissed. They fondled each other. They were really very nice young people. Didn't have a chance. Then Sheila took off her dress and, in white half-slip and bra, picked up a pillow from the couch and went into the bedroom. They

*I first heard this tune at a party in the Dakota. The rich bastard ran out of ice. I hate the rich—perhaps I lie when I say he ran out of ice.
**I honor Don Byas here because he was impeccable on the reverse side of the first record I ever heard by Charlie Parker—"Ko-Ko."

made love. (They didn't make love?) Let's assert that they "made love" but that they didn't "make it." Lou couldn't maintain an erection. He'd never been in bed with a girl before thcugh he was no virgin. But he adored Sheila, and so she frightened him. The love was so powerful that he was crippled by it. She lay waiting while he knelt between her legs, his soft penis brushing her lustrous bush. It was too embarrassing to continue for more than five minutes, so he rolled over and lay next to her, lit a cigarette. (The lighting of a cigarette in this situation is a fictional convention and who am I to deprive Lou of his rights as a bona fide character?) Sheila was angry but she told him that it was all right, she understood, it was all right. He lay there. *Poète maudit.* He hated this apartment now. Of course. To write funny stories about this is limping magic to ward off the disaster. It was really a beautiful dress that Sheila wore. Orange is my favorite color.

So they were married. Which we certainly know by now. And Sheila began her long round (her perhaps permanent round) of affairs. When Lou found out that she was occasionally sleeping with Dick Detective, he was somewhat pleased, since he admired Dick—in a way. He always made sure to compliment Dick's careful poems, and wrote about them on more than one occasion. His criticism was of that sort which is subtly idolatrous, i.e., it found fault. That is, Lou never praised Dick's poems extravagantly, rather, somewhere in his conversation or comment, he would interpolate something like, "this poem is perfectly wrought, but for . . ." and go on to some totally unimportant nitpicking concerning a line or a phrase. (Some fool's comment on a book of poems may concern his admiration of the use of the verb "implore." This is the reverse procedure, but it works the same way. This man doesn't like the poems, but admires *a thing* in them; Lou didn't like Dick's poems, but *didn't* admire *a thing* in them.)

Anyway, Lou made an effort to concern himself with clothes, as did the Detective. This was difficult for him—he gave it up after several months—because Lou was essentially a slob. He didn't do this in order to rival Dick for Sheila's affections, but in order to compliment Dick on his choice of a sex partner. In a word, he was flattered that Dick should select Sheila. I'm not speaking of monsters here, though it may seem so to the casual or sheltered reader. As a matter of fact, I'm inventing things that may pass as probable or at any rate, possible. If I were to record absolutely the facts about these people, nobody would believe me. You think of Thoreau and his remark about men leading lives of "quiet desperation." Number One on the list was, of course, Thoreau. The great writer, Edward Dahlberg, has pointed out the fact that Dear Henry fucked trees. (I take liberties with Dahlberg's note, but I take him to mean that.) Quiet desperation, to be sure. I would like to have a long talk with Lou and tell him what I've made up about him, except that he would laugh at me, and tell me about my novels . . . how much they mean to him. The Lou I make here is absolute. There is no such thing as "Lou-ness." If there were, I'd give you a man who would react perfectly to all the things that trouble him. But the poor bastard strives daily to make sense of his life, that is, he tries not to die all at once. Let's get a psychoanalyst in here to figure Lou out for us (and figure me out for us). Well, the hell with analysts. I admit that I fear them because they hate my powers. They want me to be an entertainer. They want to "understand" Lou beyond what I tell them about him—what they mean is that they want a key to art, and they think, in their professional arrogance, that the whole thing is a trick, learned process. A friend of mine, the other night, told me of the time, in his youth, when he worked as an attendant at a mental hospital. One day, another attendant, after staring for a long minute at a flower growing on the grounds, turned to a doctor who was, in his own estimation, one step removed from godhood, and said: "I think this flower needs a lobotomy, Doctor." This is a good story, and strikes directly at the heart of all psychoanalysis. They want to dissect or remove the artist's brain to see what makes him compose. What they find, of course, is another troubled man, in the case of the artist, a man who is perhaps more deeply troubled. There is no place for an artist here any more. He has been officially dismissed in favor of the entertainer. Smile, they say. (Good writing, good writing, indeed, but . . .) When you get around to an artist *manqué*, like Lou, you've got the same sense of hopelessness, but none of the strength the artist's craft bestows on him. It's no small thing to make a poem. There aren't many men who can make them, and if you can, you've got something they can't take away from you. We all know who "they" are, too. Don't give me any of that wise-guy undergraduate talk. Why is it that people want to be around artists, sucking the powers out of them? Or even be around the artist's wife? Sucking the powers out at one remove. This is such a common occurrence that nobody even mentions it. Wouldn't it be strange if Dick Detective laid Sheila so that he could obtain what he took to be Lou's genius?— after all I've told you about Lou's incompetence. But perhaps Dick wasn't of this opinion.

Here are two anecdotes: Lou once got lost on Blake Avenue in East New York, on a bitter cold night. He began to cry in his frustration and fear. He had enough money for a cab home but since he hadn't planned to take a cab, it was at least ten minutes before this idea proffered itself to him. He was lost, absolutely lost, for ten minutes. Now tell me what a jerk he is. This is all fiction. It is my own problem, Doctor. Why do you think I made this anecdote up? I was never lost on Blake Avenue. Thank God. This is an anecdote about childhood.

Lou had a picture of William Carlos Williams taped on the wall over his desk. The morning after a night in which Lou had failed in love with his wife, an argument developed at the breakfast table, concerning the fact that Sheila had made the coffee too weak. She had. The argument was, of course, not about the coffee. They lapsed into a bitter silence.* After Lou left, Sheila drew a black handlebar mustache on Williams's face. When Lou saw it that night, he laughed. It was another laceration in both their hearts. Sheila spent the evening drinking with Dick Detective, giving him a very hard time. Then she went home and cried all night, begging Lou's forgiveness. This is an anecdote about marriage.

I've got a few more comments to make about Lou, a few more things to say about him before I get rid of him. Prose is endless. It strikes me that I could go on and on, into a thousand pages, about this poor man. (How poor, compared to the rest of us?) For a moment, I thought of having him step off the curb in front of a truck, or drown in the bathtub, something simple and accidental. Just write him off so that the long future of academe would not be his and Sheila would be free to be unhappy with somebody else. End him with a brief paragraph, E. M. Forster-style. Would that be too literary? No such thing. People who make such remarks admire the prose of Jimmy Breslin.

Prose is endless. Tell it to the Marines. It is the texture I love. Imagine Lou going on and on, the writing of an entire life, thousands of pages, his every day recorded. Useless. You want to do it though. Art is selection. Which doesn't mean that the writer is content with what he selects. Maybe Lou should leave Sheila for another woman? But that would force me to bring her in. He could have an affair with April Detective. She would never have an affair with him—with others, yes, as we shall see, but not with Lou. It will be a kind of fine pleasure to have April unfaithful to Dick. There is nothing more ironic than the cuckolding of a chronically unfaith-

*I have the feeling I've read this sentence somewhere.

ful husband. The irony becomes particularly sharp at those moments when the husband confides his feelings of guilt and remorse concerning his affairs to a close friend who is among those who have given him the horns. Or let's have this really exquisite situation: the wife's current lover makes her pregnant, whereupon the husband, accepting with pride and responsibility his role as prospective father, gives up his sexual adventuring and becomes a model of fidelity. At this point, the wife, if she be particularly venomous, may castigate him by reciting a list of her grievances against him, thinking the while of her lover's naked body. Matter for tragedy there.

Best to let Lou run down—and out—as he will. Peter out as the book ends, or stops.* Maybe I'll meet him someday —he's not that rare. If someone like, let's say, Larry Poons is endlessly reproducible, then certainly Lou Henry is. I'll say to him that I think I've met him before, no? I think I've met your wife—Sheila? That will not be his wife's name, of course. We'll have a Robbe-Grillet conversation, infinite boredom. He'll have read this book, and will not have recognized himself. People who "recognize" themselves in books are never in the books. It is the meticulously woven fabric of the ruthless imagination that makes them think they did what the artist says they did. We'll have a drink together in Max's Kansas City, or some other brothel of success. He'll say, "There's Larry Rivers," and I'll counter with a story I've invented about John Chamberlain. We'll sit down among the Mao jackets and miniskirts and he'll show me a poem called "Helen Sleeping." Sitting among the aroma of lobster and the dimwitted conversation of up-and-coming molders of stainless steel and styrofoam, I'll suddenly realize that I am a middle-aged and unsuccessful writer. Lou will know this and so talk to me as if he is my peer. An oaf. Look him up in *Esquire*. He'll be telling you about the New Left. In the meantime, "Helen" will come in and she

*More likely this book will just stop.

will of course be Sheila. She is attractive, elegant, desirable, etc. Slight Brooklyn accent in nasal "a" sounds, drops a "g" now and then, and occasionally hits you with an "n-g" click. Lou introduces us, she gives me a peck on the cheek and her eyes are fluent brown on mine for a moment. I'm flustered, and she laughs, "Well, why not?" It's Sheila, all right. I leave, I wonder what in hell she ever saw in him and go back to my book to see what I had to say about this. Of course. Who else on Ocean Parkway had read *Paterson?* This is not so ludicrous as it sounds. It is after the fact, say ten years after, that it may seem insane. I know a man who married a woman because she understood ice hockey. I'm making this up.

So let's finish with the real Lou. The one in this book, married to Sheila Henry née Ravish. Time to get on to someone else.

A Clutch of Things Lou Henry Liked Before He Became
   a "Serious" Writer.
Lord of the Flies
Coney Island
Café Figaro (the good old "Fig")
The Botanical Gardens
The poems of Dylan Thomas
"Sweet Lorraine" by Joe Venuti*
Italian opera
Stravinsky
New York City Ballet production of *The Nutcracker*
Rum and Coke
Fabian
Audrey Hepburn
The "Tonight" show
Glittering crowds in canyons of steel
"Mending Wall"
H. G. Wells
Victor Mature**

   *Totally inexplicable
  ** *Victor Mature!?*

Ogden Nash
Tortilla Flat
Li'l Abner
A fireside when a storm is due

June 10, 1966
Dear Dick,*
    Just a note torn off between another reading of *A Dream of Love,* and lunch with Guy Lewis. We're sort of playing around with the idea of Guy doing some drawings or collages for a little book of my poems. But what I wanted to write you about is your two poems in *Paris Review.* I was pleased, more than pleased, *moved* by them. I think it's your use of a longer line and the fact that you've started to rhyme inside the line that makes them work so well. They are gutsy poems, and perfectly clear. Anyway, I just wanted to write and tell you that I think you're really into something here and I'd be pleased to see more of your work. Why don't you call and come over to see Sheila and me? Maybe for dinner with April?
Yours in poesie,
Lou

Allow me some comment on the foregoing letter. Dick never published in the *Paris Review.* So far as I know, he sent work to the magazine's poetry editor on more than one occasion, but was never acknowledged. You will understand that at the time the rumor about town was that the poetry editor was busy selling sweatshirts and lapel buttons. Whatever, Dick's poems never appeared in those pages. There was also a rumor that George Plimpton, connected with the *Review* for many years, liked the poems enormously, but I place no stock in that. Secondly, the reader will note that Lou's invitation to Dick and April smacks of the bizarre. Perhaps he had a possible sex orgy in mind. What I think is that Lou wrote this

---

*"Detective" was not Dick's surname. I call him that for reasons which (I hope) will become clear. None of these names matters in the least, and it would certainly have been preferable to use letters for all of these people, even though I've already done that in a book. Someone said that this device (a "literary device," he said) spoiled the book for him; it seemed affected. In this book I have invented such nonliterary names as Sheila Henry, Guy Lewis, etc. But allow me my one frivolity.

letter in a kind of subtle and ironic anger, and never sent it. I'll ask him when I see him. Certainly Lou must have been aware that Dick never published in the *Paris Review.* What two poems? Yet the reference to Guy is plausible, since Guy eventually did linoleum cuts for *Sheila Sleeping.* I have a feeling that Lou is getting away from me—and about time, too.

One of the accepted clichés of our time is that marriages fail because the secret desires of the partners remain unspoken. That's a good way out of the problem. Psychiatrists get fat on it. But after the orgasm, there are the underdone eggs, the Sunday football games, all that detritus of life. And how is the sun coming in the kitchen window today? Take Lou. Take Sheila. They didn't do too badly on the sexual front, as the reader knows by now. The "sexual front" strikes me as being incredibly vulgar —but I'll let it stand. They also probably did a lot of things I don't know about: all in all, they had their adventures, more than most, I'd say. Probably more than the manager of the supermarket in your neighborhood, or the woman who taught you in the fourth grade. But look at them. They are, as they say, in bad shape, they'll never make it. I can't see them in dazzling Color, shaking their white heads wisely at any Golden Anniversary dinner, while Walter Pidgeon looks after the wine and José Iturbi rips into "Clair de Lune."
   All right. Let's assume then that their sexual fantasies, at least insofar as they concerned each other, were largely assuaged. What they could discern and invent, they tried out. Their marriage is bad. Lou, staggering around in some dizzy imitation of an artist. Sheila, well. The familiar flesh. Does the quality pall? Sade, in that heartless madness of his, attempts to break this lock by substituting quantity for quality. Not one girl, but a hundred. So that the lust be continually wakened. The lingerie fetishist's new lover is naked sweet. As her body is more thoroughly learned, so is it progressively adorned. If he could avail himself of each woman that he desired,

his aberration would disappear. Then sexual experimentation and finesse become ways to make the flesh new. It is love, new love, in its dazed sweetness, that is satisfied by simple orgasm. So that Lou, in the first rush of his desire for Sheila, thought himself rid of his sexual obsessions. It was only later that he allowed himself to think of them and to ask Sheila to perform them with him. I have been speaking of destruction in this book. There is nothing funny about Lou, you will understand. He should be happy, I have no desire to make him suffer. What is true is that there is no one who could have rescued him. He has no need for anyone but Sheila, but the time will undoubtedly come when he will look on a young woman and think of her as his salvation. He will think that Sheila has made him unhappy. This new girl! A sparkling affair! He'll show the bitch of a wife of his that he's still got it! Taking to this third party his huge, lumpy bag of tricks. All the filth and knotted string of his life. Twenty years her senior, which means that his sexual fixations were constructed and annealed at least eight years before her birth. God help this man, blundering through his bad poems, reading Williams, whom he will never understand, so tortured was he by love and sex all his long life. "What power has love but forgiveness?" "What good is it otherwise?" I see Lou at about fifty, swept by lust as he turns a newspaper page to confront an ad for a new style of girdle. The model has the dark, soft features of Sheila at eighteen.

The Promised Fragment of Lou's Folk-Rock Song. (Reproduced in its Proper Place.)

. . . on Route Ninety-Four!
Ain' gonna fight no more
In no war.

'Cause it's love
An' the green green grass,
Lemme hear it, baby.
C'mon an' knock out the jazz!

Not gonna s'lute no flag,
Gonna hear sweet Harley roar!
Cookin' along on Route Ninety-Four!
Ain' gonna fight no more
In no war.

'Cause it's love, etc.*

After Sheila went to work for the Marvelous Magazine
Corp. (we'll call it), surrounded by old drunks and the
like, Lou became what he liked to think of as a "full-time
writer"; as in " . . . for four and a half years in a pet shop
catering to French poodles while he wrote *Bouquet of
Lovers*. Now, with the paperback sale, and the acquisi-
tion of the novel by Warner Bros., as well as its selection
by the Book-of-the-Month Club, Mr. Drogg has quit Pru's
Pampered Poodles to write full-time. 'It's a little scary,'
he admits. 'I mean, I got used to using the job as a defense
against the novel—now,' he says, not unhappily, 'I guess
I'm on my own.' "

If *this* were only a novel, I could punish and reward
these people as I see fit—send them to Hackettstown in
August, to sit in the Warren House in the cool of a 1939
taproom, drinking Trommer's on draft. Steamed clams
and polkas on Saturday nights. Not even the DL&W
stopped in that leafy burg. Marry them off to eighteen-
year-olds who sing "Satisfaction." Let them walk on Fire
Island beach in October. Permit them to buy pieces of
some patsy fighter who can't hook off a jab. Stay them
with flagons.

So Lou became a full-time writer. Light breakfast in
the morning with Sheila, the *Times* for a quick scanning,
alone, over a second cup of coffee. Then—to the typewriter. He thought. He said. Looking out the window,
leafing through books he would one day reread. He
thought. He said. The poems were really coming along,

---

*I seem to recall that this song was set to music by a student of
Balladic Structuring in Contemporary "Movement" Songs at the College of Musical Knowledge, State University of New York at Petard. His
name was Julius Orange—later the lead singer with the Orange Julius.

he would sit and look over the previous day's work. Disastrous. He set himself the task of writing a sonnet a day: one had an opening line, "Atop the roof from which the bomb was hurled." That will give you an idea. Reading Williams again: tell me, Doc! What is the secret? He learned the names of flowers he had never seen and had no desire to see. He began a novel about his childhood (no part of which will be inflicted on the reader). Not a bad guy, old Lou, as you have seen, just not a writer. He wrote a lot of letters to other writers. Full of literary allusions and references. In them he always had to get out of New York. How can anybody work here? Insane, noisy, so many people, parties, readings, visitors, the phone always ringing.

What can I do with him? Here he is, getting away at last, on the way to his ripe middle age. Good luck to him. At the moment he is reading *The Debauched Hospodar,* the first stanza only of a villanelle in the typewriter, and masturbating. Maybe the phone will ring and he can go and drink ale all afternoon in McSorley's with a poet just in from Cleveland. I think that probably will happen.

3

The Butcher Cut Him Down

To BEGIN to understand Guy Lewis the reader should
know something of his attitude toward Hemingway. Do
I hear you say *arrgghh?* You can skip to the next chapter,
if you wish—there's no plot here to worry you. You won't,
of course, understand him, since I don't understand him
myself. I haven't seen him, or the man who passes for
him, for some time, socially at least. I've run into streams
of his particular madness in bars and at parties on occasion. Caught in his wake, as it were. But Guy is not Studs
Lonigan, that I can trick you into thinking you know
something about him. Hemingway, at any event, was responsible for wrecking Guy's gifts—such as they were—
for the writing of prose. When I read the impacted, abstract prose that Lewis writes, I always think of a letter
he sent to me some ten years ago. There is a paragraph
at the end of it that has the sort of sweet clarity that
presages a distinguished career. It is monstrous to think
that he has spent those ten years meticulously destroying
the contours of that style. But he was someone else then,
even his name was different. At that time he even believed that other people lived lives not answerable to his
analysis of them, that is, he believed that other people
existed outside of his opinions of them. Now he writes of

himself in the most claustrophobic terms. He is Chicken Little, the sky forever falling on him, particularly *on him*.

The prose of this letter that I speak of is photographic. It is, as a matter of fact, a photographic passage describing a photograph. I love writing of this sort, because I love photographs. I don't speak of movies: they are either diversion or art. But the photo, if it be not taken by some intelligent and knowledgeable professional, is absolute revelation. The faces of those dead bourgeois, meaningful and famous only to the dead photographer—they are enough to wrench the heart. Absolute pictures of mortality. To see one's mother, now putrescent in her grave, at the age of sixteen, quiet in a field, or standing before some long-uprooted shrub of hydrangea. Faded and brown. To describe such a photograph in prose is a mark of excellence.

Along with this letter, Guy sent me a photograph of himself, which I no longer possess. Full of summer. He is in white ducks, a white shirt, the collar open and the sleeves rolled up, white sneakers. In the living room of his mother's house in Kansas City. In his hand a big drink that looks to be, by its tone, bourbon or rye over ice. You can feel the cold, wet glass. Guy has a new haircut and smiles at us, here in New York. That was a killing summer, viciously close and humid. Now he is the king of the little magazines. With what bitterness he thinks that. An "experimental writer." God, that dreary psychoanalytic mumbling. Masturbating in the mirror, his glass eyes. His drunken eyes. I met him a few months ago, almost unconscious with booze, and in his furious despair he told me that girls to whom he is introduced walk away from him in fear. His glass eyes on my face, the confiding light grip on my forearm.

We'll ramble around here. Didn't he ramble? Came out of summer and leafy suburbs of America. White shirts and flapjacks, banana splits and the American Legion band. The smell of cut grass in the lambent evenings of

Kansas City. Mother and father proud of his talents, incredible. Shaving brushes with mugs of savory cream. How could he not absolutely understand Hemingway, and grow to loathe and fear the man's specific honesty? At this moment he is standing over his beer in a bar on downtown Sixth Avenue. The Beatles are singing "Strawberry Fields" and he thinks it's for him. Telling the bartender about the great new story he's writing. Or about the time he saw Ted Williams go 5 for 5 against the Browns. Did Ted Williams ever go 5 for 5 against the Browns? Not that it matters. The Browns are dead and gone. They wouldn't even allow the Browns any more. They are outside the concerns of money. They had a one-armed outfielder, Pete Gray was his name, who batted .218 in 1945. George Plimpton could conceivably do better against such wartime pitching. The Browns are redolent of American innocence, and I am being neither romantic nor sentimental. They literally would not be allowed now. The fan of today who mistakes movement for action demands a more brutal address to sport, swift and vengeful: witness professional football. Guy, in the bar, boring the bartender with this tale of Williams, going 5 for 5. Soon he will tell him about Pete Gray and the bartender won't believe him. A one-armed outfielder? Can you imagine Schaefer or Bud standing still for that? CBS? Pete Gray on the Game of the Week at $17,000 a minute? Guy plays "Strawberry Fields" again and orders another beer. The bartender is reading about Joe Namath's white llama rug. Rambled till the butcher cut him down.

With a jeweler's care, destroyed his natural gifts. It took him ten years. Picking and scratching away to expunge from his prose every trace of what he took to be Hemingway's influence. And so grew to loathe the man's work, and from that, came to a loathing of the man. When he blew his brains out, Guy felt relief that he was gone and that he would no longer have to beat responses out of his mind and emotions to handle new writings. And, along with the relief, bitterness that he should so die, as some specific character in one of his stories. You will understand that his attitude toward Hemingway was not unique. The other day someone spoke to me of that writer's anal-obsessive character. By which he meant that he was troubled when he was writing badly. This conception of the artist's fears for his fertility is indicative of the times in which we live. The fears are amusing, since they have nothing to do with a greater reality. (Read: "Social Reality.") The artist is a contemporary pariah because everybody understands what he is, and what he is doing, and thinks he should go straight to hell. Fifty years ago they didn't know anything about him and thought he should go straight to hell. It all falls out the same way: snake eyes.

Now let me "extend" my character, Guy Lewis, a little. Guy's essential problem was impotence: erratic impotence, that is, so that he never knew when he would fail in love. He was married, briefly, to a girl named Bunny, whom we shall speak of later on. He married her so that she could help him. She married him so that she could help him. Catastrophe. Fresh from her studies as a psych major—into the real world. When Guy confronted her with limp penis, tears, and thousands of manuscript pages of unpublished fiction, Freud tottered and fell on top of Jung, Adler, and Stekel. The man smelled of sweat, dipped his toast in his egg yolks, and died on his feet in front of her eyes. The psychopathology of everyday life, indeed. But we'll deal with this in more detail later. At the moment, it is Guy's impotence we must consider—its relation to Hemingway. Guy knew what many literary critics do not know, and that is that Hemingway's concern was not with destruction, war, violence, or action, but with impotence and how one confronts the fact with dignity and courage. Do you think Jake Barnes is a "symbol" for a destroyed time? I don't care what they told you at Columbia—Jake Barnes can't get it up. Nobody can get it up in anything that Hemingway wrote, albeit their rampaging loves. They are all in some absolute way, impotent, and this was the writer's obsession: to challenge this in his work. So Guy hated him and feared him. Came to think of him as sick and bloodthirsty and lacking in love—while the man's work, the best of it, is full of the grace of honesty. And terrifying in its ability to expose his secret fears. Do you think for a moment that an artist selects his theme? It is all simple obsession, which is why no professional reviewer will tolerate for a moment a deviation from what he takes letters to be. The artist gets on the maniac nag, rides him into the flames. Goes mad. Rots in obscurity. Destroys his gifts by finally selling them and himself. "Consumes himself in bitterness." Blows his brains out. Or pretends that nothing fazes him and dies over and over in his imagination, doing his best not to smash those close to him. Or writes, like Hemingway, a book of weary, desperate bitterness, *Across the River and into the Trees,* delightedly assaulted by the corps of hacks, whom he placated, with what staggering cynicism, with his last book, *The Old Man and the Sea.* And won the Nobel Prize, and lost his mind, and blew his head off. Nothing strange about that.

So Guy, who could not confront his own demon, battered and chipped at his prose until it changed from a clear, yet strange modeling of his particular sense of reality, to a shambles of abstract egoism. That each leaf should fall for Guy! That a paraplegic should roll into a bar at 3:00 A.M., escorted by a dyke dressed in a tuxedo, to terrify Guy! The sky falling on Guy's head. Couched in dense psychological prose, narrative of Guy vs. World, a fictional Guy whose affairs with women were sullied in every way but that way in which they were truly upended. Impotence equaled Hemingway. Or, impotence begged to be defined in a prose that would reveal it: and so conjured up Hemingway. Dear God, help him to destroy himself with dignity. Yet he grows older, his hair is gray, face collapsed, his hangovers shred him, while his prose grows worse, hysterically egocentric. He has reached a point, so he has told other writers, at which he has discovered that the use of the first person automatically releases the truth. "I just finished writing this fantastic short story," he says. "Christ, a knockout!" The gentle grip on the forearm of some hack sculptor who is thinking of how much it will cost to repair his Mercedes. While Guy buys the drinks and runs his bar bill up another thirty dollars. God give him the strength to fail with dignity. I see him looking out of Kansas City summer at me, in fresh white clothes. The living room is shaded from the sun, one of his early collages on the wall over the mantel. His collages are brilliant. Were brilliant. No one can tell him that any more. His face twists into a vicious scowl: at the memory of his own life.

One of the first things Guy did upon reaching New York from the school of fine arts he had attended in Chicago was to fall in love. We'll call the girl Lucy. A good time to fall in love, it was 1957, New York art world vivid and fairly clean. There were in those days men of great courage and greater gifts, the world being broken open and European weariness wrenched and throttled. Guy was painting delicately, but with great strength, a strong surface, impasto, following Guston's work of those years, yet using darker colors. I particularly recall a small painting of his done at that time, called "The Assault." A figure in crimson bursts out in severely controlled whorls and slashes from a flat background of Prussian blue. It is Guston, but it is also Guy. He painted well. (Face scowling at the memory.) He fell in love with Lucy, living at the time on Grove Street. I understand that now she lives in Los Angeles with a painter who constructs giant vulvas out of brass and sheepskin. She is doing very well, as is the sculptor, he sells to hip young stars of films and television. She lived, thirteen years ago, on Grove Street, a pretty girl, blond hair, casually sloppy, a watercolorist of no talents at all. She had lived with a poet, a play-

wright-director, and two painters before she met Guy. In
those years he wore caps, rather elegantly cocked over
his left eye, gray tweed, old-fashioned, the sort that cab-
drivers and longshoremen wear. I think I visited them a
couple of times, in their chaotic domesticity. Or that
might have been another couple on Grove Street. In all
events, I am certain that I met Lucy, Guy loved her and
her schizophrenia to the point of madness. Their argu-
ments centered on whether or not she had flirted with
other painters in the old Cedar Bar.* Or on his drinking.
Lucy thought that his drinking was responsible for his
erratic sexual performance, and Guy encouraged this belief.

She had money from her parents and attended the Art
Students League and a modern dance class. She liked
men and had had many affairs outside of those that she
considered "serious." Of these affairs Guy was in ignorance, but he simply assumed that they had existed. In
the middle of his love for her he wrote a letter to an old
friend, who, with his wife and new son, was living in the
south of France, doggedly writing short stories and as
doggedly reading. It is incredible that writers spend their
whole youths in such activity. In the letter he told him,
almost as a postscript, that he was living with a girl,
Lucy. Wondrous, intelligent, with such a delicacy of
movement, her voice, etc. The hyperbole of new love.
Two weeks later, a reply, Guy to this day remembers the
swift, vertical hand on the pale blue of the air mail envelope: addressed, as usual, to Guy Lewis, c/o The Cedar
Bar. Malice in the hand. Wit and malice. The end of the
letter read: ". . . it is good, etc., that you are happy with
a new girl, and that you are working steadily. New York
can be hell without anyone at all. I remember when I was
there in 1954, it was such a relationship that kept me
sane. The girl I knew then lived in a little place on one
of those quiet streets in the Village and her apartment

*No attempt will be made to describe this famous bar, thank God.

was always a delight, airy, bright, coffee in the morning with her, etc. I don't remember too much about it except that in the tiny bedroom she had a really good print, I thought, of a Hopper painting. Somehow, the combination of the desolation of that painting and the snugness of that room, with her, always gave me the strangest sense of safety and happiness . . ." Guy looked up from the bed on which he was sitting to stare at that blank, silent, midwestern street on the wall above him, hopelessly American, dream of sterility. Ah, to be so knifed, over the entire sea. It was not jealousy that held him, nor anger, but the sense of absolute futility: Death in the road, dark-shadowed in the shelter of the trees. He never told Lucy, nor did he ask her anything about this. No doubt she would hardly have remembered—the adventure of a month or two, three years before. That night he got drunk in a White Rose bar in midtown on Lucy's money, watching the Yankees against Detroit, the love running out of him, blood.

The way he stood on the rubber before putting the fast one across. Tried out for the White Sox, but his mother saw the arts in his future. His tiny uncle would make him laugh, mugging, in the bathroom, then pop his soapy shaving brush in his open mouth. These bits of mica. Cap over his eye. Painters' softball games in P-town. With what fear and joy he struck out those famous men. Sodden with beer and his sloshing gut, still his change-up was a marvel to see. Then he died and returned as someone else. His name changed? His face old, hair gray. Filled with self-pity. His prose a viscous green. The sun, the sun! around which all revolved. Linoleum cuts for Lou Henry's cycle of poems. That *he* should appear! That his name would again be in print! With what a suppression of literary taste he did those delicate cuts. He fell in love with Sheila, he fell in love with April, he fell in love with Lou. Drew pornographic pictures and exhausted himself in masturbation. Bunny left him and returned

and left him again. He wrote a long story about it. Occasionally saw flashingly that his grace was gone: turned to
gesture. A memory of youth. Went to Provincetown in
January and wept on the dunes. Came to hate his peers
and so became a teacher of youth. Gathered his legend
about him as if he had come out of the Côte d'Azur after
a season with Scott and Zelda. Romantic configuration of
the blasted thirties. All his finest prose wasted in oral
stories. That clear sense of a gone America. Turned to
analysis and maudlin denouement. That he should never
have read Jimmy Cannon. That he should never have
read Raymond Chandler. Martell for the drunk on the
wagon, how could he help but assimilate that relaxed
romance? He went back to Kansas City for a visit and was
seduced by the mother of the boy with whom he had had
a raging affair when they were both sixteen. And compared it later, in his head, to something in Dashiell Hammett. Thus his lucid sight of his own past became tangled
with the violent paradigms of these men. Someone in
Chandler has violet eyes. As had his mother. This fact
stewed in his head with the energy that moves astrologists to their interminable solipsisms, so that those characters in his fiction who were most important, or who
carried the vital thread of the narrative, all had violet
eyes too. He would type, smiling through his hangover at
the words, in his delight of working, "It struck Benjamin
that the handsome girl had eyes the color of perfect violet." Yet in every story, a flash to show what he could do:
stepping out toward the batter and releasing the sweet
change-up. So that even those who had come to despair
of his writing continued to read him, waiting for the
moment when he would show pure his basic gifts. I have
watched, as a matter of fact, once-young pitchers of enormous promise grind through year after year of the most
unsatisfying seasons. To see them, at the most meaningless moments, in relief, and with the greatest authority
and arrogance, break off a vicious curve on a cleanup
hitter for a third strike . . . ! To see that. Dear God, with

what feigned aloofness they wait for the next batter—to be lacerated by a long triple on the first pitch. But the strikeout curve, the way it broke . . . sudden blush of those one-hitters in Amarillo.

All those chestnuts roasting on those open fires. Damned silent nights. Joyous, joyous holiday seasons—Christ, the lives that fall down and apart under the weight of them. It must be specifically American, and specifically Christian, this Christmas despair. A time for madness and weeping, divorce, separation, cruelty, and sexual hysteria. Behind the dazzling fronts of the parties and the booze-dulled sensibilities, what a stewing of terror and fear. The manic commercials and ads, the weary bluster of clergymen, the chipped and faded ornaments on the trees in slushy parks in Brooklyn and the Bronx. Did you ever see Christmas on Baltic or DeGraw Street? If you haven't, you haven't begun to live. Stick that cucumber sandwich up your ass. Home movies, television specials, the clutter of gifts. I remember standing in bitter gray courtyards waiting to go in to the nine o'clock Christmas mass, the kids shivering and lying about the toys they didn't get, the nuns, red-cheeked, slapping their animal-trainer wooden clappers together. Full of joy at Christ's birth. The devastating strain of appearing happy. I knew a man who for years got sick when he drank Scotch because it reminded him of Christmas office parties. It was his problem, do I hear you say, Doctor? And so it was. I remember Guy Lewis at someone's house on a Christmas Eve, or a Christmas night, it might have been my house at the time, some ten or twelve years ago. It might have been someone else's house, with me there as a guest. Full of booze, we listened to Billie Holiday and Dexter Gordon —shamans to ward off the black terror of the season. Pretending it was just another winter night. Taste of Scotch. I used to get sick when I drank Scotch because it reminded me of a man I knew who used to shake cringingly the boss's hand at Christmas office parties. Guy

Lewis entered this house, a bottle, three-quarters full, of Jack Daniels, drunk and grinning, he kissed me. Or he kissed the host. I think. Let's state that he certainly kissed the hostess, a woman who would later devote her life to the attempt at destroying her children. Thought that to live, others had to die—and why not children? I love children because of their incredible gallantry in the face of the assault leveled at them. Guy kissed this hostess, in any event. That's that, now forget her. He had this huge box that he had picked up a day or two earlier at the post office, or the Cedar Bar. A big box from Kansas City, from his mother. Brought it over, intact, so that he could open it with his friends. Or, with "his friends," or, with his "friends." These are fine distinctions. What is the difference between a coaster and a caster? Right! Now, spell Parchesi four different ways and you get to "date" the new file clerk. Second prize, a copy of *Portnoy's Complaint* autographed by Moshe Dayan.

Guy opened his box. Christ, with what bitterness! Then he threw all the stuff on the floor, shaking his head, drinking the booze out of the bottle, saying, for each item, "Looka this shit fuck shit!" Hello! Merry Christmas. I knew a guy when I was a kid who used to send cards that said "Merry Xames." Why not? You don't have to know how to spell to be full of that old spirit. Have you ever gone to a house where they have Hanukkah lights, a Christmas tree, and serve you spaghetti and meat balls just prior to smashing open the piñata?—which always includes a copy of the Koran? Neither have I. I just might write that story, though. That's what they call black humor. No sense in going on about this. Following is a list of the items that Guy took out of the box from KC.

1. Copy of the Oxford World's Classics edition of *The Poems of Robert Herrick*.
2. Small cloth sack of old-fashioned licorice pillows.
3. Small cardboard box, wrapped in red tinfoil, of sour lemon drops.

4. Star cut out of a piece of orange construction paper.
5. Copy of *The Little Red Book of Baseball.*
6. Two packs of Balkan Sobranies.
7. Individual-serving bottle of Strega.
8. Jagged chunk of blue glass.
9. Number 5, number 9, and number 12 paintbrushes.
10. Tiny magnifying glass.
11. Sterling silver penknife.
12. Simulated black leather diary for the coming year.
13. Small sliver of gold leaf.
14. Sprig of holly.
15. Bottle of Higgins India ink.
16. Round Venus typewriter eraser with attached brush.
17. Copy of the Kansas City *Star.*
18. Key ring with a small compass attached.
19. Amber glass ashtray marked: Welcome to Kansas City.
20. Pair of black woolen gloves.
21. Small bottle of Elmer's glue.
22. Spool of lavender thread.
23. Sheaf of fine sandpaper
24. Package of Cryst-O-Mint Lifesavers.
25. Cellophane bag of Hershey's Kisses.
26. Clipping of a particularly stupid review of *Paterson Five.*
27. Paper-Mate pen.
28. Jar of pickled cocktail onions.
29. Miniature watercolor done by Guy at twelve, superbly matted and framed.
30. Crumpled sheets and strips of crepe paper of varied colors.

This list is a bore to read but was interesting enough to compile, based as it is on a hazy memory and on the imagination. You will see that what I am trying to do is set a tone so that the reader can determine the sort of home life from which Guy flung himself into booze and impotence. There are hundreds of things that might have served in the place of this arbitrary list of thirty. But one of the basic reasons for this list is to allow numbskull reviewers to tell their readers that it is merely an avant-garde convention, employed since Joyce. Further, that the use of these lists is a method whereby the writer avoids the responsibility of narrative and plot. But this book has both narrative *and* plot. Subtly disguised, I grant you, but there. What they really loathe is prose. You remember prose? I'm rereading *In the American Grain.* You remember that book, right? You *don't* remember that book. Well, you remember *Herzog?* Right! That's a *great* book. All about America—the reality of America. I'm tired of all of you. Take the list or leave it. This book is for me. My next book will be a novel, for you, tracing the fortunes of a typical American family, from the years of Depression up through the Swinging Sixties. It will be written in Abracadabra, have a number of brutally candid sex scenes, and the hero will be an alienated Jew who likes to Suck Off Christian movie stars and Fuck black girls in the Ass. Confronting Contemporary America in a Big Way. There will be no plot and I will exhaust everybody in sight by listing, at every opportunity, the contents of anyone's pockets and wallets and handbags. There will be an interesting scene detailing a luncheon between Wyndham Lewis (what?) and a *Playboy* interviewer. The latter will ask Lewis a number of questions the answers to which he will not understand. Seems this Lewis "makes no concessions to his readers." A Fascist pig anyway. We showed the creep where his bread was buttered.

Thank you for listening. Now that you've been patient with this apologia, you can once again dip into your beloved copy of Sir Thomas Wyatt. I know you're anxious to get back to him. I really didn't know so many people still read Wyatt. When I was a young man there wasn't a shopkeeper in my little town who didn't have his battered, dogeared copy behind the counter. Wyatt and Campion, Campion and Wyatt—one would think there were no other authors! Those were the days. If it hadn't been for the ambience of that little town I'd probably be a revolutionary in Washington Square Village by now instead of a poet's poet. Tell me about Cuba. Are the mission bells still ringing there? Got a long letter from Fidel the other day on the ultimately unsatisfactory politics of Rimbaud. Fascinating. Right now, he's reading Defoe's *Colonel Jack.* Introduction by Louis Auchincloss.

To finish this section, let me state, for the record, that Pee Wee Russell just died. Nobody could touch Pee Wee on his instrument. Don't tell Ishmael Reed I said so.

Then there is the story of Guy and Lena, I think her name was. I invent this to give the mood of the fading years of the Eisenhower Administration. When this idea first presented itself to me I thought of formalizing it into a short story, or a tale. But there is no point to that. I have certainly no moral to draw, and it is somewhat difficult to bring such a tale to a satisfactory conclusion. So. We shall posit the fact: a party for Dick and April Detective at somebody's loft on Broadway. I see that loft now, from the front windows the miniature perfections of Grace Church. A welcome-home party for them, their return to New York after an extended honeymoon in Mexico. Mexico was very big in those years, probably a hangover from Lawrence, some weird idea about being free. Many people went down there to write and disappeared into the dust. Do you think it a mistake that *Under the Volcano* was ignored for years? How could such a book be taken seriously in that fever of wrong notions about Mexico? This is beside the point, however, the party is the thing. A party, lots of people, booze, etc. Marijuana, etc. This was a time when people drank, smoked pot, took pills, all at once. Get into it, get out of it, fall down, anything to change the shape of the reality around them. There was no sense of a "pure" high. That came later. The party.

Let me interpolate here the fact that in those years, the late fifties, there used to be dozens of people in New York for weekends only, and that most of them seemed to come from Washington. I grant you that this is a subjective view. But nonetheless true. They fled from Washington agencies, miles of bureau desks, with their incredibly cheap booze, by the gallon, in the trunk of the car, their aging twice-divorced women, manic in what they took to be a last assault on love. I can see these same women now, married to master sergeants who have been shipped to Vietnam, drunk by noon and showing their thighs to the gas man. America is geared to infidelity. You can think about that and see that it is beyond argument.

This girl Lena in the fashion of the day, toreador pants and a sleeveless sweater. Not pretty, an angular, mannish face, she struck Guy. He wanted her. It happened that the host had a painting of Guy's on the wall, a large, gray-and-white action painting. Lena looked at this painting, got closer to it, looked at it some more, with interest, drinking bourbon from a peanut butter jar. Her hip thrown out, so that her buttocks protruded, beautiful in the tight pants. Born to be buggered. Guy went over, drunk now for three days, and said something, Christ knows what. I wasn't what one can call self-possessed in those days, so I can't remember too clearly, but he said something, the artist to his audience, etc. You like the painting? I see you've been looking at my painting . . . does it interest you? She didn't seem to hear him. She didn't hear him, in fact, because she was deaf and dumb. By some accident, she turned toward him and lip-read, let's say, the words "my painting." And then there came from her mouth the most fantastic, guttural sounds, so that in my scattered state, I took her to be speaking German. I am of that vulgar segment of my generation that grew up on war movies, in which "Germans" barked and coughed. Such prejudices run deep and no amount of education can ever completely eradicate them. Guy paled at the infirmity. (Figure of Death in his dreams, a calm man in the road, some miles outside Kansas City, in small hills.)

Some hours later, now incoherently drunk, Guy danced

with Lena, close, to a Frank Sinatra record. And whispered in her ear, I love you. How explain this madness? I love you, he whispered, while she danced with him, his breath in her hair. Guy danced badly, with a graceless movement learned in roadhouses, his feet splaying out, a shuffle. Perhaps he was better that night. I seem to remember myself sitting in a sling chair, drinking ice-cold beer at the time, talking about Dexter Gordon or Gene Ammons in some arrogant manner. I love you, he whispered. Then he said it aloud, and then he was shouting it into her ear, Lena smiling into the smoky air, locked into her silent world.

This can be taken as a weary metaphor for Guy's search for love, i.e., that no one could ever hear him. But it is more to the point, as I said earlier, as a comment on these inelegant years. What a futility. Guy, feet moving in the drunken steps learned in Henny & Mary's as a boy, you can imagine him perfectly, the blue suit and spread-collar shirt, knitted tie with Windsor knot, in his hip pocket the pint of Imperial. What is most amazing is that any of us are still alive. It is the masked pride in surviving at the edge of despair that holds my generation together. We pity and love each other even now, years later, estranged and at odds, and lie to young people that we understand them. While what we understand is that America fell apart in those years. The smallest wisp of absolute vigor and madness became visible then, traced in air above the ruins. Guy, dancing with this deaf mute, in his head the boyhood image of muddy CCC camps. The allegiance one has to Kline and Charlie Parker is secret and almost inarticulate. Certainly beyond aesthetics. They explained our childhood. When the tune ended, Guy bent Lena into a graceless Glen Island dip and we laughed and cheered, surprised at this atavistic gesture, borne suddenly back into bitter adolescence.

Guy at the bar with April Detective. He has had many dreams about her lusting for him, April in his bed, the

two of them sweating over each other's genitals, sweat
and drool in the deadening humidity of August, or warm
in the winter together, ah dear God, his rigid penis
thrusting on and on for hours, she moans and blas-
phemes in her passion and gratitude. At the moment he
is drunk, talking about—talking about what? What can it
be? Exactly. Let me say that it is staggering conversation
about *Pierre*. Why not? April nods, smiles, crosses her
legs, Guy's glances on her thighs and knees, he is bitter
toward Melville's failure, in his drunkenness, more bitter
because of his desire. All this is absolutely possible. Melville's genius suffers for Guy's needs. April is aware of
this lust, she is delicately careful not to arouse him further, but hides, as it were, her body behind that brittle
mask women can put on when they are made cognizant
of the beauty of their flesh. A sort of shrinking, a particularly strange sexlessness that they entertain, or aspire to
—ah, I don't know how to explain it, but it is so. April does
it, she makes small her sex. A few laughs, a look of intense concentration, etc. Guy is grateful for this, senses it
and is grateful. But her thighs are beautiful, shining and
firm in the black nylon. If April could only *see* her own
beauty as Guy saw it, just for a flash be aware of the
gentle curve and swell of her crossed thighs as they were
there in Guy's vision, she would—what? She would be
even more maddening. But all this is surface. What is
going on is subterranean anger. Did I say that April is
waiting for Dick? She is. They will have dinner and go to
the movies. Dick is late and April knows that he is late
because of an assignation with Sheila Henry. She thinks
it is Sheila Henry, but isn't sure. She doesn't care, nor do
I. Let's make it Sheila since we already know her, and can
imagine her with Dick, whom we don't yet know. (And
never will, I say to myself.) But Sheila is fine with me,
they were in the middle of their affair at this time anyway. He comes in, finally, late. Monstrous to April that he
should be unfaithful *and* late. One or the other, but this
is a double insult. Of course, Dick is angry before he even

gets to the bar. To have this tryst cut short, to have to rush, to wake up and throw his clothes on and run, Sheila smiling, dozing, warm. This is all April's fault, right? Her thighs are not beautiful to him. And there is Guy, Jesus Christ! To have to put up with Guy, who will tell him something he doesn't want to hear, who will tell him about—Melville, tonight. And *Pierre.* What he tells him about is Guy. Of course. Suddenly April drops her reserve and by the subtlest turn of her hips, the movement of her buttocks on the barstool, a smile, she is available to Guy. She smiles secretly at him and at the same time pulls the hem of her skirt down, with that modesty which is so utterly provocative. Dick is still between Sheila's legs, this brilliant charade is lost on him. Guy takes the hem of April's skirt in his hand, the backs of his fingers warm with the flesh of her thigh, he winks and smiles and pulls her skirt down as she has just done. This takes a second and Dick, in that time, takes Guy by the sleeve and—says nothing. Looks at him with contempt and anger, the smell of cunt off him. Guy is the classic victim, why not? He falls into the trap, so they shoot him. It is a truism that the married couple at war will doggedly wipe out all those who stray onto the battlefield, it is a way of delaying their own final destruction. I suppose that it goes without saying that they do not have dinner, but finish their drinks and leave, Guy weaving at the bar, not quite sure of what has happened, it was friendly and then it wasn't. April is shut in again, Dick is glowering, bitterly hurt that the bartender might have seen this. Should he have struck Guy? What will the bartender think of him and his act? Or his lack of action? It is very important to him that the bartenders think highly of him. We'll talk of this social façade later. At home, April comes out of the bathroom in her black pantyhose and shoes to prove to herself that she cannot arouse her faithless and depleted husband, and she is right. Dick looks out the window, smoking, while she puts on her nightgown and gets into bed. Guy is now talking to a painter about *Pierre,* looking at a young woman who has just come in with some creepy fuck hip bastard aware phony relevant shithead radical prick men's shop proprietor, who is carrying a copy of *Caterpillar.* He thinks vaguely of April and is delighted that she is angry at Dick. It is a high-school dance in the forties, the girls are unbearably, amazingly lovely under the Japanese lanterns. All the boys look like yokels, absolute yokels. To be a woman, to be a woman warm in that soft flesh, the incredible power of the very shape God has given you. Flush every pimply face in the room, stiffen every penis, as you bend and gracefully pick up the dime that you have dropped. Guy looks at the girl. It is a high-school dance and he is there in the smell of must from his rented dinner jacket. Then home alone, drunk, puke down the lapels, through the blank streets. Through the Hopper canvas. I have a vision of him at sixty. It is fearful and excruciatingly sad. It's as if he had one chance and didn't take it, didn't even know of it: a falling star while he was making a model airplane in the attic.

Guy's old friend* in the south of France was finally published by a commercial house in New York. His reputation had grown through his appearances in little magazines, and the publisher had finally decided to take him on to show that he wasn't afraid of publishing "fresh, young voices." You could die laughing. So that the friend, importuned by Guy, acted as a go-between for him with his editor—a "hip, young editor," you of course understand. Every publishing house worth its salt has one. They're the ones who find books like *V.* Very hip, indeed. Very young. In all events, Guy's book, a collection of short stories, as if you didn't know, was rejected. I don't want any surprises in this book, everything must be telegraphed. If you've been surprised, I didn't want you to be. Guy was dejected and depressed. In his American trust,

*The phrase may be read as an example of *lingua franca.*

in his mad naïveté, he thought that the editor would see him for what he was—what he thought he was—the direct descendant of Scott Fitzgerald: young midwestern writer clashes with the City, booze, sex, love, art. The editor read a couple of stories and was bored. Now, let me say immediately, that although I have harshly criticized Guy's writing, this was a book of better than average work—especially for the short story, which is still in the throes of "surprising" you. Dear God! Guy, at this time, was writing a severe, yet elegant prose, and was attempting to get at a specific thing in his work that nobody else was attempting. A friend of mine described it as pushing reality so hard that it fell over on its back and became a kind of fantasy. Of course, the editor didn't see it. Maybe he read the book on a couple of vodka martinis. Which, may he drown in. I was an editor myself some time ago and have little sympathy for them. The very best of them can read, the rest (you'll pardon the vulgarity) talk a good fuck. But Guy was crushed. Visions of Max Perkins. It's really too bad that old Max ever lived. His activities have perpetrated and perpetuated the myth that editors are somehow on a par with the writers whom they edit. Fitzgerald and Hemingway didn't need him. Wolfe would have been better off without him. One can see that wise smile now as he talks about some exhausted novelist's book as if it were a piece of meat. You cut here, you put this there, chop a little here. But what did Guy know of all this? This is New York!

This bored editor, how cool he had to be. No offend the signed writer. No insult Guy. At the same time, be sure to keep Guy sure of himself (ha-ho) by inviting him to send on future work. This is all such old stuff that I'll make up the letter that Vance Whitestone sent. I'll try to include all the elements of a good rejection letter. Those of you who are writers will recognize the stink immediately. You readers will understand slightly the boredom of getting one of these letters. O.K.

Dear Mr. Lewis:

I'm sorry—and I really mean sorry—to have to tell you that your book of stories, *American Vector,* is a project that we can't see our way clear to publishing at the present time. Both the second reader and I were impressed at the way you handle the shifting locales and characters that reoccur throughout the book, and we both felt that many of the scenes really came alive. But the intensity of the title story as well as the longish concluding story, "Bath of Snow," isn't really matched in the rest of the book. In the very tough fiction market of today, we think it would be only fair—both to us and to you—to present a "package" (if you will excuse such a word) that would make its own way.

I know that it must be small comfort to you, but I want to tell you that you certainly can write, and that I would be very interested in seeing any of your future work.

Thank you so much for letting us see your manuscript. I'm mailing it back to you today. Please give my regards to Jim when you next write him.

With best wishes,

Vance Whitestone
Fiction Editor

There are a number of phrases in this letter that can be regarded as having taken their place along with such jewels as "raining cats and dogs," "snarled traffic," and "incredibly naïve." The reader will see them for himself, and must not be surprised if I tell him that there is no rejection letter ever written by man that does not contain at least one of them. Guy believed this letter. Oh, he didn't *believe* it, but he thought it sounded—right. Sincere. (As if an editor would not sound that way.) And he was flattered that Vance thought that he certainly could write. Here is a test for editors to see if they are fit to pass judgment on books. They must get six right.

1. What contribution to jazz drumming did Big Sid Catlett make? Jo Jones?
2. What is uniquely excellent about Paul Goodman's fiction?
3. What is a swizzle stick? A swizzle?

4. Name the great trombone section in Ellington's 1938 band.
5. What is Jack Kerouac's best piece of writing?
6. Explain how a critic like John Simon cloaks his ignorance.
7. Recount two legends on how the Gibson got its name. (This should be easy.)
8. What is Kenneth Patchen's best poem?
9. Point out a failure of tone in *The Sky Changes*.
10. What is the basic flaw in Norman Mailer's fiction?

But I am amusing myself here—perhaps cruelly, I admit. There's no reason to dump on editors like this. Guy himself told me many years ago that it would be difficult for me to become a cult figure—my secret heart's desire —if I insisted on railing against the world of publishing. I ceased to rail for years, just occasionally trying my hand at old Sicilian spells to persuade their Dobermans and German shepherds to bite the asses out of their pants. A jolly surprise on those bright mornings when one rises to greet the day, etc. Down to the beach with a jug of Screwdrivers, etc. Hey, there's Larry Rivers, and there's Leo Castelli, son of a bitch! I hear Bruce Friedman may be out for the weekend. I mean just once, in the middle of that, to have those expensive mutts tear some ass.

I see that my problem is identity, i.e., my problem is that I *know* who *I* am. This is a big drawback to the writer of today who wants to sell his books. It's a kind of necessary poormouthing not to know who you are. The other face of that problem is the fact that I don't know who my characters are. It's *their* identity that proffers such difficulties. Sheila Henry once told me that I could be a great novelist if only I could create character—that's how she put it: "create character." That was in a little cabana out in the Hamptons where I had gone to dig clams. I called it "getting back to my roots." On the other hand, my characters all know who they are, too. If they could only stop from bumping into other people they'd be all right. But in my next novel, already sketched out for you, my first-person protagonist will be a publisher with a crisis of identity. He will be an uncircumcised Jewish publisher with a harelip who wants to "have" Jewish girls and marry a *shikse*. Title will be: *They Laughed When I Took Off My Pants*. I wrote to Guy about this some months ago from the comparatively safe distance of Rio, where I'd gone to buy a couple pairs of shoes. He thought the idea was good, if a trifle anti-Semitic. I tried Dianetics and Scientology for a while to see if this was so, but fell asleep during a particularly relaxed session and they took my tin cans away. But this is supposed to be about Guy. It must be obvious by now that I'm having a great deal of trouble making things up about him. (I feel as if I've been looking out the window at Stuyvesant Town for fifty years.) What I'd really like to do right now is read *Tristram Shandy*—but with this fifty-thousand-dollar advance half spent, it's write, write, write.

None of these wisecracks will help Guy. What I'm doing is trying to soften his defeat. That is, to make it seem as if his defeat doesn't matter, or that everyone is defeated. But everyone is *not* defeated, and because of some perverse twist of my mind, my literary concerns are not with them at all. We are measured in America by the graph of specific losses and individual disintegrations. You can go all the way back to Columbus and see that. Read Hart Crane. The poets know all this, that there is no winning at all for them: the times they live in receive their impression, and years later, someone will trace it, and recognize the enormity of their defeat. Not that Guy is a poet, but, as I said above, who knows?—perhaps an acceptance of this early book of stories might have changed at least some aspect of his life. Vance Whitestone still plays tennis twice a week and fills his gut with expense-account booze and steaks. Guy reels through his days, eaten with the loss of his manhood, his artistry, and with his bitter insistence that his prose is the finest being written.

Allow him to be loved.

Give him a stiff penis.

Make him realize the value of his early collages.

Let the deaf-mute Lena hear his voice, a miracle.

Let him fail with some grace.

Let him not see himself in this prose.

Allow him to strike out the acknowledged slugger of the barroom team.

Let him see that those particles of language, the bones of the very letters themselves, that are particularly his, in his imagination, can be marshaled, crafted, shaped, molded, urged and sweated into the absolute image of the old photograph. That lances the heart. Let him reread Hemingway and understand the man's harsh obsession with impotence as the engine that drives his people to their nightmare dialogue and rush toward death.

I had thought to give you some examples of Guy's current prose style but it would be too much to expect that the reader would willingly plow through such stuff. And I haven't got any of his current writing here anyway. Instead of that, I'll tell you a final story, which is not to be construed as any attempt at an ultimate revelation of Guy's character. I don't know anything about Guy's character. What I mean is that this story is no clue to Guy. There he is, drunk again. All I know is that he used to be great to be with. My opinion, of course. I could dig you up a number of people in and about New York who will tell you he was always a wrongo. In all events, whatever he was, he is now a drunken bore who forgets what he just said from minute to minute. Yet hath his mind entire. Some radium glow deep in the brain, making sense for him of all phenomena. Guy's character. What is that? I don't even know who he is. There is, in fact, no Guy Lewis. This is a novel. He used to have a different name, anyway. I told you that, too. Right now, under that old name, he is living in Santa Fe with Lena, on welfare and writing imitations of Chandler. Santa Fe is very good for that, you get into all that mysticism about space and mountains, after a while those lumpy metal sculptures look good. Smell the air! Look to the mountains! The Sangre de Cristo. You know why they call them the Sangre de Cristo mountains? No? Well, just wait till sunset and then you'll see. (Later: sunset: see?!—that's the event for this day.) So Guy is there. "I just wrote this *great* story about the Empire State Building, 'Bitter Tower.'" The Indians in their J. C. Penney blankets don't give a damn, nor do the chicanos. That's all right, he'll publish it in a new mimeo magazine out of L.A., filled with fresh, new voices and a twelve-page poem of Robert Kelly's—something composed in the bath one morning before he sat down to *really* write. Don't let me get off on any literary criticism here. Ruin my good name.

But Guy Lewis is gone. Guy Lewis is fixed forever on a fire escape, no gray in his hair, on West Twenty-first Street. Drinking gin and tonic on a humid, windless night in August. We should leave him there or else he'll press on you the prose I have devotedly spared you from reading. Let's say he's drinking out of a big pickle jar—plenty of ice and a half-pint of gin, splash of Schweppes. A new taste thrill! Liner going down the North River toward the bay and then the Atlantic. That is the scene. Let's say this is the evening of the day he got the letter from his friend in France about the Hopper print.* You'll notice how carefully the threads are pulled together in this book. I don't want to hear one more word about formlessness. And, at the very moment, Lou Henry is adjusting his wife's garter belt around his waist. Now, what else do you think is happening on this hot night? A famous novelist is giving a party in P-town. There's a girl there who is an old friend of Sheila's. She is living with a sculptor who now makes movies, movies that are, in his opinion, just possibly the best movies ever made about the erotic life. (That's, The Erotic Life.) Into the party there has wan-

*What about the Yankees vs. Detroit?

dered an uncircumcised Jewish publisher with a harelip, a-ha! In his hand, a copy of *Pudding Junction,* just published. The bio note says: " . . . in *Esquire, Playboy,* and *New York.* At present, he divides his time between his home in Brooklyn and a fishing cabin in Maine, where 'I loaf, read, drink,—do everything but fish. I hate fish.' He is married and his wife is both a fashion designer and street-gang worker." As Guy takes his second sip from the pickle jar, the Jewish publisher is rubbing his erected penis against a black girl who once read *Dutchman* in manuscript. Now, on to this final anecdote that will fully and totally reveal Guy's character to you.

First, though, you must know that this anecdote, in a novel, would serve as either that action just prior to the climax, or the climax itself. I tell you this in the event that Guy interests you enough to make you want to put him in your own novel. You can have him, and all his paraphernalia. You'll have to make up your own description of him, though. Give him violet eyes, to be sure. I wrote a novel called *A Time for Snickers* once, filled to the brim with descriptions. Publisher loved it, and advertised it in the real estate pages of the Fresno *Bee.* Sold eighteen copies in the Central Valley. That was fifteen years ago, the book's still in print, but you have to go to the publisher's warehouse in Anopheles, New Jersey, and get your copy out of the cartons on the third floor. But the plot was sketchy, and none of the threads of the novel seemed to come together, so Craig Garf said in the Amarillo *Scorpion.* "While Mr. Lewis* shows a real talent for sheer writing, there is a curious lack of compassion for his characters in these pages, and a seeming inability, or refusal, to bring the loose threads of his novel together. The reader is obliged to follow Lewis up dozens of blind alleys . . ." None of this has anything to do with me, of course. It does, as a *writer,* have to do with me, as a *writer.* That is, to paraphrase Cocteau: *"I* am Guy

*I wrote under this name in my youth, when Guy was someone else.

Lewis." And so, to this anecdote. Epiphany. This shatter-
ing climax. I joke because of the utter sadness of this
whole chapter.

To set the scene. Guy is in his studio on West Twenty-first
Street. A hot day. This was back in 1956, before I knew
Guy. The whole thing has been reconstructed in my head,
as is the novelist's wont. Not to say that it isn't true, but
it is pulled a little this way and that. Guy is very hung
over, trembling, sitting on a broken straight chair and
getting a cold beer down for breakfast. There is a large
painting on the wall in front of him, not completed. It
looks completed to the casual eye, but there is something
lacking, a touch or two to give it the tension and balance
it needs, and Guy has been looking for this touch for two
weeks, in a kind of despair. I have always envied painters
because, in my ignorance, I think that they never face the
problems of a writer—that their work is somehow
healthy and ongoing, to see the picture come out right
under the brush, moving out of the arm and hand, directly, as if nothing happened in the mind. This is all
rubbish, of course, I know that it isn't so, and I'm glad to
be able to invent Guy here, with his unfinished painting,
driving him mad. The hangover is not helping, this July
morning, the studio is hot already, the booze coming out
on Guy's forehead and upper lip, he stinks of it. Sweat,
you damn painters. I love your problems, they make me
feel better about *this* insane business. Sculptors are even
better, crashing around, the big bears that they are. I
always think of them as saying, HO-HO-HO!!—swinging
a twelve-pound sledgehammer. They're probably the
healthiest, the whole thing like making a tree. Guy looks
at the long painting, it is six feet by four feet, and moves,
in its browns and whites, toward the center, and is there
unresolved. He opens another can of beer and straddles
the chair. Another cigarette, looks at the battered metal-
top kitchen table, packed with cans, tubes, brushes, rags,
jars, and bottles, and gets up, puts on his carpenter's

apron. Two hours pass, sweat, beer, curses, adding, wiping off, scraping, nothing is happening to bring this wretched thing off. He runs down to the bar and gets two more cans of beer on the cuff, comes up again, drinks them, his hangover gone now, he's feeling a little better. (Guy was really much more interesting and valuable when he painted. I'll never know why I decided to make him a writer.) The studio is really hot, no breeze coming in the shadeless windows, the john out in the hall stinks. The bar downstairs is cool, and the ball game is on by now. He goes down, something will come to me, is maybe what he thinks, eating raw clams and drinking draft Ballantine. All in all, a good afternoon, the Yankees beat themselves on the bases, a small miracle in those days, believe it. Fucking off in the bar, didn't he ramble? Then, it's six o'clock and he has to go and clean up, change, there's an opening at the Tanager he's got to go to, Walter Pirogi. Puffs of primary colors on raw canvas. (Later showed at Martha Jackson and Howard Wise and is presently making films.) Guy owes him fifty bucks, so figures he ought to show up.

There is the goddam painting, as Guy gets into his chinos and seersucker jacket, and he is suddenly against it, absolutely against the whole painting and wants to rip it off the wall and kick it around on the floor, but grabs for a brush, stuck in a can of black enamel, and smashes it, loaded with paint, against the center of the canvas— of course, you're right, it makes the painting, everything coheres. But bear with me for a moment. After he hits the canvas in his anger and futility, he turns from the painting and chucks the brush back into the can, pats his pocket to see if he has his cigarettes. Then he turns, black paint is running down the center of the canvas in a thin stream from the heavy, triangular splash that is its source. The painting is forming, it is moving, and Guy steps back, really terrified, looking at the sliding paint in the mellow sun through the dirty windows. The painting is absolutely being opened by something inside it, the black center is the demonic face of some creature that has been inside the painting, inside the canvas, all this time. He knows this. He watches the thing open the canvas as a curtain is parted, so that it can look out at him. Face of Death. The shrouded figure on the road, silent under the trees. There is almost a rustle as the paint moves slowly down. Dear Jesus! he says, and steps back, looking into the eyes of darkness. It has come for him. Why not? Art is magic, that is true. This is a sign. When he told me this story, I believed it, saw how it could have happened. I've seen the painting as well. It's very strong, there is something uncanny about that glossy blackness that separates the undulant browns and whites. A girl who once held it for Guy for six months took it off the wall after two weeks because it frightened her. She didn't know the story either, nor the title of the painting: "The Valley of the Shadow of Death." Don't give me any lip about this being melodrama. Don't you think I know what melodrama is? This is Guy Lewis, lost in his bitter life, it happened to him. In those days he was a good-looking young man, before the booze wasted him. A year later he met Lucy—you don't want to hear about that. That one's already been written. A thousand times. This anecdote demonstrates that painters can be very weird. The painting is now in the library of a wealthy young man who is married to the first wife of a dear friend of mine. He's one of the intelligent and educated rich. You know what I mean? God save us all from them. I hate the rich.

"Today I went through old photographs of the family, my grandfather and mother and father and me and my sister and I am bringing some back to NY and I will show them to you. They are so full of love and trust I am terrified to move for fear I'll hurt them. There is one of my cousin Ella, my sister and my cousin Jean. They are sitting in the front yard and my sister has a pullover on and short pants and Ella and Jean have dresses on and my sister has one of those propellers where you pull the string and it sails up into the air; it dangles in her hand and touches the grass. She is sitting crosslegged. Behind them is Uncle Weston's old Chevvy coupe, parked by the yard. Weston took the picture and they are smiling into the camera. In the background, across the street, is the house where Ann Taylor Redding grew up. It is impossible to describe the lost sweetness of this old photo."

4

And Other Popular Songs

Bunny Lewis, Christian name Joanne, née Joanne Ward. This is going to be a tough one, because there is something of the archetypal about her. Which is to say, what I have in my hands here is a cliché—before I start. This will not relieve me of the necessity of presenting this woman to you, of course. I could leave her out of the book, but there is much of interest here, she at least will illuminate something of our friend, Guy. When Guy met her I was in San Francisco. You know about San Francisco, right? Dedicated provincialism, I mean, they have made of their isolation a thing of heroism. But it's a beautiful place, you can rot there in the most delicate comfort. Physically, it's incredible. Looks like a lot of cupcakes. Bunny's brother, after he was discharged from the Marines—he was a first lieutenant—opened an ad agency there. Branch in Berkeley, and a home in Sausalito. You can buy a lot of Eighth Street cups and pots in Sausalito—terrific! I was there when he met her. What was she about?

She was born in a little town in New Jersey named Boonton. I know this town, it's very grim. It will be better to have her born in a Long Island town, for our purposes, which will soon become dazzlingly clear. Frightfully

clear. So, she's in Long Island, you can pick your town,
let's put in on the North Shore. Her mother was the kind
of woman who served all her meals off unmatched tableware. "Each piece chosen separately, and with love."
You know what I mean. Also, put up those damnable ears
of Indian corn in October. That was the official mark of
fall. Little Picasso reproductions in the foyer. Not the
run-of-the-mill trash you see about, tasteful stuff. Listened to Bach. Watched the documentaries and Channel
13 only. Papa was an amateur astronomer, collected
rocks, grew a kitchen garden. He taught Automotive Me-
chanics in a vocational high school in Long Island City.
Too good for it, of course. But he was humble and never
put the job down. God bless him. Dignity of labor. "Give
the kids *some* chance to make a living in the world."
Bunny was vivacious and cheerful, a strong, healthy sort
of beauty. She drew, she painted, she could play the clari-
net and piano, she took ballet lessons at Miss Edna's, who
had studied with a New York teacher for years. She was
a cheerleader. She was voted the most popular girl in her
senior class. All of her friends were the sons and daughters of professional people. But she was taught not to be
ashamed of her own modest background. Her father
thought she would turn out fine. She did, I guess. Guy was
a brief aberration. She took him on as her father took on
the sons of janitors in his classes. Straighten them out.
Ah, that Indian corn! Oh, that roaring fireplace! Thanks-
giving dinner with relatives and friends from far corners
of New Jersey and Bay Ridge. Mama had a strong person-
ality, voice to match, and thought of herself as the daughter of a farmer. I don't know why. She and Bunny's father
had their children late in life because of the Depression.
If that isn't a clue to their characters I don't know what
is. In the ten years or so before Bunny's brother was born,
they went to leftist political meetings in New York, saw
Sovcolor films in the old Stanley. Her father wore blue
work shirts with subdued paisley ties under his tweed
coats. In those days he spoke of automotive trades as a

kind of art form, the machine, gleaming pistons, etc. Lay
a lot of Léger on you. Not on me. They felt good about all
this, ah, why not? It hung on, and hung on. The Wards to
this day, speak, half seriously, about their phone being
tapped because of their antiwar activity. A household of
warmth and beauty, deep understanding. I have trouble
with this stuff because it is so far removed from my ken.
What I'm trying to say is that they lived on the imagina-
tions of other people. I don't trust those harmonious
households, not an inch. There's a broken heart for every
ear of Indian corn. When Bunny married Guy, both her
parents were in their sixties—and still, well, still *young!*
Strike two! Give me a minute and I'll give you a few facts.
Some more data to put in your head. They deeply missed
"Omnibus." What ever happened to Charlie Chaplin's
Oscar? Did the Jew really understand the aspirations of
the Negro? Bunny was studying psychology. Along came
Guy, cap over his eye, drunk and disorderly. She was a
mark for him. Oh, she'd done a little wild-oat sowing in
college. An art major here, a Student for a Democratic
Society there, some law students, some medical students,
a couple of athletes. Some were O.K., some were not. But
the mark of doom was not on them. I don't know how she
met Guy, but we'll imagine it was in Provincetown, after
Labor Day. The dunes, the sea, the wind. Guy told her
about his dreams of death and within the hour she was
blowing him. Guy's penis kept getting soft and she
thought she was doing something wrong. That was even
better—she would have to work, hard, to give Guy all her
love and understanding. This isn't heartless of me,
though it may seem so. These are people born to decent
families, the fact of their helplessness is a human fact,
i.e., don't tell me that you have to know what happened
to Guy in the garage one day? Or, what secret terrors
Bunny was exposed to when she was eleven, when she
realized that her father and mother . . . Isolate flecks. To
understand the particular configurations of total disaster. How slowly it comes. Bunny would have been hap-

pier marrying some doctor with liberal politics and that mixture of contempt and respect for money that so marks hip, middle-class youth, i.e., money is only good for what it can buy, *ergo,* give me my share. By "happier" I mean within the terms of that kind of marriage. People like Guy shatter people like Bunny because they fall apart from the inside out. The people with whom she might have been "happy" flake off in pieces. A mistress here, a little favor there for some lout, and thisa and thata, and all of a sudden they're giving you some reasoned thought about Richard Nixon, or they're telling you about the essential nobility of Nelson Rockefeller. If they run through their salad days with consummate speed, they tell you why they deserve to be the victims of Eldridge Cleaver. But Guy just went blooey. The novelist's task is to tell you why all this happened. That's why I won't tell you. Isolate flecks. Is it totally ludicrous to say that we are all paying for Cortez and Cotton Mather? Every kernel of that Indian corn represents a dead Indian. I say, give them all the muscatel they can drink. Don't give them jobs, but allow them to sponge off the government forever. You know what you can do with automotive trades, right? These are all non sequiturs.

Concerning Bunny, I find that I have varied possibilities. The joys of art. I can send her to any school I want, give her any sort of first date. How about her first real affair? This is all the most deadening tripe.* A gossip-column style would perhaps most exactly limn her and be amusing as well. "Dining in the Pavillon yesterday, Bunny Lewis told of her first meeting with Guy Lewis, the painter and author of *American Vector.* Shocked at seeing Lewis eating a ham sandwich slathered with red paint, she was reproached by the artist, who said, 'I've always maintained that paint is in my blood.'" . . . "Bunny Lewis, skiing at Aspen last winter, took a rather

*"Deadening tripe" is a Deep Image.

nasty spill and wound up in the hospital next to Sheila Henry, the whore, who had also had a mishap on the slopes. 'First time I ever hit the ground with my legs closed,' Miss Henry quipped." . . . "Bunny Lewis, flying to Israel for a benefit performance in honor of the Stern gang, found herself seated next to Adolph Hitler, the ex-Nazi leader. *'Ist mein Zimmer fertig?'* Hitler said, firing a Luger into the ceiling of the pressurized cabin. Miss Lewis, calmly inserting her finger into the puncture, called for the captain. 'I've never been so fuckin' scared in all my life,' she admitted on landing." Why not? A life encapsulated in quips, anecdotes, and dull-witted PR releases. It would be a kindness to her, and her life might turn out better. The ups, the downs, and the ultimate comeback before her death in a bathtub full of vodka. In some Los Angeles motel, a copy of *Airport* half-read in the bathroom. She could be an actress and star in a Ronnie Tavel play, "dance," "sing," and "shit" in her hat. That's "Gut Theater," babes, don't you ever forget it. Why, oh why, are we presented with this immovable life? Desperately normal, and filled with the most incredibly uninteresting phenomena. A leader of cheers, a beautiful girl, the belle of her high sɔhool. North Shore High, well-integrated, a good football team, an Arista, which Bunny made in her sophomore year. Political science was her chief interest. One day she fell down and scraped her knee. One day she had her period and her mother told her she was growing up. One day she gave a boy a hand job under the stands at the football field. His name was Ralph and he came all over her skirt. One day she read *The Sound and the Fury* and cried. She did a lot of things, every day. Said a lot of things, conversation, they call it. You put it into quote marks and demonstrate your ear. "God, what an ear for the language!" She was a very nice girl, a good human being, and she met Guy Lewis. Guy took her to galleries and showed her how the painters did it. This was later in her career, when she was going to Barnard, majoring in psych. She wore a silver friendship ring that her first lover had given her two years before. She said to Guy, "Oh, that? That's a ring a—friend—gave me." Guy wasn't curious in the least, and they had their first argument. Bunny wanted him to be jealous, she waited to see flakes scale off him. But Guy was wasting inside, into his third novel now, and writing film criticism for *Flikk*, a magazine of mixed-media arts. He took it for granted that Bunny had played around. Hadn't she gone to Barnard? Isn't that where the girls eat shit and bark at the moon on Zig-Zag Day? But I am making light of Bunny. Underneath this fashionable rig, she was strong and womanly. She wanted to help Guy, oh, not in any corny way, but be his Wife, be his Mate. She believed in his stories, his novels, and his criticism. She typed out his *Flikk* reviews for him, clearly and honestly marveling at his insights into the movies he handled. All in all, he wasn't bad at it, to tell the truth. His particular magic was to see American violence in everything that Hollywood made. She learned a lot of sex from him, not corrective sex, but opulent sex. It was healthy for her to get out of that early madness that had led her to believe that sex was all blissful orgasm and free bodies. Guy made her realize that there is a great darkness to it. His own, of course. She wept as he told her about his blasted affairs. Barnard seemed smaller and smaller. Somewhere around this time Guy changed his name and got old and Bunny left him. The story around town at the time was that Dick Detective was fucking her. That may be true. The Dick thought she was class. April was O.K., she knew how to dress, but Bunny had a speech pattern and look to her that was strictly Bonwit Teller, from panties to handbag. Dick was impressed, even I know that, and I was not even conversant with the scene at that time. (Now that I think of it, I haven't been conversant with the scene for some years. Is the mission bells still ringing but?) Then I heard that Bunny went back to Guy, then left again. At the present writing she's seeing a young discotheque owner who has part interest in a haberdashery on St.

Mark's Place, by the name of Kama's Ultra. Smoke a gang o' boo in the back room, Jim! Then fall by the Electric Circus. They know it's a phony, though, don't get me wrong. She is deeply unhappy, and is known to her new friends as Joanne. This is all conjecture on my part. She may still be with Guy, for all I know. I saw him last summer pitching a softball game, but I couldn't bear to talk to him. They were knocking the hell out of him. Curiously enough, I saw Bunny the same day. She was with three or four ugly Beautiful People, laughing, crackling, full of life, but underneath . . . ! It was clear that her heart was broken. She was carrying a torch, she took a lot of time out for tears, she won't die, she'll live on, she gets that old feeling, there'll never be another Guy, she won't forget the night she met him, the songs of love are not for her, she dances with tears in her eyes, her love for him meant only heartaches, she'd like just one more chance, willows weep for her, every street's a boulevard of broken dreams, she covers the waterfront, she can't show her face, she smokes, she drinks, she never thinks about to-morrow, sometimes she can't even think of his name, sonnets she writes of him, she's aware her heart is a sad affair, their love went out just like a dying ember, she'll never smile again, half a love never appealed to her, she rushed in where angels fear to tread, she has those blues in the night, she's got it bad, she doesn't want to walk without him, she'll remember April, he'll never know just how much she loves him, she falls in love too easily, she should care, it was like a trip to the stars, he came, he saw, he conquered her, oh, how they waltzed, it's just her luck to be in love in vain, she wishes she didn't love him so, haunted heart won't let her be, don't cry, Bunny, she didn't see her in his eyes any more, her heart cries for him, she'll never be free, she talks to the trees, she won't cry any more, he's unforgettable, that's what he is, she wishes he were here, she needs him now, the night is bitter, she'll never stop loving him, and, frighteningly manic, she says, "Drink up, all you happy people!"

It was a sad day for Bunny when she first read Carl Jung. This is not surprising. There are hundreds of people who have been wiped out by a reading of the old man. She thought that she understood what he was saying. Right after this she met Guy, who was also reading Jung, whose influence was stampeding into his prose. Together, they analyzed Guy. They analyzed Bunny. They analyzed their relationship together. They went crazy with the heat, as the old saying has it. If you can't stand the heat, etc., etc., as some doddering fool had it. In the middle of this Jungian orgy, Guy went out to meet Bunny's parents in Katydid Glade, or whatever. You make up the name: Smoky Chicken, L.I. That was a scene, from Bunny's point of view, it was fine. She always had this good relationship with her parents, as we all know by now. I.e., nothing to pin her misery on. I don't like people like this, it is sheer envy, of course. It was amusing, of course, a scene by Terry Southern, right? Hollywood satire, sharp and bitter as a jelly doughnut. Shake up the folks down in Amarillo and bug Judith Crist. Gotta hand it to Hollywood, they've really come along in the last ten years, yep. So, our scene. Both Mr. Ward and Guy were wearing blue work shirts. Mr. Ward would show him he was nobody's dumb old father . . . a copy of *Evergreen Review* and *Tulane Drama Review* on the canvas beach chair, etc. Bunny was particularly lovely, a crocheted dress, white, white sandals, all this against her golden tan, honey-colored hair tied carelessly with a bit of white silk. There was a long talk about the dignity of labor (I swear to God) along with a couple of pitchers of daiquiris. Guy put those away like Pepsi, aha, aho! A little Léger, a little Picasso. Into the particular mystique of the southern Negro in the North. Mr. Ward knew about that, you better believe it. They wanted work, they wanted dignity, he was doing his bit—always had. He got a little juiced too, started coming on about the Spanish Civil War, and so on. The Depression when he worked etc., etc., here and there, etc. Oh, those fuckin' daiquiris, that Puerto Rican light, pale rum. Bunny and her mother were making a salad, he's nice, a writer. And a painter, Bunny said. Don't get them like that out here in Two Car, L.I. Why don't you and Papa move back to the city? You know that Papa has his work here, the school, the house is finally paid off. The bones of life are unutterably sad. The two men were zonked, Mr. Ward ruined the spareribs with enormous thoroughness. Plenty of beer, they pitched horseshoes. Bunny changed to shorts and a blouse and Guy hated her for it. She was apart from his concerns, this house still filled with her life, she had changes of clothes inside. And the house reminded him of his mother's in Kansas City, the very way the shade fell on the garage roof. When they got back to the city they had very unsatisfactory sex, why not?—then dressed and went out for a drink or two. Guy introduced Bunny to Lou Henry and Dick Detective, standing at the bar. It may well have been this night that it was settled that Guy would do the linoleum cuts for *Sheila Sleeping.* Guy was full of warm words for Bunny's parents, especially her father, because he had got zonked with him. The clear values of the lush. Bunny was still lovely, if a little strained, and Dick was imagining her thighs. A night, a night, yawn, they all went to get hamburgers about one o'clock in the morning. Years later, Guy would write a story about this late snack, full of oblique dialogue, the point of which would be that Bunny liked to make love more than he did, and was therefore at fault. Bunny should have met Lucy at this time, but Lucy had already left town, and was living in Taos with a gallery owner. Bejesus, sold those snowcapped-mountain paintings still wet. Someday I'll tell you about Taos, which I know little about. I've got a good title: *Piñon Fagots.*

Speaking of Taos, let me invent a story about Bunny spending some time there before she met Guy. She was in, let's say, her sophomore year at Barnard—about nineteen. It was in Taos that she recovered from her first really serious love affair. It had been with a married man, a young Englishman who wrote serious historical novels. You know the kind. Those in which nobody picks up a halberd when he should be picking up a quarterstaff. Reviewers love this muck. ". . . has made the long-maligned 'historical novel' not only respectable, but has fashioned a work of real literature." And so on. This ace was, all the time he wrote these novels, working on his Real Book. Of course. In the meantime, he enchanted his faithful readers with what *really happened* behind the official façade of the Third Crusade, etc. He was in America to help promote a movie that was being made out of his second novel, *Unicorn Crimson, Unicorn Grey,* and met Bunny at a cocktail party given by one of her history professors. A hip academic crowd.* Wear you down talking about *Pale Fire.* Bunny and the English novelist left, they went to a Riker's for a bite, then to Bunny's apartment for coffee and another drink. My wife, I love her, yet. I never knew that I could meet. But you're so young. We've been somehow estranged since I've begun writing my *real* book. And on into the evening and so to bed. Bunny was thrilled, guilty, frightened, sorry for him that he should be so sensitively lost. In the morning, she made creamy scrambled eggs for him, with oregano and parsley, bright and beaming in her robe. The coffee was weak. Perfect. Sara Lee Cheese Danish. This can be called a Breakfast à l'Amour. Middle-class girls are known to serve this to convince themselves and their fuckers that they are not simply whoring around. The whole thing has a different connotation than it has if, say, the girl gives one a cup of coffee and a cigarette. What the curious connection between breakfast and virtue may be is a task for the sociologist. He started to talk about a divorce. You'll love London. And so on. It was another movie, the same one Lou and Sheila were in out on the Coast.

*There's no need to be venomous.

He left. Letters, letters. London in the fog. The Cornish coast. I met Mick Jagger at a party. Bunny in school, Jung & Co. flying over her head at incredible speed. She talked it over with her mother and father and they warmly and understandingly told her to lay off this guy. Now we come to Taos. The reason I mention this Taos sojourn is because it points up a really rare coincidence in the life of Bunny Ward. The reason that Bunny went to Taos is that she read a book of poems by a young man living in the Southwest: the cover of this book was a line drawing of the Sangre de Cristo range by Guy Lewis.* Bunny didn't even notice his name but the drawing moved her, there was something clean and powerful in it, the mountains seemed close, a presence to move her from her preoccupation with her tragic affair. Far from New York and London. She would cleanse herself there! I personally know a lot of people who have gone to this area to cleanse themselves, to breathe clean air, to paint, to write, to see, really see the Indians, to live cheaply and well, to relax. After a while they disappear and turn up, years later, in the Bay Area, or Los Angeles. The few who stay drive around in station wagons to see each other and complain about billboards and White Sands, and congratulate each other on the blue sky. They make a lot of herb tea and the women weave blankets and give their visitors *ojos de Dios* to take back to New York. It's a good life and curiously destructive of art. Or let me be clearer: everything is art, so that the blanket, the pot, the dinner on the handmade table, and the poem and painting are all one. A wish to be tribal, an insistence. They show you the Sacred Mountain of Taos, it is somehow theirs. Their poems are about mountains and sky and desert sunsets. The place is filled with hack painters who live off rich summer tourists, and they come to be friends with these painters. Why not? They must be friends with these painters, or die of loneliness. Against this they set the corruption of the city:

*The reader may assume that Guy had gone, at some time, to New Mexico to make this drawing. I am not aware of any such trip.

or the City, i.e., New York, as if that fact is news. What I am trying to get at is that the corruption of a community like Taos is more interesting. An endless Christopher Street, or Georgetown. But somehow True, and Real, and Beautiful. Because this rotten art comes out of these breathtaking mountains, its rottenness is ameliorated. When it comes out of Fifty-seventh Street, ah, *then* it is rotten art! In any event, it can trick the weary traveler. It tricked Bunny. She even kept a little notebook.

So there was Bunny in Taos. She walked around, she sat in the Taos Inn, went to some parties given by rich men from Oklahoma who came to buy paintings and look at the mountains and do whatever the rich do on vacation. I hate the rich. She also wrote letters to her mother and father, telling them about the smell of piñon and the marvelous adobes, Indians, etc. Another thing that she did was drink a lot. As a matter of fact, she got herself a little habit, and had plenty of very bad hangovers, sick to her stomach, trembling hands, cold beer for breakfast. Nothing dirtier than a booze addiction, even though she just touched on it. Later, this brief excursion into the world of drinking would give her an understanding of Guy's problem with alcohol. And would make her sympathetic to it. Too bad. It would have been much better if she had retained that TV idea of it being a kind of manifestation of wit and charm. I'd really like to see Dean Martin puke on his tuxedo, that would be a show to remember! She even had the horrors a couple of times. And she kept her notebook as faithfully as she could. When she had nothing at all to say, she'd jot down a comment or two on the weather—always the same. One of the glories of New Mexico is that you not only forget that you're in the United States, you forget *when* you're in the United States. You get the idea that you might bump into Lawrence at the post office. Hello, Lorenzo! How's the new book going? How's the old dark secret blood? Instead, the earth shakes every once in a while as the AEC gets on with its underground testing. It's America all right. But it is not my task in this novel to ruminate on America. I'll leave that to Europeans who have been here about five years or so. They'll tell you all about it, starting with the essential nonseriousness of its art. Then they hit you with packaged food, bad movies, dirty air, and so on. The polite thing is to listen as if you didn't know about any of this, then agree and add some indictments of your own. Works like a charm.

She wrote a couple of letters to her Englishman, but threw them away the next day. She was simply articulating her thoughts, getting them in some sort of order. It distressed her that she wasn't really unhappy about the abrupt conclusion of what had promised to be ... here she was in Taos. I was going to send her to Taos with a girl friend, but it's better that she stay alone at this period of her life. She'll have plenty of time to be with friends when she comes back to the city to meet Guy. The young man who had written the book of poems for which Guy drew the cover was not in Taos any longer, she had half hoped to meet him, although it was the drawing she liked, not the poems. Not that she disliked the poems, she simply didn't remember them, or, let's say she remembered them as a kind of genre poem she had read before; that seems fair enough, and certainly possible, considering the book. I know this book and it has those poems in it, all about Being Alive In The Fresh Air And Living With Your Woman And Eating Good Food And Smoking Pot And Watching Your Woman Getting Dinner Ready The Way Her Simple Skirt Molds Itself To Her Full Hips Outside The Voices Of The Children As The Evening Comes Down On The Mountains Fuck You America You Can't Change This. With a lot of Mexican friends (Spanish friends, that is, in the Great Southwest), and Indians drinking tokay and muscatel. Plenty of battered, dusty VW buses in evidence too. But the poet had gone away, gone to the Coast, I think. Lou Henry said he met him out there when he had occasion to go to San Francisco on a business trip.* He was living in Haight-Ashbury where he was considered something of a freak because his poems neither rhymed nor scanned. But you'll have to take Lou's word for that. I don't even know what Lou was doing there. Business trip, indeed! I'm getting into trouble with these people, as soon as I stop watching them, they start moving around on me, and acting in an utterly uncharacteristic way. Now I've had Lou out in San Francisco and Guy has apparently been in Taos or environs. When they made these trips and for what reasons I have no idea. The prose obeys me, but these people that hide behind the letters are doing God knows what. At this very moment Sheila may be in Miami Beach, watching the dog races. But that's Sheila outside my concerns; the only real Sheila is in Chapter One. The girl with the long and lovely legs. For now, I'd better get back to Bunny before she leaves for New York.

But before we go back to Bunny in Taos, let me say a word or two about her marriage to Guy. The slow decay of that state. What she wanted out of the marriage, outside of helping Guy, I don't know. She loved him, indeed. What sort of chance did she have with him? Or with marriage to anyone? A nagging dissatisfaction afflicted her as it afflicted most young women of her education and class. She wanted love, and a good man, eventually children, but more, more. Not to grow old surrounded by housework. To be something, herself, not Guy's wife, but herself. Life made into a progression of startling events, so that each day there might be a party or a new friend, something to offer brightness and interest. There was Guy, drunk, his impotence becoming more fixed by the week. Bunny began to misread his prose, to softly criticize it, so that he seethed and snapped at her. She wasn't helping him, and she felt old, at twenty-five. There were girls with whom she had gone to school whose lives were

*A business trip?

dazzling in their excitement and fun. On the surface, in any event. What to do with these women? What is it that has made them so dissatisfied with themselves? Why do they marry either erratic neurotics like Guy, or young lawyers and doctors who send them off to Long Island all summer? Out of commercials, they walk on the beach, slim, tanned, lovely, their children playing in the sand, they swing their beach bags cutely, they die in front of your eyes as they guzzle their Pepsi. Before thirty, their lives have run into the most barren ground so that you feel as if they'll hang from a nail until sixty, when they'll die, quietly. Sheila Henry is not unlike this in her dissatisfaction. But the remedies are not there—to marry Sheila to Guy and Bunny to Lou . . . just as impossible for these women. Bunny, imploring Guy to be her husband. She would have long talks with her mother and father about this. Good advice, they'd give her, voices from the clouds that had nothing to do with her life. Amazingly enough, she didn't start drinking. But God, how she wanted out of the whole thing. She left him and came back after he had sent her a dozen letters, long letters of despair and devotion. He loved her too. He made her a brilliant collage and mailed it to her and she came back to him. Nothing was settled. She was "seeing" Dick Detective, who explained Guy to her in long, understanding talks, as they lay in bed together after making love. Watched the smoke from his English Ovals slide along the wall. Dick wanted them to stay together, it wasn't his funeral. That is the expected task of the friend called in for advice, anyway. I once told a woman that she'd be better off and happier if she left her husband and she struck me in a real rage of exasperation. I had overstepped the boundaries of friends' duties. Dick, though, really wanted them to stay together, at least until he had eased himself out of this desultory affair. He didn't want a free Bunny in his life. She thought Dick was fine. And he made love to her with great finesse. She didn't like the subtle references to his love for April, but she herself was going on and on about Guy, so it was all right.

She was dressing well. As the marriage got more and more impossible she looked better and better. She took to going to parties alone, and dancing with all the youngest men there. She didn't care at all any more about what anybody had to say, and Guy could go fuck himself. But how bitter it was to stay out all night and find that Guy hadn't been home either. She'd take two-hour showers to wash herself away. Sometimes he'd be in the apartment when she came out of the bathroom, starting in on a fresh drink, snapping his fingers to Frank Sinatra or the Beatles. She left again, packed everything this time, Jesus Christ, to save her life. She moved back with her parents for a while to observe the niceties and to observe their marital secrets, study what they did and didn't do. She went so far as to write to her English lover of five years before, a friendly letter. Perhaps England? But got no reply. God help her. She went to Paris for a year, at her father's insistence, and had an affair with a Parisian artist. He didn't paint as well as Guy and bored her to tears talking about the political complexities of abstract space. That's what he painted, his "trademark" a black heart in the middle of each canvas. When she left Paris, he was about to have a new show, verbal descriptions of paintings that he had never done. She saw herself in the mirror on the plane back, and thought she looked younger, cosmopolitan. When she got to New York she found she was out of style. It would have been better had I simply not got involved with Bunny, she's hopeless. I'll bet you a dollar that she gets a job in a publishing house assisting a hip young editor, or one in an ad agency as a Girl Friday to the Creative Director: you know, the trimmed Van Dyke, flowered ties, conservative bells. Smokes black cheroots from Holland. And is working on a novel. She's one of those bright, lovely, intelligent people who should have never been born. We'll finish with her postmarital career by putting her in a Connecticut motel one December afternoon, with a gang of young, creative profession-

als, half-drunk. She's in the middle of a laugh, those perfect white teeth. They're all watching the Giant game.
Bunny, who is now called Jo, suddenly recalls Guy's absolute contempt for football. "For morons who like pain."
She looks around at her friends and hands her empty
glass, smiling, to her escort. Her heart a chunk of burning
metal. She'll marry this man.

Now we'll go back to Taos for a bit, to end this chapter.
I want to give you a story. Of course it's literary. Did you
want life? This story is atypical, which is why I tell it. It
doesn't strike me as being true, but it appeals to my sense
of the grotesque. A friend of mine told me the story and
swore that Bunny herself told it to him. I give it to you
here, with some embellishment, to be sure, but the essential structure is right there. I had planned to write this as
a short story called "Sexual Liberation Front," but the
knowledge that the fiction market of today is very tough
prevented me. I am nothing if not a cunning author.
  The Taos Inn. This may well be the cutest place west
of the Mississippi. We find there, one day, a bright blue
day, of course, Bunny. She is sitting with a man in his
mid-forties, a chunky man, with a beefy, gross face. They
are drinking bourbon and dark Mexican beer, and are
both a little drunk. This man is dressed in that fashion
that *Esquire,* some twenty-five years ago, dubbed "the
Bold Look." Padded shoulders, wide lapels, a spread-collar shirt, large-figured tie in a Windsor knot. The suit is
of that fearful color called electric blue. He's everything
he wants to be today, i.e., back to Taos where he was born
and raised, to buy land and houses, he has big plans, open
a gallery. Yes, indeed, he made his money in oil up to
Oklahoma and now he's ready to come back home, ran
away when he was fourteen, saw the world, combat in-
fantryman, paid his dues, painted for a while. Jesus, the
Adam's apple on him, bobbing up and down as he lied. I
would assume he lied. I think he was probably a salesman out of Abilene, come to Taos to rest after an opera-

tion. Bunny thinks he's eccentric. He is. Not in the way she thinks, as she'll find out this very afternoon. The booze goes down easier all the time, the bartender is reading a two-weeks-old copy of the *Village Voice* behind the little bar. The man crosses his legs and jiggles one foot. Now he's into some lie about the South Pacific, Bunny likes this man. There's something so—western about him. Open, candid. There is a kind of character about his face, the lines in his forehead, his hard mouth (with a ready laugh). His speech is direct, and not a little gauche, it sounds as if he's reading a long poem by Anne Waldman. "Sometimes I like to make real hot chili, you know what I mean by real hot? Well, that's the kind of chili I like to make. My guests all say, Harlan, you make a real hot chili, maybe a little *too* hot! And I just laugh, because you know, there's no such thing as chili being too hot. I have oysterettes with it, and sometimes make my own tortillas, real Mexican tortillas, and serve ice-cold beer . . ." That sort of talk. Makes you fall down in a faint of ennui. Not Bunny. This was O.K. with her, but I grant you she was in pretty bad shape at this time, drinking her sweet ass off. Well, when they were pretty well zonked, Harlan asked her to come up to his house, he'd like to show her around, etc., etc. He let her assume that it was his house, but he was renting it, cheaply, because he had agreed to make some minor repairs on it. They got in his car, a Jeepster, Bunny liked that too. A workaday car, covered with dust and clay. I must tell you that Bunny looked fine this day. Harlan had his hands on her breasts as soon as they were in his living room, stroking and squeezing them gently as he called her attention to the rough *vigas* on the ceiling of the room. The original *vigas!* Maybe as much as 150 years old! His hand on her buttocks, and she moved her legs apart so he could work his fingers up between her cheeks. I submit that this is indeed a strange sight. This young woman, fashionable, very Bonwit collegiate, and this meat-cutting-machine salesman, last seen in Lawton or Wichita Falls, in this suit that could bring eighty or ninety dollars on St. Mark's Place. Electric blue! Even the color is precious today. Think about them, swaying in the center of the living room . . . wait a minute, by now on the couch, her skirt is up around her waist, the sight of her white lacy bikinis has him slobbering, his hand covering her plump, moist crotch. One must admit that her hand is stroking the bulge in his electric blue trousers. In a trice . . .

Now, maybe ten minutes later. Harlan is on his hands and knees on the oiled adobe floor of the bedroom, naked. His penis is extraordinarily stiff, and jerking up and down spastically. Is Bunny beneath him? Is Bunny kneeling before him as he prepares to service her? Where is Bunny? At this point I suggest a pause in your reading so that you may dream up your own fantasy concerning Bunny's whereabouts. Does her whereabouts have any redeeming social qualities? Perhaps you would prefer to bring in a third protagonist. I would prefer a maid in the shortest of skirts, wearing black nylons and high heels. But I am not writing pornography, so I'll have to save the maid (Annette). The truth of the matter is that Bunny is standing up, behind Harlan, in her shoes, stockings, garter belt, and panties, and she is beating him with his belt. His back is full of red welts, the skin is broken in a couple of places, and Bunny is gagging, trying to stifle her nausea. Harlan is not completely happy, because Bunny is wearing simple brown low-heeled shoes. He would prefer her to be wearing glistening black boots. But she is whipping him, which he never expected, I mean, he thought that he would be able to lay her, but he never thought that she would gratify his most secret desires. To tell you the truth, neither did I. You may infer from the fact that she is becoming nauseous that she is not a sadist. There's something about this Harlan, the way he stroked her crotch, such pleading, such an incredible shyness. She is sorry that she is not wearing boots, for him. It must also be said that she is masturbating herself as she whips him. She is only flesh and blood, and she is stirred. Sex is basically incredible, i.e., the body help-lessly goes down the line with it. By which I mean that even priests have the most voluptuous wet dreams, and a woman's hand can make the most flagrant queen have an orgasm. His penis doesn't know that he's a homosex-ual. These are truisms, thoroughly investigated by Sade.

At last, his body releases itself and he comes, ah, dear God! The face, blessed purity, the sunset scarlet on the snowy mountains beyond the picture window in the bed-room, their flesh the rosiest color, aglow in the soft light in the room, gouts of semen spurting on the packed adobe floor, his thighs and belly quivering as he is emptied, Bunny retching, her arm tired, furiously rubbing her clitoris. He lies down on the floor, blissful, she stops mas-turbating as he turns to look at her. She drops the belt and sits on the bed, ashamed of herself in her underwear. Her garter fasteners gather her stocking tops in a bunch and she feels that the sight is ugly and puts her hand over her right thigh.

He drops her off at the Taos Inn, and she goes in, alone, to have a couple of quiet drinks. She gets up and goes into the ladies' room and throws up, then sits on the toilet and brings herself to a long unsatisfactory orgasm. In the morning, she wakes up with a vicious headache and a delicate stomach. In her mind sees Harlan's back, his face in the rich light of evening. Harlan is gone, the bar-tender tells her that afternoon. He's left him enough money to buy Bunny a drink, "with his respects." The young woman is moved by this. A couple of nights later she goes to bed with the bartender. This seems to me to be a curiously American story. This yokel masochist, this simply perverse act carried out in that lavish sterility of the Southwest. In later years Bunny would think of it every time she wore boots. She told Guy about it once and he started to read to her from Stekel.

5
Images of K

It is only fair that the reader know that I once deeply loved Leo Kaufman—oh, for many reasons. The reason that I state this here is so that as I investigate and reveal certain aspects of his character and life to you, such labor will not be mistaken for malicious zeal. There is nothing the matter with Kaufman. He surrendered, that's all. There's nothing dishonorable about that, it occurs every day. But in a book like this, a slap here, a dash there, a couple of anecdotes mixed with gratuitous opinion, a figure can emerge that has little to do with the figure as it really exists. Not that Leo exists, but even the invented Leo has a set in my mind that is different from the way he will turn out here. All these people are follow-the-dots pictures—all harsh angles that the mind alone can apprehend because we have already seen their natural counterparts. I'm saying that if you know Leo, you'll see him plain. If not, you'll see what I let you see. The beauty of fiction is that it goes two ways, at least. Out, into the world of the reader's experience and in, into the stringencies of the writer's tyranny. The more harshly the latter is exercised, the purer the prose, so that as Ford builds his overwhelming lie, Christopher Tietjens, we move, with each word, into a realm of total truth. More real than the most meticulous conversation of John O'Hara. Prose will kill you if you give it an inch, i.e., if you try and substitute it for the world. What I am trying to do, through all this murk, is to define certain areas of destruction. I mean, we are surrounded by dead men. Who put them there? Why are they dead? Why are they dead, yet have their minds entire? Men turn the corner and disappear. How about the man who took the garbage out and threw himself away? When he came back down the alley with the empty garbage pail in his hand he looked real. Didn't he? Was he you? Was he Leo Kaufman? Was he my imaginary Leo Kaufman? He would someday soon go to a party and joke with Frank O'Hara. I remember Frank that night. He came to a party that was down on Avenue A and Second Street to welcome Ed Dorn to New York. Dorn never showed up, and Frank came late, very drunk and with two of those pink-faced kids in well-cut jackets and faded levis. Leo puked in the sink that night. The swan song of the Beat Generation. Paper-cup party. Let's say Leo puts the garbage pail down in the kitchen and his wife looks at him—this is his first wife, Anne. She's in her burlap skirt baking whole-wheat bread. Ah, God, I wish I were joking. She thinks Leo is there, but he's turned into prose, and has lost all control of his life, or, let me say, the little control he had. Now I own him. I even gave him this name, Leo Kaufman. I thought about it for a while and rejected the original name, Leo Marowitz, preferring to make that his second wife's (Ellen) maiden name. He hasn't met her yet, but she's out there waiting for him, as in the legends of love. At this time, 1959, Ellen is only fourteen. She's been reading *Arrowsmith* and Kipling. "What are the bugles blowin' for?" Leo, is the answer. He is standing in the kitchen, Anne is baking bread. He runs his hands up her legs to her crotch

and buttocks and grins with that most difficult of male
grins: that is, the grin says that he means it and that
he doesn't mean it, or, more precisely, he means it, but he
won't be annoyed if she rejects his advances because he
doesn't mean it all that much. I don't know what she does.
That night they either make love or Anne goes out to the
movies and Leo zonks himself out on a fifth of muscatel,
listening to Civil War songs of the Union Army. Or they
have a talk about the trouble with their marriage. Perhaps friends come over. The important thing to remember is that Leo is out at the end of the alley with the
garbage. This guy in the living room is l e o. He is a poet
of brilliant gifts who writes directly out of his life, that
is, whatever is happening to him becomes the stuff of his
poems. Anne hates his poems because they are all about
her and their marriage. They are edged and poignant,
and held finely balanced between bitterness and tender-
ness. To publish them or read them to friends in their
white candor is the major reason for the fact that Leo has
been saved from utter despair. Anne, of course, cannot
understand this. Or perhaps she can understand it, but it
doesn't matter to her whether Leo is saved from despair
or not. When Leo reads, she feels insulted and humiliated. She has her point. But Leo is struggling for his
very life. If Anne knew this, she might feel more charita-
ble toward him. But what can he do? Can I have him say
to her one night, "Jesus Christ, Anne, I'm struggling for
my very life"? That would bore you to tears, even in the
context of a controlled narrative. Leo would bore you,
perhaps he does already. Most artists bore you to tears in
their lives, anyway, because they refuse ever to forget
how things felt. They don't know how to play "New Day,"
nor can they successfully turn memory into sentiment.
This trait of the artist is often confused with bitterness or
cynicism, but it is simply an insistence upon remembering the specific emotional responses that were once actual. All frozen in the artist's nerve centers, so that at any

moment he may embarrass the company by some remark
better left unsaid. His life a clutter of dead event, pre-
served with the exquisite care of a master taxidermist.
Never can tell when some of those dusty birds up in the
attic might come in handy.

Let's put Leo back in 1956. A day in late May, humid and
overcast, depressing New York weather, when nothing at
all seems possible. A great anger over living in the city
that grinds you into fine pieces, and makes you pay for it.
Leo in the Bronx Zoo, on a bench, drinking from his third
pint of muscatel, in a seedy raincoat, corduroy cap.
Three-day beard. An old friend of mine wrote a story
about Leo in this very situation, but was ultimately kind
to him and ended the story by putting Leo down into the
African plain, where the lions live, at which point the
story ended, as Leo fell asleep in the shelter of a great
boulder, warm and somewhat content in his drunkenness. This did not really happen, but the story made its
point. It's not a bad story at all, except for the fact that it
ended, and stories that are replete with sadness and despair never end at all: they stop. The way this day ended
was with Leo going home, sodden, to Anne and his
daughters. She said nothing and he fell asleep on the
broken-down couch. You can't solve any of these things
by fiction. Or, let me say that you can make sense of them,
and even solve them, if what you mean by fiction is prose.
Prose. If you pay enough attention to the way the sen-
tences fall, and if the events are presented in only the
clearest contours—what is salient—you will have a perfect fiction: reality. On the contrary, the attempt to make
a photograph gives you reportage. Read "The Knife of the
Times." It ends, "Why not?" 1932. Imbeciles ranting about
proletariat fiction. All the keys that brilliant artist presented us with—scorned. Look to the poets or suffer the
death of the imagination: then the sensibility atrophies,
after which the beast arrives. In various guise.
Leo was in the Bronx Zoo, drunk. He is looking for his

totem, the black bear. I should make the black bear a kind of symbol for Leo, but it's too obvious. Dancing, performing tricks, garlanded with artificial flowers, every once in a while the trainer giving him a swig of sugar water out of an old Three Feathers bottle. But extended metaphors tend to fall apart and one is left with a problem of mere engineering. Leo was no black bear, but in his particular kind of sentimentality, he thought of the black bear as his totem. There was a reason for this, based on childhood experiences and his reading. A lot of wishful thinking thrown in. The problem with accepting primitive beliefs is clear. You see this man going along with them, step by step, you know, sun, stars, astrological signs, spooks, and the rest, then one day, with a grossly vulgar realization, this son of Ra-Set, this Capricorn, discovers himself on line at Key Food, in his shopping cart such things as Cap'n Crunch, Broadcast Corned Beef Hash, Tide, Kool-Pops, a carton of Silva-Thins. All the gods are falling under the table in drunken hysterics. Anyway, there was a reason for this black bear business, which it is too boring to make up. Believe me when I tell you that I really could make it up, but I don't want to. I'm interested in Leo. Follow the dots.

It just occurred to me that I could make Leo into Guy Lewis before Guy changed his name. Then I could talk about this novel being an inquiry into the nature of reality. What is the Nature of Reality? Whatever it may be, this poor son of a bitch in the park, name of Leo Kaufman, is suffering. We'll take one thing at a time. First of all, Leo is really Leo (invented, of course). I mean he is not, was never, and will not be (I'm almost certain) Guy Lewis. Now, for another stroke of the brush on this panoramic canvas. Leo knows Guy, and knows him quite well —has known him, in fact, for some seven or eight years. They met in a roadhouse near Lake Hopatcong, New Jersey. Or near Budd Lake. Leo taught Guy the Glen Island dip this night. The name of the place was the Blue Bird. Or maybe the WigWam. The Hi-Top? Harry and Mary's?

The Seven Gables? The Blue Front? Five Vets? They ate pizza and danced to "Again," "Haunted Heart," "It's Magic," "On a Slow Boat to China." Maybe Guy taught Leo the Glen Island dip. I was there that night with a girl named Diana Glick, whose favors I passionately craved. It's very strange that these two men, whom I didn't know at the time, should turn up as characters in this book.

Leo was in the Bronx Zoo, drunk. He can't bear to go and see the black bear, because the wine is breaking his heart. The day doesn't help either. His hair needs a washing so his scalp is itchy, which increases his misery. None of this is meant to be funny. Let us take the case of the man whose wife leaves him. That's one thing. Now, give him a toothache. That's another. I can hear him wanting to say to her as she packs her bag, "You can't leave me! I've got this fucking toothache!" Is that funny? Now, let's have him really say, "You can't leave me! I've got terminal cancer!" Laughter is markedly decreased. The wine is breaking Leo's heart, everything is brutally sad. Anne has told him that she is going to San Francisco with a jazz piano player, a friend of the family. She has never been unfaithful to Leo with this man, Duke, she tells Leo. Perhaps that is true, in any event, Leo believes her because he must. She loves Duke. Leo is a better poet than Duke is a musician. This fact never enters Anne's mind and if it did it wouldn't matter. Yet she married him because he was a poet—as will Ellen. Leo pukes on his scuffed shoes, bitter wine streaming from his nose.

Leo saw her standing in the sun. Just like Dick Haymes in the old movie. She was something to see, etc. The value of the popular song is that it deals in superficialities that release the emotions. Scratch the veneer of those pedestrian lyrics and you look into a crystal ball of the past. Anne was part of a group of women students come to Leo's college for some senior dance. Leo tweedy, in the fashion of the day, with a polka-dot bow tie, cordovan loafers. Anne went to some sort of teacher's college and excelled in athletics. It's hard to describe her overall look, because I can remember only how she looked later, when she was Leo's wife and the mother of two daughters. I always see full skirts, sandals, peasant blouses, hair in a thick braid down her back. She always looked as if she was going out to some wheat field in the Ukraine with black bread for the harvesters. But her face escapes me —a bright, glowing, Scots-Irish face, the father of such a face could easily grow tobacco in North Carolina and serve as lay minister. Sunday suppers of fried eggs, red beans, lettuce and tomatoes, coleslaw, cucumbers, sourdough bread, cold ham, apple pie, tapioca, iced tea, and lemonade. Blue haze in the valleys, smell of magnolia and honeysuckle. To marry Leo! There was a Jew in the town at the bottom of the valley, owned a dry-goods store. He wasn't a bad feller, extended credit and had developed a slight drawl. But Leo, Leo Kaufman. From Tremont Avenue. Anne's father knew about the Bronx, of course. The Bronx Bombers. And the famous Zoo. He was dead, though, before he ever met Leo. A break for both of them.

Shall I talk about Leo's father for a moment? Just for a moment. He was a sheet-metal worker, became a foreman, a good boss, knew his business, looked like an Italian. Short, solid, bald head. A virile-looking man. Leo's mother hadn't satisfied him sexually for fifteen years. He masturbated and occasionally got himself blown in East Harlem hallways by Puerto Rican and Negro whores.* In a remark calculated to explain his marriage to Leo, Mr. Kaufman once said: "All I ever wanted from your mother, Leo, is that she should once, just once, make my eggs over easy." Don't laugh. This story is only funny to young lovers, to whom the world is a popsicle. As a parenthesis, let me note that Mr. Kaufman hadn't satisfied Leo's mother sexually for twenty years. It would be simpler to say that Mrs. Kaufman was frigid, aloof, insensitive, etc. The

*Here, one of my readers must remark on the sexual exploitation of black women by Jews. This is called "reading between the lines."

truth is that the old man was a bad lay. He even had trouble in the hallways uptown, his mind full of bits and fragments of images of VD films he had seen in the army. All this serves to explain Leo's life, right? What a bore. Another thing: Leo's father thought of himself as a craftsman. Oh, God. Dignity of labor business, Jesus. So that Leo, in his maturity, also equated working with the hands with innate nobility, and reconciled himself to his own poems by pretending that they were products of mere craftsmanship: otherwise, he would have thought art effete. How anybody ever gets out from under anything is a puzzle. I have made my own father into a legend in order to prevent myself from finding out anything true about him. It is difficult to accept a life as nothing more or less than the pattern it makes.

So, Leo in his tweeds. And Anne. Smell of Castile soap to her. In that sultry June evening, he spoke to her of his poems, his arm around her waist. Anne made pots and ceramics, and wove. Craft. Her own strong hands. One here begins to see the configuration that will soon lead to love. That was love already. He saw her standing in the sun.

After Anne left for San Francisco with Duke and the children, Leo married Ellen Marowitz. Not right away, of course. They met about two years later, after Leo had placed himself in the way of three or four devastating affairs, refining his suffering with enormous style. These affairs are too banal to go into here, but can be taken care of by a swift gloss on their basic characteristics. The art freak was the first girl; then the passionate divorcée, older than Leo, a woman who would be perfectly set in a Greyhound bus station coffee shop, 3:20 A.M., Galveston; the bright career-girl from Long Island (looked and acted much like Bunny Lewis); the political activist, last seen visiting her parents at Passover. Then came Ellen. Lovely, stupid, and gleaming with health. Looked like a Northern Spy. After washing her hair, the resemblance

was more to a Golden Delicious. Leo was later to defend
her brainlessness by quoting her opinions to friends and
acquaintances: "Last night Ellie was saying about Mo-
zart . . ." "Ellie *liked* Eric Hawkins—except for his dancing." "Ellen said this great thing about *Metropolis* . . ."
And so on.

They met at a party given for Leo after his first reading
at the Guggenheim Museum. She came with a friend, a
young man who had first persuaded her to read Leo after
he himself had come across a long poem of his in the
Minimalist: "Raincheck for Fidel and Che," written after
the Bay of Pigs. Up to this time, it was the worst poem that
Leo had ever written, so it was greeted with enormous
enthusiasm. Why not? His disillusion with America, his
ironies, his bitternesses. Jesus Christ, a professional
poem, indeed. Beginning of Leo's surrender.* Along with
the reading of this poem, Leo also read his Woman-Wise
poems, if I may so designate them. These were poems in
which Leo triumphed over invented love situations.
Came through the muck and mire of heartbreak invented. He had this audience agape. A far cry** from
Leo's first reading at the old Seven Seas coffeehouse back
in 1957. Heyday of the beatniks, and everyone walked out
on him during intermission, disgusted by this square
shit. They had some idea they were going to hear a
Jewish Ted Joans. I was there that night and recall the
owner of the place (who later edited—edited, mind
you—a magazine whose first issue was devoted to
the works of Guido Caesar Matarazzi, the well-known
Pastelist) saying, with some pique, "I didn't know
you wrote real *poetry!*" So much for the artistic fer-
ment of the fifties, a time filled with sweet cats. (Not as
sweet as they are now, of course.) The difference is
that the old sweet cats conned the citizenry, whereas
now they con divers foundations. The level of incompetence has remained constant, although the haber-

---

*Not the absolute beginning, as we shall see.
**I am indebted to Sir Walter Scott for this phrase.

dashery of the poem has been altered.

This party was in the midtown apartment of a man we shall call, for that is a useful phrase, Horace Rosette. There's a rumor around that he used to hang around under the boardwalk at Coney Island, but I place no stock in it. I place little stock in it. I tend to believe the rumor has some foundation to it. Of one thing you *can* be sure —he is, indeed, that same Rosette who has memorized all of Kenneth Koch's plays. He's a sweet cat. Some would call him a sycophant, but I prefer to think of him as an ass-kisser. At the time, he was going with a girl he had met under the boardwalk, who was now Eastern District Coordinator for the Committee to Disseminate Contemporary Poetry. So much for American mores today. The committee had arranged for Leo's reading at the "Gugg" (as we call it), paying part of Leo's fee. This committee also published *Seed,* a journal of the arts, edited by the lady coordinator and a promising young poet named Biff Page, who had once interviewed Ron Padgett for the underground newspaper, *Akimbo.* As I recall it was a brilliant interview, replete with Padgett's playful and witty (and unorthodox) gibes.

Rosette made his living compiling anthologies of verse —clever anthologies, to be sure—none of your run-of-the-mill offal: *One Hundred Poems on the Daffodil; Bridges: Poets Express Their Love* (picture of—you better believe it—the Brooklyn Bridge on the jacket); *The City in the Poem* (beginning with passages from Homer, Rouse translation, on Troy). Cute as a fucking button. He also lectured on his own books, helped arrange reading tours for poets who had a certain flair for jollying the audience, and wrote reviews for various journals. He was, as you might have guessed, on the advisory board of *Seed.* This was an entrepreneur, brother. Imagine Henry Ford giving you a stanza of "Among School Children." Help, help! Climbing the book-lined walls. "My books are my tools," he was fond of saying. "A good book is like a good awl," he would sometimes say, young guests gathered around

him. "Yes, a good awl—or plane ... one can ... shape one's
life with a book." He was quite a case, a specimen of the
times. I might say here that he smelled Leo Kaufman, the
first subtle aroma of putrefaction.

But let's give Leo a break, that is, assume that at the time
of this party he was coming out of the emotional som-
nambulism of the two years he had spent without Anne.
Oh, those were fantastic times for Leo, most of the hours
spent drunk, staring into his glass, or at the floor. He
snapped at friends and got himself into the most hopelessly alien beds, with women whose sole duty in life was
to comfort artists. There's never been a satisfactory name
for women like this except for one that was current about
ten years ago to describe women who clustered around
jazz musicians: "tune freaks." The women whose nifty
little apartments Leo found himself in were poem freaks.
Came from every walk of life. Following are twenty
things that Leo and some of these enraptured girls did
during those two years.

1. Ate a mountain of paella.
2. Went to the Art and the New Yorker theaters every
   time the picture* changed.
3. Struggled through a hell of a lot of those creamy
   scrambled eggs I've already spoken of.
4. Lost a raincoat in Dillon's Bar.
5. Found little Italian restaurants tolerable only if the
   diners feel each other up during the antipasto.
6. Spent $1,457.70 on cabs.
7. Went to Stony Point, the Hamptons, and Connecticut
   for a lot of warm martinis and burned chicken.
8. Watched the dawn come up in Tompkins Square
   Park.
9. Got drunk on Virginia Gentleman in some rich man's
   house in Great Neck.

*I should say "film."

10. Got drunk on Gallo Burgundy at an opening at the Tanager Gallery.
11. Got drunk on J & B, Jack Daniels, and Seagram's V.O. at an opening at Martha Jackson's.
12. Met hundreds of roommates, friends, ex-lovers, college buddies, people who danced and acted, filmmakers, directors, and junkies.
13. Smoked a lot of marijuana with that serious, intense look that characterized the heads of that era.
14. Went to parties at the Artists' Club.
15. Bought flowers "spontaneously" so they could feel like characters in a bad French movie.*
16. Were on hand for Ornette Coleman's opening at the old Five Spot.
17. Went to innumerable readings in coffeehouses, bars, galleries, churches, and lofts.
18. Stained a lot of sheets at the Albert, Brittany, Marlton, and Van Rensselaer hotels.
19. Read *Kulchur* and commented on the arrogant clique that ran it.
20. Painted four apartments.

If the reader will take all these things, and imagine for himself the events leading up to them, the places through which Leo and his various loves passed to get to do these things, and the events that followed these things, he will have a general picture of the hip New York scene during those years. In other words, the reader is asked to write the book that I have no interest in writing. I don't give a damn about the scene during those years. Most of the time I was in Hoboken which town the residents insisted was even hipper: which is why they spent all their money on the Hudson Tubes. Got a lotta clam broth! Got a lotta beer there! Got a lotta . . . clam broth! Got a lotta . . . bars! Very hip scene. A lot of actors went over there to find out who they were. Never seen or heard from again—a small

*I should say "film."

blessing. The fewer actors the better. Leo wrote a play once, very flimsy. I told him so and he told me that I didn't know anything about the theater. Who does? I don't trust a verbal art in which the language is held in contempt. Even the dance is better if you can bear to put up with all those symbolic twists and floor stampings. Dancers are simply stupid and go with it all the way down the line— good for them. Actors think they know something. Have you ever talked to an actor? It's like calling up Dial-A-Prayer. This is very intolerant, but who can care about an audience?—which they do. Well, this is another digression, I'm trying to give you an outline of Leo's basic activities during these two years. I've left out most of the important things, i.e., the black terrors, the weeping, the self-pity that made him, so many times, an object of contempt, and someone to be made fun of.

One of the things he would do in those years would be to fall asleep at parties. He'd drink so much that he would simply fall asleep, in a chair, or on the floor, sitting leaning against the wall, his warm drink next to him. Before he fell asleep he'd mutter and grumble into his drink, or talk to the floor for a while. When I think of him doing this, I always seem to hear bongos, or Sonny Rollins playing "Wagon Wheels." There sits Leo, his drink in his hand, people dancing around him, talking, Guy Lewis nervous and anxious lest the booze should run out before morning. Here and there in the room various poets and painters, musicians, tune freaks, smashed girls from Antioch and Bennington and Bard at this, their stopping-off place before Westchester or Brooklyn Heights. Always some young man who just got out of the happy house: attempted suicide. Ah, these seminal years, with everyone trying to get into everyone else's pants. As a friend of mine once wrote, Brook Farm. Revisited. One man at these parties used to bait Leo unmercifully over his dozing and his misery. "Oh, for Christ sake, Leo, stop bitching about Anne—get yourself straight!" He gave him the name of the Flake-Out King. The fact of Leo's undis-

guised misery enraged him. This same man, when he
was cuckolded, put his fist through a plate-glass window
on Fourteenth Street. Standing there at four in the morning in his undershorts, screaming and weeping. The
"moral" is clear—misery is totally democratic. Another
man who was insanely in love with a beautiful girl
dancer was powerless to prevent her from sucking a lady
poet's cunt. Oh, this is a vulgar way to put it, I know. You
know what I mean: ". . . powerless to prevent her from
becoming involved in a lesbian affair with a genteel lady
poet." This man too tore at Leo in his stunned and
drunken misery and when confronted with his own poi-
soned love turned the girl in to the police for possession
of marijuana, then cut his wrists. Tell me about the
fifties. The shoulder patch of the 2nd Armored: HELL ON
WHEELS.

We should get back to the party at Horace Rosette's
house and have Leo meet Ellen. But there's time for that,
I have it sketched out in my notebook* and can drop it in
here whenever I like. Plenty of time to send Leo down
life's road. (Figure of Death outside Kansas City.) Leo
keeps sliding around on me. I'd like to keep him in these
years after Anne left him, eating his eggs at dawn in
Riker's, puking in dozens of bathrooms with Museum of
Modern Art postcards on their walls, looking for a clean
shirt under piles of magazines and filthy socks. But he
seems to insist on fading back into his first marriage.
What about that? I don't know anything about the early
years of that coupling, I met Leo and Anne after they had
been married five years. Anne was fine, warm, solid, self-
reliant, a good cook, a patient mother. Served her meals
off unmatched tableware, each piece chosen separately,
and with love. She put up ears of Indian corn in the fall.
The reader will see how the images of this book persist
and reappear. That is because these things themselves
are the plot. They carry all the meaning. Isolate flecks.

*A notebook! You mean this thing is planned out?

Even Vance Whitestone saw that, one day when I happened to bump into him in Buenos Aires. I must say he
was a bit embarrassed, because the young lady he was
with was most decidedly not Mrs. Whitestone. He smiled
a lot and introduced her as a colleague. O.K. What do I
care? I was there merely to buy a couple of pairs of shoes.
I am nothing if not fashion-wise. He started to talk about
Guy Lewis's *American Vector,* apologizing, etc. Somehow, he seemed to think that I had sent him the manuscript. I let him think it and hid behind my daiquiri. He
said that he'd heard a lot about my new novel—he said
"Novel." At that time it was called *Isolate Flecks*—still a
good title. His colleague thought I was Biff Page. She was
very hip and one and a half sheets to the wind. (These
kids don't know how to drink.) I told him that it had been
turned down by seventeen publishers so far but he said
not to worry, it would surely find a place. Why didn't I ask
my agent to send it over to him? My agent *had* sent it over
to him and it had been rejected by one Lee "ZuZu" Jefferson. The reader can well imagine my surprise when,
after another drink, Vance said that he and ZuZu would
have to run along: they were down there trying to sign up
Manuel Gordo y Chingar, the Argentine concretist.

Ears of Indian corn in the fall. In the spring, white
curtains with a daisy pattern in the kitchen. Burlap
skirts, paisley blouses. Shoes from Fred Braun. Baking
her bread and hoeing her kitchen garden. In a moment
of uncharacteristic candor, Dick Detective told me that
she wore a red satin garter belt, trimmed with white lace.
For months, my image of her was rocked. The Dick may
have been lying—you can never tell with him.

A word or two about Leo's apartments during this two-
year period. How many he had I don't know—three or
four, I would guess. Those apartments, dear God. He
moved from a bad one to one a little worse, until finally
he was in some desperately wretched railroad flat on
Rivington Street, or maybe it was Suffolk Street. The

harsh overhead lights, the dirty dishes, clots and gobs of garbage in the sink. The brown toilet and the kitchen bathtub with the smears of dirt on the bottom and sides. In his inviolate isolation, linked to the world by telephone and taxi. He would take girls back to this place and get them into bed without putting the lights on. In the morning they woke up screaming, so to speak. Off to Ratner's for breakfast. Afraid to go home at night except by cab. That key in the police lock: image of loneliness, as we all know from Baudelaire. You remember Baudelaire. Good-Time Charlie, they called him in Paris. One of them symbolists. The bear in his apartment, crashing through the empty whiskey bottles and beer cans, looking for a clean shirt. The places would get so dirty that he'd be ashamed to hire a woman to clean them, and he'd move. Bags of rubbish in every room, grime on all the furniture. He had mice but wouldn't get a cat because "men don't keep cats, man!" God, the image of manhood that he had formed in his brain—out of which warped conception would ultimately come his famous poems. Whatever was left of Leo, the composer of those cruelly lucid early poems, retreated, until what confronted you in his later years, after his marriage to Ellen, was an invention—some doggedly romantic figure with the ethical equipment prescribed by the legion of Mailer imitators. Journalistic man. Poems to please the hacks who ground out columns for the *Post*, the *Voice*, *New York*.

You could crawl on your hands and knees behind some packing cases to avoid saying this. I could, that is. But it's valuable to investigate, however superficially, the destruction of a poet. Or of any artist. Leo, you will understand, is not Lou Henry, the man without qualities. At this moment, I'm looking at Kaufman's name on the cover of *Poetry*—last month's issue. In this issue he has a poem about his wife's ass. Christ, it's a bad poem. I can name you twenty people who like it—and there must be hundreds more like them whom I don't know. On the other hand, maybe five people know that Leo died. As he came to be more of a poetic figure, so did his poems shed their strength. Poems of manhood, they became. Their essential burden something like, "if there's one thing I've learned in the last twenty years, man . . ." and then what he learned would be something like, "chicks dig cooking." Or "chicks like to go down on me when I'm sweaty." That's how chicks are, saith Leo. Football, baseball, basketball. Telling you on the phone what Joe Chooch said about what Gil Hodges said down in St. Petersburg after Tommie Agee said something to somebody about something . . . "so that was the final batting order, man." Your mouth open, what to say to him? Leo, Leo, leave me alone. We are not friends any more. Tell it to the Marines, tell it to Pete Hamill, tell it to some sweet cat who just got out of the Airborne, tell it to Joel Oppenheimer, who knows more about baseball than you'll ever learn.

What is this phenomenon? This death that comes about? Of course, it is because the artist is not needed, but what has that to do with the artist? Rimbaud, we don't need you. Hear? Rimbaud! I say *we don't need you!* Uh-huh, just a second, let me finish this line . . . OK, now, what was that? Fail, fail, you dead letters. Lovely in defeat. Don't tell me this is romanticism, you idiot. I know all about romanticism—that's losing with a fat check in your hand. Then you tell everyone what a whore you are. Yes, I understand you, you whore. Then they get angry, you get it? They want to be whores in a sweet-cat kind of way. One lies down in front of the new XT-14BQL Medium Flame-Thrower Tank, then later writes a screenplay for Otto Preminger. What a Whore I Am! One makes a commercial—why not?—all that bread, man, I might as well get some. Oh, What a Whore I Am! Some "aware" broad interviews one for a big slick and misquotes one. That lousy bitch! Oh, What a Whoooore Iiii Aaaaaaa-mmm! Art is very harsh, i.e., it doesn't care what you meant to do.

You will understand that nobody sells out the way it happens in the movies. It comes in bits and pieces, for whatever reason. Dream of fame.

   Curse of art. Terror of art. Only you know what you did, maybe a few others. I'm trying to get at something here that pertains to Leo and to many others: if you must fail then fail in the terms of your art. Don't abandon it for something that looks like art but which is apple pie to you. So that, in the pursuit of its easy crafting, you become a Great Man. It then becomes sour grapes for anyone even to breathe that you once had something real occurring in your work. Because now, ah, now, you have dazzled the bushers. Norman Mailer knows what I mean. What is the difference between twenty shiny armies of the night and one failed deer park? Fail in the terms you are helpless within. Terror of art. Consider Dexter Gordon. I'm talking about gifted men—Leo is not Lou Henry. What a long time, what labor it takes to make an art. Takes just as long to make a failed art. Hart Crane, Weldon Kees, Scott Fitzgerald, Hemingway. I honor those men because they fell apart in their own work. I grant you this is subtle. But the artist knows what his own work is. When Leo went to Horace Rosette's party, the aroma of decay about him, he went there as a man who had succeeded—in work other than his own. He knew it. But it was some bad and muddy painting that was in his apartment as a child. Vague browns and brackish greens, a lake, some monstrous globs of trees hanging out over the water. Far away. He saw it but he didn't see it at all. The false manufacture of some manhood that had nothing whatsoever to do with his life became the mine from which he excavated these pleasing poems. Ellen knew this work, then, she met him, as someone utterly different from the man who had put out a first book of poems the clarity and loveliness of which are stunning. I look at that book today and the man (whom I loved) who wrote those poems appears in my recollection as some young figure who may as well be buried in one of the bleak cemeteries that break Brooklyn into divers territories of the living and the dead. It was his true, gentle manhood that was killed in those years. Took the garbage out and threw himself away. He himself thought that he himself came back down the alley with the empty pail. But that figure merely looked like Leo. Science fiction. I'd rather not say any of this. But a poet is no common thing. I'd rather he were simply defeated, that his sweet line lost its charge and power. What do *you* know about my life? I hear him say. The poor bastard doesn't know that I invented him, he thinks he's real.

Here are three anecdotes* of Leo Kaufman, prefaced by his most famous quote, which I took down verbatim. The occasion for this memorable saying was a hot night when a friend of mine and Leo's—who is now supporting the saloons in Los Angeles—Leo himself, and I, were drunk in one of Leo's disastrous apartments. In a fit of drunken candor, our friend told Leo that he had never seen such a dirty place in his life, whereupon Leo said: "All the dirt in this house is dirt that blew in the windows."

Leo was giving a reading one night at a grim little coffeehouse on the Lower East Side, known as the Blue Whale. He was nervous, as usual, before he read, and, in the Cedar Bar, where he was sitting with Dick Detective, Guy Lewis, some redheaded tune freak who wore huaraches and ate candied orange peels, and a closet queen who had once published in *Trace,* Leo decided to eat something bland to avoid further upsetting his nervous stomach. He ordered spaghetti with butter sauce. When it came, Guy, who had decided to irritate Leo that night, made a number of unkind remarks concerning such a dish. Why don't you put some fuckin' garlic on that, Leo? How about some pepper an' a little cheese? How about makin' the fuckin' shit edible? Leo, more involved in preserving his façade of dignity than in any actual fury, shoved the spaghetti, untouched, over to Guy and said, "You eat it, you cocksucker!" Guy took the plate and put

*This book seems to me to be merely a *collection* of anecdotes.—ZuZu Jefferson.

salt, pepper, garlic powder, red pepper, and Parmesan on the spaghetti and ate it, with such remarks as "Hey! This is good fuckin' spaghetti, Leo! You want some?" etc. After a minute or two of this, Leo got up, went to the bar, and had a double pink gin. This is an anecdote about the failure of tactics.

On a night of the most intense heat, I walked from the Cedar Bar, which was air-conditioned, down to Dillon's, which was not. I don't remember why I did this, but it might have been to avoid being stuck in a conversation with Ward Willis, the editor of *Found Object Review,* a quarterly that would send you screaming into the night. It was, incidentally, in this journal that Sheila Henry first published, in an issue given over to an interview with Guido Caesar Matarazzi. Let's say it was for this reason, anyway. Dillon's was always at least twenty degrees hotter than the street, and on this night, it was almost empty, except for a few bowling-machine fanatics, a drunken potter at the first table by the door, and Leo Kaufman, who was hunched over the bar, swaying to the jukebox. As I recall, the tune was "Are You Lonesome Tonight?" A bad sign. I walked into this steam bath and touched Leo's arm. What would one say? I must have said something like "Why are you in here? It's so *hot.* Let's go." Whatever. Leo looked at me, the sweat running down his face, his shirt soaked. "That's why I'm in here. Doan you understand? The reason I'm in here is because it's so fuckin' hot you can't stand it!" He looked at me with utter contempt and ordered another boilermaker. This is an anecdote about the success of tactics.*

Years passed. Leo was married to Ellen. They were invited to a party at the Dakota, or some other elegant place, to celebrate the arrival in this country of some brilliant young playwright who had done something or other. Somebody fucked a chicken in one of his plays, or something. Young English instructors talking about Phil

*I'm afraid I don't know what the author is getting at here.—ZuZu.

Whalen. A forty-five-year-old patron of the "Y" who waited at the door to see if Ornette Coleman would show up. Beatles records, bad dancing, a lot of imported cheeses. Buffet supper with rice glop.* Leo was not at home here, and the fact that Ellen was a great success, dancing, being groped, etc., did not seem to help. He reverted to older form and drank himself blotto, then sat in a little straightback chair in the corner, where he tried to assume the air of one who has a benevolent contempt for all. This doesn't work with the rich, and the rich in manner. The rich possess sensibilities that extend to the exterior surfaces of their garments. Then Leo, after telling Ellen, for the fifteenth time, that it was perfectly all right with him if she danced with somebody in bell bottoms and a work shirt, got sick and puked in his lap. Later, he would say that he didn't want to give the bastards the satisfaction of puking on the carpet. Some spectacularly retarded Englishwoman from Springs, L.I., married to a very rich painter, went up to Leo and told him that she thought it was marvelous that he had just thrown up like that—just *thrown up!* It was really marvelous. Marvelous. It was marvelous. Just marvelous. This is an anecdote about the absence of tactics.

About eight months after the party at Horace Rosette's, Leo and Ellen married. The ceremony was performed at the Ethical Culture Society chapel, and Ellen's father, who was not altogether pleased at this, was in a better humor than he would have been had they been married at City Hall. Leo trimmed his beard, got a haircut, and bought a new blue suit for the occasion. For the past year or so, he had been a wild sight indeed, his hair standing out around his head in a great salt-and-pepper corona, his beard long and untrimmed. Ellen was bursting with health and vivacity, in a pale tan suit, white stockings

*I am indebted to Joel Oppenheimer for this word, used by him to describe near-unidentifiable food. It is usually applied to dishes made with tuna fish.

and shoes, and a white silk kerchief around her neck. You will understand that during the months of their courtship, Leo became more shabby and disreputable-looking than ever—to prove Ellen's love for him, perhaps. He met her once at Lincoln Center to see the New York City Ballet and was twice chased away from the corner by policemen, who thought he was panhandling. To see him, in his unbelievably rumpled suits, broken shoes, his wild-haired head, with Ellen, this little Golden Delicious, this Eskimo Pie, in her immaculate and expensive clothes, her eighty-dollar boots—it was fantastic. Beauty and the Beast. Lou Henry wrote a poem about that time called "Beauty and the Beast," but it was about himself and Sheila. Thus do hacks find their inspiration. I doubt if Leo had ever met Ellen's father before the ceremony, and a good thing it was. Ellen's father was pleased that his daughter was going with a Jew, although certainly Leo was not the "nice Jewish boy" of song and story. If he had seen Leo, he would have sent his daughter off to a kibbutz, or away to Paris, another good place to turn into somebody else. He knew that Leo was a poet, but thought of that as being something like a television producer, you work and work and then you get your big break. Mr. Marowitz was in the business of manufacturing drapes, curtains, etc., for very chic and expensive specialty shops, and was worth about 150 grand a year. Ellen had gone to Smith and Barnard, and liked her father. Her mother was dead. I was at Ellen's father's house once, quite recently, at Christmastime. They were celebrating Christmas and Hanukkah together. A fucking piñata that would break your heart, hanging from the ceiling. Mr. Marowitz was feeling his Canadian Club that night and made leering advances to a very attractive maid who had been employed to serve at his little holiday party. (Her name was Annette.) Leo put his hands on her a couple of times as well, smiling, smiling. It was a nice party. Played Beethoven sonatas, some Irish folk songs, and danced to the Beatles and the Stones.

There's no sense in going into the whole marriage ceremony. Nothing untoward happened, and everybody went
downtown to a friend's loft, a painter who had begun to
sell very well out of Martha Jackson's, with shaped, ar-
chitectural canvases. He wasn't a very good painter, but
he had an idea, right? What is art if not idea? A dullard
I know took a picture of his wife's torso from belly to
knees in fishnet tights, blew it up, and sold it to the Modern's photography collection as *Grid #1*. That's what
you call involvement. I can hear him now: "When I first
got involved in a . . . a . . . photography of—detail, I was
concerned that . . ." and so on. Dime a dozen. At the
wedding party, Guy Lewis fell into the bathtub with the
ice and champagne.

There were a lot of people at the party, artists, film-
makers, writers, poets, owners of hip bars, boutiques, antique stores, writers of satirical comic strips. A reporter
from the *Voice*, a star of the underground cinema, a director who was out on bail after his cast had shit on the
stage at one of the performances of *Eros Depraved*. After
the party the newlyweds went either to their new studio
apartment on Christopher Street, or to a suite that Leo
had rented in the Fifth Avenue Hotel. It doesn't matter.
Ellen dressed herself for him as a maid, tiny black skirt,
black nylons, heels, and they had a marvelous night of
lust and champagne. They were very much in love, and
it is good to report that Leo was happy for the first time
in five years. Ellen felt very good pleasing him, and
rather admired herself in her beautiful flesh, provocative in the costume Leo had bought her weeks before.
Dozing on the bed, smoking, Leo thought of the time he
had "delighted" Anne with a cucumber, one night after
they had got home from a party at which she had flirted
with everyone there, most especially Duke. Even in her
laughter, she came four times, then Leo mounted her,
and they had a really wondrous coupling, apologizing
through their gasps and groans. It might be said here that
Anne began to miss Leo's sexual ornamentations, now

that she had been with Duke for a while. Duke was a good, solid lover, who thoroughly satisfied her. But Leo had ideas, he was pornographic in his sexual imagination. Duke gave her her gift, as it were, mutually delightful. But that cucumber. And Leo buying her that red satin garter belt.*

The reader may think that this is weird and abnormal, but I assure him that it is not. This is America. If anything, Leo was beating the rap. America had got him hot, and he was alleviating it. If Leo's father had brought a French maid's costume home to his mother, in their burning youth, his father aflame because of some dirty pictures he had seen at work, say, would she have worn it for him? No, I would guess, no. She would have thought him filthy and sick. He knew that, so he wouldn't have done it in the first place. This is America. Women putting plastic in their breasts, right? Wearing skirts up to their crotches, showing you their legs. Leo beat the rap. Happy with his wife. They experimented, they tried their best not to be jaded with each other, his Golden Delicious bought herself waist-cinchers, garters, high-heeled boots. Of course (I don't know why I say of course) later, as the reader will see, this turned into something else, as Leo assumed the role of the "old cat" with the "young chick" wife. Preparing himself for his dread of being again given a fine pair of horns.

Here is a poem in Leo's "later manner." It was published in *Tenochtitlan,* a journal of the Workshop for Multi-Mixed Media of New York Artists, funded by an annual grant.

FOR ELLEN AND OLD FRIENDS

in just the last year,
one has decided to go back on
junk, another to leave his

*So Dick Detective *was* telling the truth.

wife, one writes for
hollywood, one dead in
a stupid accident.

i survive
here in my comfortable
apartment, my beautiful
young wife in her bath as i await
her. my penis hard. this fact
will not help my friends, when
will i ever learn that, i
who trust the poem as my life.

in the 30's we were thrilled
and astounded to watch a seaplane,
something she has never seen. how
do i make her understand
that my lost friends have
disappeared as gently as that
somehow gentle machine. will
her innocent breasts make
their lives more possible.

i grow older
in the clothes i didn't
dare to wear 15 years ago. i
prefer to think my current
taste a mark, not of courage,
but of the inevitable. yes,
a man ain't nothin'
but a man. believe it, friends.

let—no—make them return, is my
wish, as bob said, with
smiles on their faces. they
will likewise all have places.*

Leo in a chair, in gloom. A dark rear apartment on East
Fifth Street in Manhattan. Anne is trying to ignore him,
getting Saturday breakfast ready. Leo has just read a note
rejecting a poem of his sent to a small anthology. This is
early in their marriage, Anne is pregnant with their first
child. The editor suggested a change in the poem, Leo
made it and the editor rejected it, saying that it seemed

*The ending of this poem is taken from "Oh No" by Robert Creeley.
"Bob" is obviously Mr. Creeley.

worse now than it had originally. A writer will understand his depression. He is hurt that his poem has been rejected, but he is furious with himself at his eagerness to please the editor by changing his poem. Perfect humiliation. I mention this unimportant event because it may perhaps be the beginning of imperfection in their marriage, which up to now, despite economic difficulties, has come off pretty well. I mean that Anne doesn't understand his eagerness to publish in this anthology, Anne doesn't really understand Leo's involvement with his poem at all. It's throwing a pot, right? You don't get your *life* entangled with it. And Leo worked late at night, didn't come to bed with her unless he wanted her. He read, lost to himself and his book, maddening, maddening, he would read her snatches of what intrigued him, then fall into silence again. I have said earlier that it is incredible how writers spend their youths. Take this Anne: she knew that Leo was a writer, a poet, but she didn't think that it would change their relationship together. It takes a certain kind of woman to live with an artist. She's got to be able to be bored and not go mad, and not blame the artist. Granted, this is desperately hard. I know a woman who married a novelist and divorced him two years later, because he was "always writing." These things are tolerable to some in the abstract only.

I remember this particular morning well. Trying to cash a paycheck in a fine, cold drizzle in a new neighborhood where nobody knew me. Leo was only a few blocks away from me at the time, but I didn't know him. He didn't know me. Nobody seemed to know anyone in the early fifties, least of all writers who were not trying to break into the *Partisan Review–Hudson Review–Commentary* circle. Faint glimmers that this was not what we were after, at all. Tell it to the Marines. Tell it to Norman Podhoretz, who made it. Scattered attempts at a freshness of assault, a new conception. Where would one put these poems and stories? Leo, that morning. Had I known him then we would have gone out and got drunk

together, to celebrate our solitude. Our various solitudes.
It is not that nobody was a known writer, it is that we
were all unknown writers without a milieu. That came
later, and was labeled arrogant. So be it. You try to live
in America, where they either hate art or try to use it. I
think of Horace Rosette. The poem as tool. Break open
somebody's door with it, or unhook a brassiere. But don't
just let it stand there, useless. "Communicate with the
people." It's sad to see young black poets making this
mistake. They are communicating with the people—
their people. Those who do, are, of course, not writing
poems. The few who develop into artists will find their
audiences fleeing wildly from their unwanted percep-
tions. But everyone deserves to make this mistake. The
artist is called. What a long and bitter battle before the
realization finally and clearly asserts itself that he is not
needed. Whatever makes him do these strange things, it
is not a necessity to tell any people anything. Discovery
of the world. Saved by his protective coloring. Have you
noticed how weird X has become? I cashed my check
buying twenty dollars worth of booze in a liquor store
that had a sign on the window, "The Bird on Ice." The
bird was indeed on ice. Tell him about communication. "None of you bastards knows how Charlie Parker
died."

I don't know where Leo worked at the time. Let's make
him a really good bookkeeper. Sense of craft, he said it,
not I. Somewhere he met a young man named Anton
Harley, a sometime motorcycle racer. I haven't mentioned him before in this narrative* because he is a lousy
bastard; but I see that he deserves a chapter to himself,
now that I think about him. The chapter will come soon.
You may turn to it now, if you wish. Years later, I met his
brother, who made boxes somewhere in Brooklyn. Wore
a beard and supported SNCC. In the casual manner for
which I am famous, I said, "How's Anton? Still racing?"

*This what?

(At the time I had heard that Anton was somewhere in the Midwest, traveling from race to race.) His brother told me that Anton would never win a race "because he's afraid to die." I make no case here for the man who is *not* afraid to die, but Anton turned out to be—I mean to me, as he was made clearer—the kind of man for which one can have nothing but contempt: he pretended that he lived a life in which his death was not important. A phony, all the way. He wrote poems too. Cellophane. But we'll discuss him soon.

Leo met him, and they became friends. Maybe it was Leo's mustache that got him, at the time, a Zapata-style. But Anton came to see them, unexpectedly, frequently, always broke, although he made twice as much money as Leo as a master mechanic. He stayed for dinner, stayed overnight, stayed for breakfast. He ate. What he was given and what he could find. Greed was his problem. Anal retentive. His father lived in Locust Valley, where he had grown up with his brother. Mother was dead. He came to see Leo and to hear his poems. To show Leo his poems. Later he would put Leo down as a lousy poet. Anne was annoyed with him, didn't like him at all. He ate, Leo defended him, they got drunk together on Leo's $78 a week. There were some good arguments over old Anton. Then came friends of Anton's, here and there, Leo knew other writers, he was alive, in some sense anyway. Sense of being there, in the world, apart from his wife. Their marriage got rockier and rockier. Anton ate. He was tall and slender, something weird about people whose gluttony doesn't show. It showed in Anton's eyes. "Thy rapt soul sitting in thine eyes," as Milton had it. From here on in, it was descent, descent for the marriage.

But I don't want to give you the impression that all this happened quickly. It took a long time, five years, to be exact. I'm just making this up, anyway, I don't know what really happened between them—oh, I know about Harley, but he wasn't the cause of the estrangement, he wasn't even the catalyst. In their early marriage, grasping for each other in their love and need. Alone together, like the old song. Sunday delicatessen breakfasts, Leo becoming more Jewish here on the Lower East Side. He'd bring in the *Times* and *Trib,* bagels, lox, cream cheese, pickled herring, sit in their little kitchen with Anne, talking about the news, scoffing at some new "Great Book" reviewed on page one of the *Book Review.* Trying to stay sane. Leo trying to write and trying to be a good husband. He and Anne had good times; sexually, they had bad periods and brilliant ones. Leo liked her to dress up for him, bought her black stockings, lace panties and bras, made her put on heels, Anne did it. Christ, she must have been terrific in them. But she was annoyed finally with this. Ritual. It went into his poems, he spoke of her in their love matches, she was appalled. It was bad enough to look like a whore, but to be written of . . . and that leech Anton listening to them with his ax of a face, devouring a slab of Cheddar cheese and a whole box of crackers as Leo read, voice stumbling out of the muscatel or beer. She thought that she was merely an agent for Leo's lust, that she might as well have been anybody. Wrong. What excited Leo was that it was *precisely* Anne in this finery— this familiar body, sprawled, or bent over, the strong, athletic legs apart. Heavy, soft bush touching the lace of a new garter belt he had bought. Her thighs sweetly packed into the black nylons. *Her* bush, *her* thighs. He couldn't explain this to her. But she became a whore for him, his whore. Not anybody, not a whore, but his wife, turned whore. At times, he would watch her talk to a neighbor, or shop, or pour coffee for a guest, solid and matronly in her burlap skirts and simple blouses, her sandals. See her stripped to luscious deshabille, for him. A pinup from *Beauty Parade.*

Time went on, it is all mixed up, how can I tell you what I don't really know? But Anne found that she attracted men who were—normal, who liked her and wanted her in her simple bohemian styles, and one night, God knows after what accident of anger, Anne was at a party alone, Leo humming drunkenly into a beer in a bar on Second Avenue. They had got Anton Harley to mind the children, and had gone to this party, where everything had turned sour because Leo wouldn't dance with her, talking with some lady poet who wrote about orgasms. Now Anne was alone, and after smoking marijuana all night, got herself into a bedroom, dark, with a young man, and she frenziedly blew him. She had a spontaneous orgasm and got home very late, threw Harley out of the house. When Leo got home there was another scene. "I know you've never liked Anton, you feel that he's a threat to you—a fuckin' threat! You've never liked him!" "A threat, a threat? You dumb bastard, oh, you dumb bastard, you are a dumb bastard!" She was going to tell him about her indiscretion, but stopped. The next week was one of cool truce, but that following Friday night, Leo brought home a bottle of Courvoisier and a pair of ice-blue panties for her. Roses. She almost got sick, and skipped her supper so that her claim of having a vicious headache would stand up. She was polite, and went to bed, leaving the dishes in the sink. Leo watched the basketball game on television, comparatively sober with a couple of quarts of beer and a box of Cheez-Its. Then he put the brandy away, looked at the panties, holding them against the light. He showered, masturbating with soap, putting Anne in his mind in the shower with him, then went to bed. Now, go ahead, tell me these people are weird. This is my America. Simply to stay sane is an achievement.

Before the amazed stare, Leo, writing these remarkable poems. An audience of other unknown poets, plus the interested lovers of art like Anton. These were difficult times to be a poet. Not as it is today, when poets are, without fail, loved, honored, and showered with gifts and cash.* Out of this slowly shredding marriage, these re-

*Rod McKuen, Donovan, and Bob Dylan come to mind.

markable poems, charged with the anger and grief Leo
felt at this staggering partnership. He didn't want to lose
his daughters, but he didn't want, most severely, to lose
Anne. But he would. She was seeing Duke almost
flagrantly now, he would come to their house for supper,
and talk and drink with Leo, mind the kids while Leo and
Anne went out to a movie or around the corner for a
drink. Leo liked him. He believed Anne when she said
that they were innocent of sex: this whole thing threw
Leo completely, so that he *came* to believe Anne. Anne
was open about it, she told Leo that she really liked Duke;
it was clear that the feeling was as intense on Duke's
part. There was little skulking, none, to Leo's knowledge.
Duke even took Anne to parties, with Leo's permission.
What it was is clear: Leo thought that if they were going
to bed together, they would tell him, since everything else
about their relationship was so candid. What do I know?
Do you think I care? Duke was always a deadbeat as far
as I'm concerned. Third-rate musician. Dull. He used to
talk about Dostoevski and Hesse a lot, and smoked pot all
the time. What a pleasure to make him up, so that I can
put him down. He had a theory that *Moby Dick* was Melville's clandestine tribute to white supremacy. One could,
with kindness, call him a yo-yo. Did I tell you that he was
a black man? I can see him now, wearing you out with
that funky piano, those wearisome phrases. What do I
care about him? Thank Jesus he's gone to San Francisco.
Sometimes I think that Leo liked him because he was
black. Only that. You must remember that Leo is a member of my generation, i.e., filled with guilt. Guilt plus
romance adds up to an attribution of wisdom to others. I
saw an article recently in *Black Nile* by Duke: all about
Charlie Parker being an unwitting tool of white musical
tastes. God, he writes a bad prose. Worse than his piano-
playing. Another innocent lost in the woods of art: he
thought that art would care about his intentions, or know
that he was black and thus saved from ineptitude. How
harshly unfair it is, how vicious, that art is remote from

one's purity of soul. Duke was a bad musician, and a worse writer, because he was not gifted. I'll say this another way to make it perfectly clear what I'm getting at. Duke was black. He was beautiful.* He was politically hip, he knew what to say, and how to say it. He was black and beautiful. He was really a very terrific guy, racially speaking. So far as I know, he hasn't left Anne yet, but that's only a matter of time. Now, in addition to all these attributes, Duke was a hideously poor musician, and a deadening writer. Isn't that sad? Leo deferred to his opinions, guilt, guilt. All the time, composing these remarkable poems. It can be said, to Leo's credit, that he never read any of these poems to Duke. He was not that sick yet. By the time he had taken to visiting the zoo, drunk, he had lost all interest in reading his poems to anyone, and had, as a matter of fact, stopped writing them. He was to start again after Anne had gone. But that Leo was the one who had come back down the alley with the empty garbage pail. He looked just like Leo. Heed the story of the man who took the garbage out. And threw himself away.

Happy days were here again. This is said without irony. Leo was happy with Ellen, now, after almost three years of marriage. Hotsy-totsy! Demons all wrestled to the ground, unconscious, dead, or anyway lying there quietly. He wasn't writing any more, that is, he was writing, but his poems were very bad. That's because he was happy. He is the house raconteur and bard in a manly bar about two blocks from his apartment. His friends are newspapermen. Who are all writers, am I correct? Bushers. And Leo, who could write a poem falling out of an airplane, dazzled these bushers. I mean, they all worked with the same tools, right? Words, words. They thought that any poem that was not "Snowbound" was an achievement. Some of them even read Yeats. Scribes together, to the end. I once knew a dumbbell, a pleasant enough guy, but

*Handsome, anyway.

a dumbbell, who insisted that it was hard to write good news copy. There was no way to convince him otherwise. I understand his point. Personally, I think it's hard to play "The Blue Danube," since I can only play a kazoo. So these men thought Leo's poems astounding. To captains however, he was no captain, as the old joke has it. He surrendered, dear. I don't want to get into an essay about these newspapermen, but they all came out of a movie. At any moment, you would expect one of them to say, voice harsh and hoarse from years of straight bourbon, "I don't know much about anything like that . . . I'm just a newspaperman. I've always been a newspaperman." That old soft shoe. Hemingway had given birth to them, Pegler as midwife. Their basic style formed itself around the weird idea that politicians have complicated human motives for their acts. If they once recognized the fact that politicians have complicated political motives instead, they would have been forced to think, which is very difficult for a journalist, or to employ the imagination, which they have spent their professional lives denying. These are the same men who fall down in adulation of Mailer's journalism, because, in their pin heads, they have some idea that Mailer has brought to his journalism the same mind that they bring to theirs. And then, by some magic, writes them all under the table. What they don't recognize is that Mailer is eating apple pie in his journalism. His artist's gifts brought to bear on these facts and figures. Shooting fish in a barrel. But those gifts, marshaled in assault on their true target, the novel, have not yet triumphed. Mailer in his journalism is Koufax, in his day, against the Columbia varsity. The big, classic breaking curve simply overwhelming. Koufax against McCovey or Aaron, however, thought about it. I'll stop this now, I've already said that the extended metaphor becomes only engineering.

Isn't art simple? "Just a newspaperman, man." It's simple, you bastards. Anyone can do it. It is de Kooning's white hair and charm that have made him a great painter. Is he a great painter? A lot of jackals have jumped on him in the last few years. One wizard has called him the last surviving member of the de Kooning school. That's what you call "a vitriolic wit." Bitching, bitching, moaning about greatness, and when they are presented with it, they spit on it. I submit that it is not Pound's politics that have denied him the Nobel. Prove that I'm wrong.

I've forgotten Leo. Back to Leo. God knows, I might have gone on in this bitter vein for pages had I not just got a phone call from him. He called to tell me that he's been invited to a party in honor of a new book by some younger poet. The book is all about his experiences as a medic down at the induction center on Whitehall Street. He spent a month there, gathering material. The title is *The Good Humor Man.* Major national advertising, streamers, counter displays. He wanted my advice on whether he should accept or not. I told him he should go, but for God's sake, this time puke on the floor. When Leo (or whoever he is) calls me nowadays, it is almost always to tell me of his fortunes in the world of success. Once he called to tell me that he had a chat with Horace Rosette who was trying to swing a deal with some airline to have poets read to the passengers on coast-to-coast flights. Another time, to inform me that he had to deflower a sheep in a new movie by Chico Zeek. Sometimes he calls to tell me that he just buggered Ellen through a bushel basket. These things relieve and color my otherwise pedestrian existence.

As I said, happy days were here again. Better that the original Leo, ludicrous, tearful, and dozing poet, was with the garbage somewhere. Better for Leo, anyway. But this happiness didn't come instantly, as you are well aware. It was with Ellen that happiness came in the door. But Ellen can't be blamed (if that is the word) for the disintegration of Leo's art. When that occurred, exactly, is unknown to me, but it was after he no longer had Anne to write about. He put together the initial model of what

would flower into a real golem: as noted, Leo the Man.
From the mouth of this frankenstein creature came the
first of what would later be Leo's famed verse. I do recall,
however, a reading at an Upper East Side gallery, a candlelight reading on a fantastically hot August night, it
must have been 1959. I can't remember now if the candlelight was for atmosphere or because the electricity had
been shut off. There were maybe five poets on the card.
A benefit, or something. (The usual seventeen dollars
were raised.) Leo, whose poems had always been greeted
politely and unenthusiastically, tore the joint up with a
poem he had written a few months before (such was the
internal evidence) called something like, "This Issue," or
"This Is the Issue." About the triumphal entry of the re-
bel army into Havana on that famous New Year's Day. I
don't wish to be snide, but reading a poem like that to an
audience like the one attendant is like singing "Return to
Sorrento" at the old Fabian Fox on amateur night. I said
nothing to Leo at the time—the poem must have then
seemed like a forgivable aberration. But I remember being resentful, because Leo's enormous skills had given
the poem a surface movement and a glitter that belied its
essential fakery. Political poetry is interesting in that it
can proffer the most marvelous radical sentiments in utterly degraded and reactionary poetic structures. Does
anyone care about this fact? Tell it to the Marines. I
wasn't seeing too much of Leo any more, he was moving
from one girl to another, desperately, working out a
method whereby his New Manhood could function. Some
time later, just before he met Ellen at Horace Rosette's,
he wrote the well-known "Raincheck for Fidel and Che,"
over which we had a bitter argument, the first, as I recall,
we had ever had about verse. It was a terrible argument,
because, being friends, it was conducted with smiles and
laughter on both sides, as if our frothy icing somehow
blunted the force of the words we used. It's not worth
recounting the argument, and I suppose it was, all in all,
a mistake. I was angry that Leo should traduce his gifts

and he was angry that I should be so presumptuous as to
tell him what those gifts entailed. So it was sour in our
mouths and continued to be. Yet this poem brought him
Ellen.

I saw Guy Lewis the other day and he reminded me of
that hot August night, ten years ago. I had forgotten he
was there. He grinned at me through his drunkenness.
"You remember that *terrific* poem Leo read that night?
Boy, that was a *terrific* poem, *terrific.*" Jesus, the anger
and contempt with which he painted that adjective.

So they met, they met. At the house of H. Rosette. La-de-
dum-dum-da. He saw her across a crowded room. Ellen
awaiting him. Peaches and Cream, Marshmallow Sun-
dae, Chocolate Soufflé. God have mercy on both of them.
I don't know how they were finally introduced, but they
were, after a while, talking with each other, the booze
was getting into Leo's head, for which he never failed to
give thanks. It was what they call an "animated" discussion. Or an animated "discussion." After a while, he was
allowing his hand to brush up against her thigh. She was
allowing her thigh to stay there. She twisted a little, in
fact, into the hand. Women are beautiful. They were having this discussion. My informants tell me that they
moved over a great deal of territory, covering subjects as
diverse as *In Dubious Battle,* Glen Gray and his Casa
Loma Orchestra, the Songs of Thomas Campion
(snatches of which Leo sang and hummed off-key), and
the essential cloddishness of the drama critic. I would
have paid a great deal more attention to what they were
up to, but at about this time, I had had enough of Leo for
a while, and did my best to stay away from the long tenta-
cles of his drunks. Had I known that this was a historic
occasion . . . but I hyperbolize. Reminds me of that snide
story I once heard about the hip politician discovered
sexually assaulting his copy of *Lolita.* I don't believe a
word of it, really. Not that it couldn't happen. A politician
can do anything, the weirder the better. I was speaking

of hyperbole. Take the strange case of *In Cold Blood.*
How about the man discovered fucking that book? No
names, please. Do you think I'm interested in the books
people love?

How did Ellen look that night? She looked good. That's
literal. A wit I know once said, "To be literal is to be
bitter." And God knows, your reporter is a bitter man.
Ellen liked cocktail dresses at the time. Tight bodice, full
skirt, nipped waist. To tie the loose ends of this narrative
together, or, I should say, *further* to tie the loose ends of
this narrative together, I'm putting Dick Detective at this
party. Looking at Ellen. Dick was drinking dry bourbon
manhattans. If you don't think that's hip, fuck you. What
would you like him to be drinking? A Clover Club? Ward
8? How about a Sazerac? Now, *that's* a hip drink. Dick
was drinking dry bourbon manhattans. April was at the
party with him, sipping at a Gordon's and 7-Up. That's
not too hip, in fact, it embarrassed Dick. There were a lot
of people there. Anton Harley was there, eating and looking sullen. Leo was the center of attention. A reading at
the "Gugg" will do that. Why do you think—I mean, just
as an aside—why do you think I put the Detective at this
party? Figure that out and close the book. The Dick is
everywhere. What I need in this book is a leitmotif. Too
late now, these people fall into their lives without benefit
of theme song. They fall out of their lives. Dick was in a
little room off the study, with two or three rich young
people, smoking pot. They were listening to Vivaldi. Of
course, he could see Ellen, right through the wall. (Who's
literal?) Leo was getting her and himself another drink,
accepting some more congratulations at the bar. There's
no order to any of this. "If you want order," Dr. Sepp
Drambuie wrote, "be a plumber." Or, "study plumbing."
I understand that this is an apocryphal remark, yet it
is exactly the kind of thing Drambuie might have
said. When last seen he was turning lobster red in his
orgone box. Changed his life, thus changed the
world. One is fascinated by these lofty mythologies.

Leo returned to Ellen with their drinks.

There's no order to any of this. Some tell me that Guy Lewis was at this party, but I don't remember seeing him, or for that matter, seeing the people who told me that he was there. I doubt if he was—he and Leo were not getting along too well, and Leo's small measure of fame annoyed Guy to a remarkable degree. Why not? Leo didn't deserve it for these buck-and-wing poems. I am reminded of the time, years later, Leo in his absolute ascendancy, happy and solid, the respected poet, a father again, playing softball with the team organized from the bar in which he drank. Guy, well, what a mess, a total shambles of a man, dear Christ. But whacking the living be-Jesus out of Leo's feathery pitches, tearing him up, so that Leo would throw the ball into the dirt, or over the catcher's head, in his fury. And Guy, ravaged, that great horselaugh slicing through the air, you fuckin' *bum,* Leo! You are a fuckin' *busher!* Who even drunk, yet hath his mind entire. The true killer was the double he sent past Leo's shoulder to drive in the winning run in the ninth. Fuck you, Leo! I didn't want to watch any of those happy Sunday ball games after that. I've never been a good sport, though. Ask Leo.

But Dick D. was there, as I've already said. These repetitions of fact* are intended. Known as an aesthetic tool. But I can't help it, this tale keeps strolling around on the paper. Dick seems to be everywhere. They didn't call him Dick Detective for nothing. I mean *I* didn't call him Dick Detective for nothing. Leo once met him in the snake house at the zoo. Now what the hell was Dick doing in the snake house at the zoo? He was with April, that may explain it—I mean, he took April out to "hip" places. Those little bistros, those charming cafés, walking in Washington Square in a snowstorm. He got around, checking up. He vexed Leo, but this particular night, Leo didn't care. He was falling in love, Ellen said that she

---

*Fact, he says.

would go home with him. What she said when she saw
that incredible apartment is unknown. You can imagine
her looking for a place to put her cocktail dress as Leo
gropes her, tugging at her panties. Finally, she throws it
down on a pile of newspapers. This is the way poets live,
she figures, so be it. It is from such squalor that beauty is
spawned. She actually said that to me once when I put
Leo down, weaving through a clutch of tried-and-true
clichés about my old friend's mode of living. "It's out of
that kind of squalor that beautiful art is born," is what
she actually said. I wrote it down in my notebook. (At the
time I was keeping a "Journal" but I gave it up soon after:
what I wrote in it, I discovered, I would have remembered anyway. The rest I make up.) We were in Max's
Kansas City at the time, which bar was invented by Jack
Spicer in his book *The Heads of the Town up to the
Aether*. The poet creates Max's in the line: "In hell it is
difficult to tell people from other people." All those
Nehru jackets and miniskirts surrounding lobsters and
steaks. If you listen closely, you can hear the mandibles
working.

So Horace Rosette acted as a subtle waft of jasmine.
Essence of ginseng. Leo take Ellen to hut. A nice Jewish
girl. It was a month or so after this that he wrote a group
of eight poems, brilliant, clearly brilliant, and they
marked the termination of his powers. Only I know this.
And Leo, too, of course. I try to imagine how he feels
when he thinks about it. The destruction of a poet is no
small thing. Although it is thought to be in bad taste to
say so, it is much more serious than the demise of a
"leader of men." Let me be clear: I mean *any* leader. I'll
give you a Mao, a Franco, a Ho, a Kennedy, and a Che for
one reasonably contented Herman Melville. This is an
obviously elitist remark.

But it's getting to be the time to let these people go. Since
I began this chapter, the reverberations seem to have
awakened some ghosts, that is, I got a letter from Anne

the other day. Speech after long silence, asking about the old crowd. Good God, that's painful even to skim the surface of. Actually, I take the liberties of the novelist here with the facts. The letter from Anne was sent to Dick Detective, who told me about it, in his fashion, of course. Hint, paraphrase, that cute ballet around the edges. But I learned enough to convince me that these people should be allowed to rest, here, in their own chapter. If I keep this up, I may awaken all the ghosts instead of laying them. Jesus Christ, Anne may come back to New York and bake me some whole-wheat bread. I'd have to send it out to Henry Miller along with some dripping vulvas so that he could make his favorite literary sandwiches: not that Miller dislikes women—what gave you that weird idea? Why, his books are full of Healthy, Bawdy Sex. Tell it to the Marines. Believe that the Pope loves you, too. One useful note to move this narrative along: Anne said that Duke left her to teach Black Music in a Black Studies program in some southern college. Those poor bastards: they'd be better off with an Oscar Peterson (the Canadian Caper) album. "Live and learn" the saying goes.

Leo and Anne five years hence. What about that? Grizzled Leo, dazzling the peasant journalists in his favorite bar. His peachy keen banana split milk chocolate frappé, Ellen, evoking a thousand erections in Leo's friends' pants. I heard a rumor that Leo invited two young poets to his house on Christmas Eve to show them the gift he got Ellen. After they were settled with their drinks, Ellen emerged from the bedroom in black underwear, nylons, and knee-high patent leather boots. Leo, grinning in his possession, and Ellen, delighted at the discomfiture of the two young men. I'm not making any case here for modesty, but I suggest that this is a symptom of Leo's decline. His loss of creative power. Sex is power, and the secrets that you share with your beloved must not be dissipated by exposing them. Leo should have allowed an orgy to develop, or he should have kept Ellen's body to himself. All right, don't believe me. You can't disparage your own sexual proclivities, or hand them out like flyers, without losing the power that they bring to your life. Puritans and libertines have full-time jobs: I mean, that's what they *do*. Read Sade. Leo ravaged the products of his powers, so that there was then nothing but for him to ravage their sources. And all the time, he thought that he was freeing himself from inhibitions. And he was. And he was happy as well. The only thing destroyed in this whole process of liberation was his art. Now don't complain or say I'm wrong. This is my book, and my Leo. I made no promise that I would satisfy you.

Those eight brilliant poems I spoke of: I went back a few days ago to the magazine they appeared in and reread them. They are indeed brilliant. The last he composed. They were composed for a woman, but are for himself. The particular configuration made by his life and by hers prevented his possession of her and these poems so eased his anguish. This woman has never seen them, yet they had the ability to act as a charm, a talisman, whereby his desire for her was stilled. Yet, in a way that artists understand, the lineaments of these poems, the fibers out of which the words came to be arranged, were taken from his love and need for Ellen. Only in his composition will his lust assert itself. His love for Ellen is so strong that it leaves him quiescent in the face of his desires. He wants to have them—both of them. So he expires in his imagination, and is reborn in the poems. They glitter: *for* one, so he thinks, and *from* the other: the fact. So is he momentarily saved from destruction. It is sometimes at this sort of crisis in the artist's career that his art is freshened. It may, however, on the other hand, grow stale and stink.

6
Radix Malorum

GREED WAS Anton's problem. I'm not interested in how he got that way. There he stands, now, in all his earthly beauty, let's say with three cheeseburgers in each hand. Why do I bother to bring him in here? One reason is that it is instructive that such a character should be involved in the arts. This ravaging mouth, involved in art! It's a particular picture, it's an illumination of the times, if you will. He made the most hopeless poems, and so had a small following. You run the chance, even now, if you frequent the places that are approved of by the hip art crowd, of bumping into someone who will say, "I understand that Anton is writing again . . . have you seen any of his new work?" It's fantastic to think of people caring about whether Anton is writing again or not, or of thinking about his old work in relation to his new work. It's like waiting to read a new piece by Jimmy Breslin, that is, *caring* about that. Aberrant. He wrote cellophane poems. He was a master mechanic and made a lot of money when he worked. But he never had any money. He was one of those rats who is always going to dinner at

somebody's house, or going away for the weekend somewhere. If you invite him for dinner, buy a steer. Ah, I see
that this chapter will be full of my own bile toward this
wretched man. I'm making him up too, but each little
piece of him is taken from the files.* And I loathe each
piece. Face like an ax. Everything was greed. I recall
meeting him just about the time he was first married. His
wife is a heroin addict now. That doesn't surprise me.
When he married her, she was a very chic Jewish girl,
looking very Christian. Model-like. You know the type.
But she was all right beyond her American lust for the
Good Things. Well, maybe she wasn't all right, whoever
she was—we'll leave her name out of this—certainly she
didn't deserve Anton Harley. Anyway, that's about the
time I met him, though I vaguely remember "seeing him
around." Probably in Riker's or Horn and Hardart, eating
something. Did I tell you that he was tall and slender?
Very obscene. Reminded me of a worm. Not that he was
bad-looking, on the contrary, he had a rather attractive
face, in that axlike way. I can't judge him, when I think
about him I see a worm, feeding. His wife. When they
were first married.

When they were first married, they would suddenly
appear at parties, hello, hello! He would have her on his
lap the whole party, except when she went to make him
a drink, or got up to dance with him. He sat and kissed
her, he felt her thighs, her hips, belly and breasts, rubbed
his nose in her hair. Something about it that struck me,
even then, when I took him for another young whiz poet.
Years passed before I realized what it reminded me of,
that abstracted cuddling, those compulsive caresses: a
man chinking coins in his hand. That was it. He handled
her that way. Of course I didn't see it then. To tell the
truth, I hardly saw them at all then, it was too embarrassing to watch them play High School Lovers. That ax of a
face into some Tab Hunter business. As I recall, at the

*The author has not explained what he means by "files."

time he had just published his first poems, two of them,
in a magazine out of Baton Rouge, *Hysteria.* I'm going to
see if I can find that magazine so I can give you an example of Anton's early work. This was about 1958. Anton
didn't publish again until about 1966. It was toward that
latter date that people began to say, "I hear that Anton is
writing again," etc. I must say that there were people who
never inquired. I remember someone asking Guy Lewis
about Anton, and Guy told him that the rumor was that
Anton had died of an overdose of meatloaf. Horrible
death. The victim writhes on the floor, a powerful smell
of onion coming from his orifices. Guy's questioner was
not amused. Perhaps he owned a hot-dog stand and truly
missed him.

Where *was* Anton at this time? He was racing his bike
somewhere in the Midwest. He and his wife were separated, and this was his way of forgetting. I should say,
"forgetting." (I don't want any spectacularly perceptive
"reviewer" to remark on how I've placed quotes around
words to invest them with "subtle" meanings. *I* know
what I've done.) "Forgetting" his wife. It was at this time
that his brother told me about the death business. His
brother, soon after this, became a pacifist, and one would
run, not walk, etc., etc. One of those pacifists who would
like to flay you alive for not believing in pacifism. Brother
Harley would even drive you into the streets howling
for mercy as he attacked the *Iliad* as an evil book, and
so on. I bring him in to remind you of his appear-
ance in the previous chapter, that's all. This novel is
subtly linked together, despite the opinions of ZuZu
Jefferson. May she perform fellatio on young English
novelists all her life! Then Anton returned, winless. It
was after his return that I began to realize his greed,
the vastness of his greed. And to be shocked that such
avarice, such cupidity, could be harbored in a man who
was intimately connected with the arts. Who thought of
himself in some way, certainly, as an artist. Ignore the
fact that he is made out of words. It's very interesting that

he should appear in this book. He sort of walked right in while I was tacking Leo together. And here he is, picking his teeth.

It occurs to me that Anton's poems have not improved in ten years. But why should they? For him, writing is the same as repairing a motorcycle. Passing the time—except that he gets paid for his mechanical labors. But it's all the same to him, as a matter of fact, he is one of that numbing legion who tells you about the butcher, the baker, etc., being the same as Leonardo. Some cabinet-maker is like David Smith, etc. The chef as great artist. I don't mind. This is commonly accepted swill in our time, much like astrology: harmless pastime for the frivolous. He knew his poems had not improved, that they were, at the center, dead. This is not to say that the poems were bitter, or angry. No, Anton had swallowed Williams—swallowed is right. He saw in that poet kindness, understanding, wisdom, all the attributes of the patient country doctor. Of course, the absolute darkness and rage of Williams's work escaped him. The poems Anton wrote were not bitter, or angry, as I have said. They were about the wonder of walking the dog, the marvel of coming in a tight vagina, and so forth. Sex, food, sky, you know—the head hits the back of the chair as you doze off. Greed was his problem, as I have also said. He had trouble giving you anything, even in his poems. If he revealed something of himself that wasn't the Official Anton, that was giving you something. So his poems were hard lumps, for all their celebration of "the good things." Have you ever read those free and open poems, filled with joyous rapture about sex and youth, yet there is this accurate and sharp odor of venom from them? As if they were written in poison. So Anton's poems were these chilled, hard objects, the emotion *on* the poem, coats of varicolored paint. In a way, I was (and am) reminded of screwdrivers and hammers, monkey wrenches, when I see these poems. You've seen them before, you'll see them again. But he had all the time in the world for producing this Bakelite. His leisure, given to Art. So could his writing develop. The silly little bastard! I've got some stories to tell you about this lame, they'll make you throw tacks and broken glass in front of his bike. Oh, his leisure. All bad writers somehow find all the time they need to further soil the world with their productions. Anton had so much time that he even started to buy things, like houses. There was some dead uncle or something come out of the blue, a happy corpse, scattering largesse. Anyway, there was money, and Anton knew how to turn a buck into two, presto! We'll talk about this later, if I don't get sick. We may even whisper a little about his politics.

As I say, Anton knew that his poems had not improved. Cellophane poems.* And he slowly—very slowly—came to admit to friends and acquaintances that his Art was in great difficulties. He quite cleverly and subtly placed the blame for this disintegration of his artistic powers to the Sickness of America. Not bad, eh? Not bad at all. Dick Detective agreed that Anton's work had not developed because of his particularly sensitive social antennae. (Dick should know about this.) It was really a beautiful thing to see Dick, Anton, and Lou Henry, tearing the flesh out of a mess of lobsters in Max's Eat-O-Mat, talking about how their poems had struggled to stay keen and sharp in this mad country. Those three frauds! Up to their elbows in drawn butter. Bunny Lewis once remarked that they looked like the Brontë sisters arguing over a dildo. Yes, America had done it!

America had done it to them—but especially to Anton. He had thought of it first. It was his con. So he kept writing, gallantly. What he didn't realize is that his own rotten writing contributed to the general degradation. There is no body of work in literature that, conceived of as some kind of diversion from the stringencies of art, will not rot and its putrescence affect the population. Those drudges

*This is the third or fourth time the author has used this phrase. Perhaps it is a "symbol."

of the Poem of Life, or the Poem of Protest and Revolution—they think they can insult the language and it not matter. I see those lusterless words putrefacting, sinking into a soured mulch that will poison the earth the writers thought to celebrate. Or, better, that the writers wanted the reader to think of as celebration.

One of my great problems with Anton Harley is that I can't make up enough terrible stories about him to make him totally unreal, absolutely fleshless and one-dimensional, lifeless, as my other characters are. I'm afraid that the reader may get the idea that some monster like this actually walks the earth. I assure them that although there are people who try to be Harleys, they can't quite make it. I'll do my best to make him totally unbelievable. I saw him on Second Avenue the other day, popping out of the Victory Delicatessen, but he—of course—looked the other way, since he had two franks in his hand. He appeared the usual way, i.e., as if he was about to bite the wall. It was seeing him that made me realize that I had to really stir this prose around to make sure that he doesn't walk around in this book with any degree of reality. That is, *his* reality. I want him to walk around in this book with my reality. Fiction. Fine.

And now, for a brief aside, while we go back a few years, to an evening when Anton visited an old college friend, married and with two children. I won't give his name, because he is still alive, and may appear in this book, in fact, in a different guise. An old college friend. An unexpected visit. The scene is set. You must understand that it is Friday night, the weekly shopping is not done until Saturday morning, the host's paycheck is uncashed, and a light supper of eggs and bacon has been eaten. There is nothing in the house to offer Anton. Now, the host is a bit upset when Anton appears on the stairs. Anton will talk about art and politics and revolution and motorcycles just so long . . . then he wants to feel those strong, yellow teeth of his sinking into something digestible. When he gets this way, his conversation falters, he becomes distracted, passes his hand through his hair. Anton hungry is like a heroin addict who is just feeling the beginnings of junk need. He must eat. He must eat! He *must* eat! HE MUST EAT! Eat, eat, eat, eat!! His eyes glaze over just a little. If you're a woman, close your legs. Or open them, if that's your pleasure. Anton eats anything. But there was nothing to give him. And, you will recall that I said that his host had not cashed his paycheck. An interesting situation. Let's observe Anton in action here.

First, Anton asks if there is anything to eat, the answer is, as we know, apologetically negative. A few minutes pass, limping conversation about some supercharger or whatever,* then silence. Anton asks if they have already eaten. Yes. He says he hasn't, he came over on the spur of the moment. (Anton has a colorful way of speaking.) Nothing left from supper. Eh? Not a thing. Silence. The jaws are working. The hostess closes her legs and suggests tea. Just tea? Anton asks. He is at the point now where all pretense toward politeness has been jettisoned. That's all I have, I'm sorry, etc., etc., said for the third or fourth time. Now, these people live in the Twenties, just off First Avenue, an area crammed with stores and restaurants of all kinds. Seafood, Italian, on the arm, Chinese, delicatessen, etc. Anton says, I wonder if I can go out and get a quick bite? Is there a place around here where I might get a pizza? The host looks at him, going along with the play. Sure, Anton, there's a pizza joint right around, and there's also a bla bla, and down on, there's a Chinese, etc., and you can, etc. Anton gets up. Now pain, enormous pain, crosses his face. Oh, Pain! Pain! But, give him his due: he says it. Can—I—bring you—bring you—any—thing b—back—? Oh, that's all right, Anton, that's all right, we ate, you know, go ahead, that's O.K., go ahead, ha ha. I'll manage something, Anton says. He's a mark, pure gold.

Time passes, and then, Anton is back with a big, brown

---

*I know nothing of motorcycles.

bag. He spreads out on the table a half-pound of Swiss cheese, a half-pound of liverwurst, a half-pound of cole-slaw, a half-pound of potato salad, a whole sour pickle, two green, pickled tomatoes, a quart of beer, and a loaf of French bread. The hostess gets him a knife and a napkin so that he can control, somewhat, the drool that is wetting his collar. He cuts the bread the long way, and starts to pile on the liverwurst, Swiss cheese, coleslaw, and potato salad. Why don't you get yourselves a plate? he says, arranging his sandwich. Christ, have some of this—there's plenty! The hostess protests, politely, but goes into the kitchen for a plate for her and her husband, and puts on some water for tea. Anton gives them, very nicely arranged, a slice of Swiss, a slice of liverwurst, a spoonful of coleslaw, a spoonful of potato salad. He cuts two paper-thin slices of pickle for them. He is sure that they'll probably drink tea, right? And the rest goes on the French bread. Eat, eat, crunch. As he eats, Anton keeps eyeing the food he has given his host and hostess, slightly—oh, just slightly—regretful. But he's a sport and hides it.

Two poems (ca. 1958) by Anton Harley follow.

LAMENT

Walked for hours
in the snow/no
supper to warm me.

If she/neglects to be
soft as piñon ash
with me, fuck it.

LUCKY STRIKE

Here she is, beautiful
beautiful. A pack
of cigarettes all

shining innocence in
her cellophane,
smooth and silk/y.

Three poems (ca. 1968) by Anton Harley follow.

ICE FREEZES RED

nothing to do smell
of cat piss faint enough
to be all right.
tick of the clock Dick
gave me on the air old
Fats Navarro clarity what
a pleasure what a pleasure.

DINNER AT EIGHT

to make a thing
strong and long/lasting,
to make a thing or
re/new it, this can keep
any man together.

after seventy years
my gourmet grand/father
found food simply
had worn out/his teeth.

WHITE LIGHT
              for D.D.

unclear/unclear usage
an assault on the soul
or brain/by subterfuge.
unclean broken
shreds still attached.

where there is no/definition
no exact grasp of word &c.
the noun is only possible clear.
                    the substant/ive.

It really would be better if he got away from here, but
now, I'm stuck for a few more pages at least, since I've
given you his poems to read, compare, and contrast. You
will see that he uses a particular poetic currency, the
distinguishing features of which are obvious. In a way,
I'm beginning to approve of my idea of having this Mouth
in the novel. There is even a possibility that this figure

could sustain a whole book, all by himself. If there is one controlling factor that today informs our lives (outside of ignobility, of course), that factor must be greed. So, the choice of Harley—I keep saying "choice," when you know as well as I that he sneaked in the book behind Leo's old benny.

To start again: so, the choice of Harley may turn out to be very fortunate, indeed. I mean from my point of view. You may be bored by this chapter, after all, there really is not much to expect from an allegorical study* of a nonexistent man. But I had a dream the other night in which a real man came to me—I was watching some sort of dull softball game between two barroom teams—the players call them (this will give you an idea of the mentality of the Nines) "saloon teams." That's really notable when you consider that after the games they eat steaks and drink champagne. This real man came to me and said: "Anton Harley told me that last Sunday at the softball game between the saloon teams he managed to get away with two steaks and three chickens." And suddenly, in my dream, I saw that the ax face that I have invented for Harley is his real face. The reason I say this is because I saw that ax buried in a chicken, blood streaming down the chin and throat, eyes closed. In the background, the saloon teams played their remarkable brand of softball.

To leave Harley for a moment, his face buried in the chicken. Let me submit a comment or two on the way this game of "saloon" softball looks to the casual observer. In this case, myself, ultra-casual, as a matter of fact, since I watched this game in my dream. Nobody on these teams can play ball very well, they are all in their middle or late thirties, fatty, windless, and rubbery with booze. They have vague memories of playing a pretty good game years ago, in their teens. So their bodies go through the

*An allegorical study? Is *that* what he's doing?

motions, but they can't execute. This is fine, but there are
always a couple of players, usually those who are slim-
mer than the rest, in better shape, who begin to play "in
earnest." They could make you puke. They've even been
known to say things like, "The only thing that matters is
winning," etc., etc. These are political liberals, right?
Some are even radicals, read Cleaver. Win! Somehow,
they become leaders. They move from a sort of vaguely
defined attitude of impatience toward those players who
still seem to be having a few laughs on Sundays, to one
of outright hostility, even going so far as to change
"pitchers"* when their team is being hit hard. Thus do
the games become less of a Sunday diversion than a great
combat of "saloons." It's amazing to think of these players as Men Over Thirty. Those few who continue to have
some fun are made to feel totally uncomfortable. There
was a rumor around that Anton Harley (he's back) was
encouraged to eat the chicken and pâté of a batter who
had not hustled on a slow-hit grounder to short.

Anton Harley is back. It should be stated immediately
that Harley does not play softball. Why is that? Let's see
if we can decide on a reason that will stand up in terms
of Harley's character. He is a rotten player and refuses to
exhibit his lack of skills. He might not have as clear a
chance at the victuals did he play. He has assumed a
spectator role for so long that there is no question now of
his ever being a participant. The players are afraid that
he might eat the bats.

It doesn't really matter at all. Even his face was closed.
Eyes closed, the blood of that chicken running down his
chin and throat. As I recall, it had been snatched from the
fire, not yet done, so hot that it burned his fingers. That
was in the dream, however. But it was really unsettling
that his face is an ax. Watching the game through those
matte, gray eyes, the words coming out along with pieces

*Nobody on these teams is a pitcher. Different players throw the ball
toward the plate.

of meat, "Get a hit, baby, a little hit, a little bingle, babe!" Good old Sunday afternoon.

So you see I've begun to turn this Harley into a beast. In that dream his face, the bloody chicken, etc. What is particularly disturbing is that the face that Harley took on in the dream—I should say, the face that he actually wore —is the face of someone that I really know. I mean he's someone who exists outside of this book, a real human being. Now, it will be very difficult to keep Harley artificial, since I see him with the face of this true and living man. I will cleave to the original conception of Anton as a figure of utter greed, and the character will distort everything it comes into contact with. Totally unreal. Nobody like Anton Harley in the world! Nobody! "The author gives us cardboard figures on which he paints ideas . . ." If Anton Harley came into your life, he'd eat it up, one way or another. But he's O.K. in many ways, what I mean is that he's a remarkable dresser, very casually elegant, hair is cut just right, well-trimmed, full mustache. Wears the very best shoes. Politics are revolutionary, master mechanic, owns a couple of houses, knows a lot of the very hippest people, has excellent manners when there is no food around, etc. Nothing about him that is square. This is a picture: he is in a rocker, a beautiful piece of Shaker furniture that he bought for his wife. He's wearing a pair of dark brown Harris tweed slacks, custom-made by Brooks, faded blue work shirt from Hudson's Army-Navy Store, around his neck a bright red, patterned engineer's kerchief. Battered, creased, and stained Clark's desert boots. On the phonograph, Ornette Coleman at the Golden Circle. On the wall, a small collage of white lace and lavender velvet by John Chamberlain, charcoal drawing by Bart Kahane, black-framed photograph of Franz Kline taken at Provincetown in the late fifties. On the coffee table, a copy of *The Long Goodbye, Studies in a Dying Colonialism, Alcools, Caterpillar* ¾, A. E. Waite's *Pictorial Key to the Tarot*, and *Axon*

Dendron Tree. With one hand, Anton is reading *Serenade,* with the other, he is pushing three slices of pizza into his mouth, there is pizza all over the floor, and from the looks of things, it seems as if Anton has been—fuck-. ing—some of the pizza. There is a banging from the bathroom, and muffled shouts. That is his latest girl, whom he has locked in so that she can't share any of the pie. He'll let her out soon and let her eat the pizza that he came over, if she wants it. He reads avidly, God, he digs Cain. Pretty soon it will be time to go over to Dick Detective's for dinner. Have I made it clear that Anton is slender and handsome? Would you really want him for a friend, though? It would be better to have one of those people from the *Character (Fiction) Directory.* Almost anyone would do, even that woman who shows up with too much eye makeup, saying "between you and I" all the time. Or the man with the frayed shirt cuffs at the faded hotel. A lot of them are probably working right now in various magazines, but as soon as they're free, they'll be happy to go and see you. Better than Anton, anyway. A few of the better-class characters might even come over from an O'Hara story. Anton will just bug you, squirming around here the way he does, telling you how to make an antitank rocket launcher. *He'll* use the rent from his buildings. How you'll finance your revolution is your problem. "A fucking *fortress* up in Vermont, man," he says, finishing off the Port-Salut. Did I tell you that he's slender and handsome and totally committed to Black Liberation? Why is he such a supreme calamity? If this were only a novel I could really explore him for you. It's really mysterious that he now has that face I know so well. Sometimes I think one simply can't attribute these things to chance.

I would give you a better Anton if I could. This is the way it falls out. This book is about destruction. Nobody is of course destroyed, that is, they go on into their divers futures, still talking, drinking, etc. So will Anton, one can see him in twenty or twenty-five years: closed. Still closed, I should say. Sexually free. I know a man from the Midwest, a large city in the Midwest, who, beneath his very fashionable clothes, and behind the sprawling and flaccid language of the poetry he writes, is a shrewd and canny storekeeper. What can Wilhelm Reich tell me about him; who has achieved a "beautiful orgasm" so as to better live to insult art? So I see Anton in the future: free and closed. The mind of a reporter. Is there a kind word I can say about this axman that will move your sympathies toward him? Or perhaps you sympathize with him already? In that case, you will adore him by the time this chapter closes.

Let's get some action here. If I'm going to hold your attention in this age of the Visual, I'd better learn something about putting together a swift-moving plot that will rivet you to your chair long into the night, that's for sure. Some action. But I really can't think of anything. I've said, I think, that it would be better if I had never bothered with this guy . . . I could go back into Leo's chapter and get him out of there, then just dump all this . . . nothing has happened anyway. I mean what do you know about Anton? That he's greedy. O.K. What else? Nothing, really, nothing at all. He's certainly not a flesh-and-blood character who shows signs of walking off the page. I've spoken of this kind of writing already, somewhere* in this book. *Prose* these figures! Prose them right into the paper and the shape of the letters. Do you know why it is imperative that words be spelled correctly in a narrative? If they are not, those things or activities, those states of being that they represent, are changed. On the page, where it counts. I speak of fiction. Nonfiction is a kind of magic-lantern show to captivate the minds of those who think it describes or reveals reality; a sort of sweet narcotic to take you to some other world. While there, you think you're perceptive of everything. But, worse, you

* "Somewhere" is a literary convention. I know exactly where I said this.

think that you can use this when you get back home to the Rock. Did I hear you say poetry? Poetry is fiction, in my specialized terminology. So words must be spelled correctly, or the reality of the true prose changes. In the mawning is not In the morning. People who write "mawning" think the language has a true "reality" off the paper. The difference between a good writer and a bad one—or, the difference between a writer (take your choice out of the millions around) and an artist—is that the former thinks the words are pictures, and so on. He thinks they "represent" things, and take their place. The artist is a slave to the fact (it takes a great while to realize this) that they represent nothing, and that you pay homage to them on their terms. This is one of the reasons artists are so politically decadent, right? There are the words, which will not come forth to greet anybody. Eldridge Cleaver must enter the tunnels of *The Confidence Man,* and the latter doesn't care. This is Melville's fault, of course. He should have so arranged his prose, etc., etc. So I am interested in the flattest of people. Anton is greedy. Now, we'll follow out the design of this chapter, which is vague before me, the periphery. I can just see the basic configuration of the pattern. Ugly.

I would really like to be social, but it is against my nature. I'm not a youth any more. What I would like to do is please you, but I want, even more, to manipulate these inventions. It's really very interesting to make up someone like Anton, and make him greedy. Now I have this character. This "character." You can think that he's real, i.e., representative of someone who is alive (outside of this book); you can think that he is real, that is, when I say "Anton walked" you think of some figure in your mind, representative of Anton, who walks. Or, and I don't think you will do this, you can think of the words. I mean, not in any dull way, but the words in relation to all the others in this book. Now, what if I were to tell you that Anton is a character in this book, based on a character in this book? That is, Anton is "really" Lou Henry. It seems complicated, but it isn't, because it wouldn't change the book at all. There is *no* character development whatsoever (I hope) to Lou Henry, so if Anton is Lou, it means nothing. But what is nice about making fiction is that I can do this. I could even write a short story, I could write a novel. But, at the moment, I'm interested in finishing this book, to see what it looks like. Christmas is coming up again, so far as these people are concerned. I really do like novels where you can build up to scenes like Christmas, and end at dinnertime, or cocktail time, or bedtime. This Christmas includes Anton. Anton and his wife, as a matter of fact. I don't remember her name. What I mean is that I haven't yet thought of a name for her. But she'll be in the following scene, for certain.

Is this book, ultimately, totally unsatisfactory? Not for me, but for the reader, who approaches it "with the best will in the world." But where is the sense in it? Plenty of sense, I'll tell you right now. Has anyone else ever told you about Anton Harley and his wife, Antonia? I met her just yesterday, by the way. It was really very strange meeting someone you're writing about. She looked all right, said she was taking the methadone treatment. She didn't ask about Anton and I didn't proffer any information. We were standing outside the Cedar, I was waiting for her to go on her way so that I could go into the bar and have a drink alone. Didn't want to hear about the old days. I'm in the middle of re-creating them—and in a very unsatisfactory way too, that's for certain. Why anyone would want to plow through this personal shorthand, etc., I don't know. But there are basic structures to the book which, etc. I mean, I'm keeping time straight, and so on, as best I can. I don't want to upset anybody. I was going to put Anton and his wife at a Christmas party at Ellen Kaufman's father's house, but Leo hadn't even met Ellen at the time Anton and Antonia were still married, and living together. But I like the idea of that party. If I had put them at that party, an astute copy editor would have said: "Harleys still together at this party? See p. 123." Or whatever. Well, maybe they're not still together, but they happen to come to the same party. I like that, it seems to take care of this scene. I said that Christmas was coming up and so it is. I've got to do something with these people.

When what to their wondering eyes should appear but a gay piñata! It was Christmastime again at the Marowitz house, and, as Mr. Marowitz had enjoyed doing for the last few years, he had invited his daughter and son-in-law to spend Christmas day with him, and to invite some of their old friends. It was good being around young people for a change. And so on.

I don't know if I can make this resplendent piñata again.

It's turning into an "Image."

Isn't that Anton Harley disappearing into the broom closet with the lovely Annette, Mr. Marowitz's lissome maid? Thank God that he's spent a half hour at the buffet table.

It isn't a very nice way to treat his wife, Antonia. But Leo is stroking her hips and telling her some stories about art, etc. What somebody said once in a plane on the way to a reading in Urbana. You would think that Ellen would be angry, but she knows Leo. It's just his way. She'll intercede if she sees him urging Antonia over to the broom closet, all right, but not before.

This is a good party, really, a good party. Holiday parties really get to be a Big Drag, and a Bore, but this one is really a lot of Fun. Really. I much prefer a party like this, anyway, to one of those terrible New Year's Eve parties, with everybody being fake-happy . . .

Annette is eating Anton in the closet. He's not quite sure he likes it.

I was at this party, I think.* Mr. Marowitz had a really

*Another literary convention. Of course I was at this party.

rotten Noland on the wall. He was talking about it. A lot of "purity" business. You can see why he has become one of Manhattan's foremost collectors. A really rotten painting, one of those targets he did before he found the dollar machine. Here comes Anton. I was, indeed, at this party. Annette went into the kitchen to bring in another tray of cucumber sandwiches. The deed was done in five minutes. Men are "beasts."

Time for the breaking of the piñata!
Time for the breaking of the piñata!
We're going to break the gay piñata, everybody!

At this, I left, and repaired to the ROK bar on Second Avenue, a great place because you never meet anybody there.

Following, a list of the things Anton Harley ate at the party:

18 small cucumber sandwiches; 21 small watercress sandwiches; 11 miniature egg rolls; 2 large roast beef sandwiches; 1 large Virginia ham sandwich; 1 large turkey sandwich; 2 platefuls of potato salad; 1 plateful of coleslaw; 2 dill pickles; 7 deviled eggs: 1 pussy.*

I don't know how to say it: it was a particular way he had of inhaling the food. Almost the way one drinks a shot of whiskey. Now you see it, now you don't.

In any event, all this is from rather haphazard notes I took in the ROK bar. There's one sentence written at the top of the sheet of paper that deserves to be set down here, verbatim. "End of the goddam piñatas!"

Whatever may happen in the future, you may be sure that Anton will survive. Quiet and anonymous on the fringes of softball games, the players of which are at this moment in grammar school. I have the idea that he will be the publisher and editor of a successful literary magazine. His poems changed, free, free, the form open and all-embracing, a graph of his mind in action. Anton dis-

*This should, of course, be "pussy."

covers sex! I mean discovers its Beauty, Power, and Mystery! All-New! Out of this will come these poems. Rotten as ever, but radically changed. They look radically changed. Sex will sometimes do that to a bad writer like Anton. The work lies there, suety, lumpish, nothing will give it life or elegance, style. But it looks different, it looks as if it has begun to move in the direction of life. This hallucination persists for a short while and is dispelled as one sees more and more of the new work. Zombie-like as ever, but in new tatters. It is sex that does this to some people, I am sure that it will do this to Anton. I'm not sure, I'm projecting this.

It would seem that *something* has to happen to Anton in every way. I meant to say that after he and Antonia were separated, he had a long series of affairs with all sorts of girls, most of whom looked slightly dazed from the shaking up they took, I suppose, falling out of trains at Penn and Grand Central—on the way to the Village! Anton scooped them up and tried to wear his cock out with them. You'll excuse my vulgarity, but there is really only one way to describe Anton's actions: when I say that he tried to wear his cock out with them, I mean exactly that. Take, take, when these girls went home, or went away, or fell asleep, or escaped into the bathroom, Anton would masturbate, their bodies in his mind: hanging on. He consumed them even though they were not present. A kind of voodoo, except that it was Anton who practiced it, so that it couldn't be voodoo, lacking that seriousness of intent: this was simply necessity, that extra chicken leg, that extra orgasm. You must be aware that Anton was profligate with his semen because it manufactured itself, free. He didn't care at all about shooting it here, there, and everywhere. He was a sport, after all. Somebody once told him that milk made more and better semen, and all the cows ran for cover. You can check on this if you don't believe me. Farmer Brown will tell you.

Orgies as well! How could I forget those? When I first heard about them from Dick D., then from Anton himself, I was astounded, then pleased, I suppose. In my still-unsuspicious mind, I thought that Anton simply needed some "straightening out" and he'd be all right. So Anton with two girls, or with girl and man, or whatever combinations presented themselves, seemed fine to me, that is, it seemed as if Anton was freeing himself of much that had almost totally stifled him. But nothing about him changed, if anything, he became more obnoxious, giving you the box scores of what he came to think of as his sexual triumphs. Of course he would think that way: sex as combat. He always came out ahead. Then, as I said, he'd run down the play-by-play of the evening, until you'd suddenly remember an appointment somewhere. Guy Lewis called this recapitulation—although it was really more elaborate than that—"suck and tell." Not bad.

As I say, it didn't change this gay blade, he still ate his way through anybody's house, putting his money in a sock and hiding it in the mattress. Why not? Bit a hell of a lot of quarters, believe it. Did I ever tell you about the time he baby-sat and ate his charge's Pablum? These stories are legend. Ask anyone the next time you're in New York—I mean hip New York, of course—about Anton. About the time he went to Rome and kissed the Pope's hand so hungrily that His Holiness had to have ten stitches? I don't know why he and Antonia separated, but I don't want to know.

Now, let's go forward again for a moment to 1980 or so . . . as I said, Anton has found sex. I mean, Sex. Power, Mystery. The real thing, as good as Wilhelm Reich gently opening your fly. Stars and all, as it is in old movies. (They had the right idea, no?) As Michael McClure has it. Stars. Freedom. The poem unshackled, follow your nose into your heart, and so on. Into your ass, your bowels. The unashamed poem, coming to grips with your closed life, etc., etc. Aesthetics as an exercise in the gym. This is also known as Art for All. Anyway, what the hell, I don't want to run this into the ground, believe me when I tell

you that this is the future for Anton. He has a girl who
lives with him in a really "terrific" loft on Greenwich
Street. An actress who is a "really" elegant lesbian this
month. Anton, the moonlight coming into the room, falling on the chair piled with her clothes, sheen of the nylon, he's balding, of course, gray hairs in his mustache,
he gets up to jot down a line or two of the new poem that
has been going around in his mind ever since he had this
evening's Holy Orgasm. He gets up for his pad and pencil,
stops for a moment, passes his hand across his forehead,*
and takes up Jennifer's pack of Chesterfields. He takes
one out and eats it. Then he eats the rest of them. His
penis is exceptionally stiff and this confuses him. He releases his confusion into his poem, which turns out to be
one of thirty-six pages.

A brown scene. Scene of umber and burnt orange, profound maroons. This is Anton's parents' house on Long
Island. Locust Valley, I have said, so we'll keep it that. A
town of deep quiet, opulence, enormous lawns. A group
of people are out there this Sunday in early November, a
kind of open house to which Anton has invited them.
This was some years ago—not too many, since Lou and
Sheila were there, as was Guy. Leo was there, Anton's
brother, Antonia as well. It seems to me, from the comments since made on this excursion, that it was a gesture
on Anton's part. He was sharing his parents' house with
his financially precarious friends. Let's assume that
there were people there who have not been mentioned in
this book, and will not be. This, like all fiction, is selec-
tive, i.e., it is totally removed from the world. You readers
must be aware that while all these people are doing what
they do, my characters, that is, there are hundreds of
people who know them, just on the edge of the narrative:
I can see them, familiar faces whom I may use. Harlan
in Taos was like that. So, you won't be upset when I tell

---

*Novelistic signal for "an anxious moment."

you that on this fall Sunday in Locust Valley there were dozens of people at the Harleys' house. Adults and children. Anton was sharing his happy childhood, his affluent childhood, with his raunchy artistic friends. It was a day partly sunny, orange. Oh, plenty of food and drink, and two maids. There was a bar on one side of the house that looked over a back lawn.

Long Island is sinister to me because I always think of Scott Fitzgerald when I'm there. What I mean is that the mood of Long Island that he presented us with is still there. The face of that island has certainly changed in forty years, and the money has moved around, but that sense of being available only to the worthy persists in certain enclaves and villages. The vulgarity that he noted, that he drew your attention to, casually, a gesture, is there, as he saw it. Certain enclaves and villages. The reader will realize that Long Island, to me, is not solid communities like Valley Stream and Hicksville; I don't speak of Levittown. But there are houses in Oyster Bay, the Sound just outside the kitchen, fine sand, fine . . . Locust Valley is a village that Scott would recognize if he today came back from the dead.

So, a day in Locust Valley. The images of the people who were there are clear, painfully so. Fixed images. Smell of barbecue smoke over the valley, the lawns, mixed with the autumn haze as the afternoon lengthened. Locust Valley, the name itself fills my eyes with bright sunlight, blue shadows on cool rock walls. These places are for those who do not have to work to eat. In a town like this one prays to stay well so that a visit to the hospital may be avoided. Hospitals in towns that stink of privilege are torture chambers for the outsider.

I don't know why Anton did this, really. I can see the faces of the guests with excruciating clarity. It seems to be the end of a period. I read into it, of course. Perhaps it is the melancholy of the season that saddens and mellows everything. It is impossible for me to castigate Anton for this invitation, since whatever faults the gesture

may have had had nothing to do with his nauseating
greed. I see, actually, that this section belongs somewhere else in this book, or that it belongs nowhere and is
simply rootless. It does establish the fact that Anton has
performed at least once in this book without manifesting
his rapacity. It may also be neatly tied to the first section
of Chapter One, since it was at the Harleys' house that
Sheila thrust her long legs out while the young drunks
played touch football on the lawn below. A darkening
November afternoon.

A brown scene, the shouts and laughter muffled. Jesus,
she is a terrible poet. But her legs. Scent of jasmine. She
is drinking Rémy Martin. It's the beginning of something
for someone talking with her, the two of them alone in
the bar. He pours her another cognac, and one for himself. The drunks play on below, deeper haze. In the shad-
owy bar, white gleam of her smile. Let me present to you
that this is Sheila's first gesture toward adultery, here, in
the autumn browns of Locust Valley. The white of her
smile, how aware she is of her long legs, they are beautiful to her. She is excited and charmed, sweet. All of this
delicious as a well-mixed Gimlet. Not far off, the old
movement of the Sound, the one that Fitzgerald knew,
almost exactly the same. I see that this small section may
as well be a gift for Scott. I give him all these characters.

I am amused by this bastard as he gets older, axface into
the future. A deep interest in politics, radical of course.
Which is not to say that his old age will not bring him to
a kind of reasoned conservatism. He has plenty of money
from the houses he owns, and has, I understand, just sold
one for $135,000. He told a friend of mine about it one
night while he demolished a roast leg of lamb that his
hostess had hoped would feed her five guests. He's going
to buy a house up in the mountains with the money, so
that he can get away from the Repression that's coming.
But—and this *is* good news—he'll be coming in to the city
about two or three days a month, for sex. I recollect Lenin

doing that, popping in to Moscow once in a while for a little gash. He always was cunt-crazy, old Lenin. And if it's good enough for Lenin, it's good enough for Harley! As I say, I grow to be amused by him.

But thank God that nobody has to put up with him, that is, he's jailed right here, and you can even skip this chapter if he's got you nervous. As a matter of fact, it occurs to me that all these people may get you nervous, but the only remedy for that is to stop reading. As a matter of fact, stop reading everything. Go to Movie. See Image Move. One Picture Worth Another Picture. Signs! Of the Times! I will not be left groveling in the dust, another writer. Did I tell you that Anton went through a period of film-making? Follows a list of his films, all of which have become examples of classic amateurism. *White Light; Strawberry Parfait; Green, Green, I Want You Green; Eating It; Tutti-Frutti Sunday;* and (with Biff Page) *Margarine Melts in His Mouth.* They're fantastic, a "pure innocence that had me almost on the edge of tears throughout," "their roughness of technique and the lack of variety in the camera angles slowly fill one with the sort of aching pity that one reserves for only the greatest clowns," "they're all candy on Xmas morning," "Harley had no peer in the ability to capture the wild, yet tender hunger of the adolescent for experience." God, they were rotten flicks! Jonas Mekas compared them to the early poems of Rimbaud, and scolded *Off the Pigs Review* for not bothering to review them. Anton told me that he was really disappointed about the lack of attention shown his films, particularly since the whole repertory was put on over a three-night period at the Cinemathèque. But Page Moses opened his *Twilight in Bloody Heads* that week and all the attention focused on that. Baylor Freeq was the whole movie, playing the Spirit of Dark Eros. And they wound up the week with *Dutchman,* which brought out another battalion of the hip middle-aged from the Village, Cobble Hill, Park Slope, East Tenth Street, the Heights, and Hoboken. So Anton was lost in the shuffle.

Someone told me that he even called the Jones film a "slick nigger play." But he got a grant that fall anyway to continue his promising experiments. He put it in the bank along with his tenants' rents.

Freedom came to him. Stars in his eyes. Suddenly, he was liberated, and open. Believed in this freedom as Richard Nixon believed in nuclear weapons. Immutable, once you have found it, never let it go. Oh, this Anton should have stayed a rotten motorcycle racer. There is something can be made of a terrible sportsman, a loser. The romantic myth is perfectly suited to the American sensibility. Crying in the movies as Deborah Kerr eats her heart out over Anton Harley, the also-ran, grime and oil on his ax. But he was a Poet. As he got more free, his poems became looser, more open, he reached out, out, understood, finally, what a well-known publisher meant when he said, "Metaphor is real. Those who think otherwise have an academic sense of metaphor, that is, that it is *not* real." This brings us all around once again to the old What Is Reality? game, now in the top of the 423rd inning. This was a very hip publisher, who spent every waking moment convincing the world at large that he was a poet. There were days when he would spend hours trying to decide how a poet should look on such a day . . . should he wear his smoke shades or his blue ones? Anton listened to him, and Yea, he understood. Published a lot of poems in his magazine, starting in about 1967 or so. Free! Free! Irremediably poor. Such work is irremediable because it has no working parts. It is a great chunk of, say, Liederkranz. Try and fix that. This product of such smug mediocrity. A Poet Who Is Alive! Etcetera. Never trust a poet, or anyone else in the arts, for that matter, who says, "Well, to be alive, to be in life, is more important than any poem." When they say this they are first of all insulting you, since they assume that they have discovered some profound idea, and secondly, they are apologizing—in an aggressive way—for the mediocrity of their productions. Smug people, dear God. Can you imagine Anton Harley believing that "metaphor is real," and so on? He may, of course, think that it's edible. Good Metaphor, slurp, slurp! Where'd you get these metaphors? Jesus, they're so fresh! On the other hand, one can see Anton spilling coffee on some metaphors. The metaphors say, Ouch! Cut it out, you free and open craftsman! His poems progress. Finally he is all blue orgones, zzzippp, zzzawww, zzzooow, crackle. He has reached a plateau, but ever onward! Art as Progress. (This is a Western idea, still beloved by thousands, though officially discredited.)

We approach the end of this chapter. I have one more small story to tell you about Anton, which will hopefully leave you with the proper feeling for him. After you read this next section, the final one, do what you will with him. Maybe we should have him meet with an accident. Or at the bottom of the last page, or in the margin, you can write in something like "Anton disappears in Coney Island," or "Anton Harley last seen entering White Tower," or "Police nab Harley in huge hamburg hijack." Whatever you like, do with him. Try and nab him yourself before he really gets on your nerves.

It's a well-known fact that painters, when drunk, or depressed, or manic, will often offer paintings to friends and acquaintances for nothing, or for some ridiculous price. These paintings should be refused and the painter, as a matter of fact, should be protected in his temporary madness.

A night in Max's. Quiet. Anton at the bar with some unknown deadbeat, a hulking man with a red beard, his hero and idol is Cid Corman. You understand this guy, right? If not, not. Anton is belching softly into his glass of Miller's, telling redbeard that he has the entire run of *Origin,* first series. The hulk is twisting so that it looks as if he wants to masturbate right there at the bar. Anton notes his envy and greed with pleasure and belches

again. He's made the rounds of the restaurant, stopping
off at tables, eating rolls and butter and salad where he
can. Now he's having a High Life on the house and driving this poor hulk mad.

The hulk leaves, or left long ago. Anton is casually
eating paper napkins and sipping the same beer. The
scene is shifting, the late-night, after-dinner crowd is
coming in. All sorts of youths with poppas who own art-
book publishing houses, young directors who can kiss
three asses at once, girls who once said hello to José
Torres, the highlight of the evening is a guy who looks
exactly like Saul Maloff, very very hip, indeed! He's with
a girl whose husband is producing a tasteful musical
comedy called *Pilgrim State Rock.*

Somewhere along the line, our old friend, Dick Detective, has entered the scene. He's been drinking Sazeracs
lately, because they're so delicately—robust. As is usual,
Dick fades in and out of focus, taking notes, picking up
whatever information he can, adding old memos to new,
stirring dull roots with spring rain. A fairly profitable
evening for the Dick; he's filled out his file for 1961 on a
girl who makes underground films.

And suddenly, to employ a trope of the novelist, it had
grown very late. Or, this way: suddenly—it was quite late.
Thank God for the first writers who used this to avoid all
the furniture between there and here. In Max's, the usual
night, arrgh. In the discotheque upstairs a woman, eight
months pregnant, danced wildly for forty-five minutes,
and everybody said how great it was, how vital, how
groovy, how beautiful, etc. Oh, dear sweet bleeding
Christ. Two fags danced, chuckle. A lot of things happened, but, somehow, and even though, suddenly—it was
quite late. A painter entered the bar, drunk, very drunk,
on the fifth day of a tear. I don't want to go into a big thing
here about this painter, let me say that he is not very
good, but that he isn't a fake. He has a gallery, sells fairly
well, and has established a reputation among other
painters and the cognoscenti. Anton still at the bar. The

painter asks Anton to buy him a Dewar's. Anton says, blanching, Ha. Ha. And what do I get out of it? To which the painter replies, Shit, I'll give you a fucking *painting* for a *quart* of Dewar's.

As a motorcycle, when taking the curve into the stretch first seems to hang back so as to gather its power for a great burst of speed, then releases that speed in a lunge like a horse falling off a cliff as quickly as jet planes climbing into the blue, so did Anton Harley move swiftly to the cashier to cash a check, leave the bar and return, moments later, with a quart of Dewar's. The reader may ask where he got this since it was "quite late." The Detective will be able to tell him, if he will write Dick at once. Anton gave the bottle to the painter, the painter put it in his jacket pocket, then reeled out of the bar with Anton steering, to his loft, where Anton picked out a large canvas. There are witnesses who say that Dick Detective took advantage of this offer as well, but all evidence as to the truth of this has mysteriously disappeared. If you see Anton, ask him to show you the painting someday. It's probably the best thing this painter has done.

Rapacity plus taste is a formidable combination, since it so often passes for intelligence. One pities the artist in a world of such predators, all of whom are deeply engaged in the arts too. I'm telling you that Anton's is the spirit that moves the times. The common enemy of all these cultivated people is art: why do you think Anton eats so much? Maybe it's because he might one day swallow this tough lump, this intransigent and despised art, and be done with it. And let the songs, dances, and novelties roll!

7
Many Years a Painter

A *brochure from the Gom Gallery announcing a* *one-man show by Bart Kahane.*

Bart Kahane's sculpture is simply deceptive. It looks joyous and frivolous, like a fading beauty from Proust. Only the serious attention it rewards reveals it to be sternly modal, harshly chaste, and complex with hidden directions.

Central to the sculptor's vision is the balance of horizontal and vertical conceptions of structured space. Each piece abounds with contradictions; each piece can be seen as a "tone row" of gay themes and unbridled mirth; or as a sort of closed, finite, totemic construct; or yet again, as a marker or signpost gesturing toward that final sculpture which will, perhaps, never be created. The pieces are static, trapping the viewer with their sense of totality. But as we watch, this seeming diamond-ness of the conceptual changes before the eye until the works translate themselves into the simple, yet brilliantly accurate figures of a dreamlike dance.

Many years a painter, Mr. Kahane shows a healthy, almost a holy respect for boundaries—the piece as conductor as well as frame for the artistic kinesis. Yet he has eschewed the painter's care for the contrapuntals and harmonics of color. The gluey black and perverse white, bitter gray metal and nagging orange plastic—all have been excruciatingly selected with regard to the colors' *colorlessness*. There is no allusive reference here, rather a totally compact extrusive force and thoroughness, a manipulation of mass and density, volume and plane, so subtle as to be almost unnoticeable. Each piece seems to be of that soi-disant gaiety associated with the receding colors a painter, in his bright craft, often makes us long for in the picture plane. Yet Kahane has achieved this special *hilaritas* without resort to the quiddities of color. The concern here is all with the maintenance of sculptural thrust, pure and unadorned, in spite of itself.

Mr. Kahane has brilliantly manifested that concern.

DICK DETECTIVE

1. ST. JAMES
2. TENTH STREET RAGA
3. LE FOU
4. LEO'S COCKTAIL
5. PORTRAIT FOR HARRY BORE
6. JAZZETTI
7. BLUE AND GRAY 1
8. FEMS McCLARK
9. ORANGE SPLIT
10. BLUE AND GRAY 2
11. MISS BROWN
12. TEN EYCK WALK
13. PLUM BEACH
14. LOTT'S HOUSE
15. THE CALIPH
16. OFFISSA PUPP
17. BLACK LADDER
18. QUIERO VERDE

We'll have to take one more really quick trip to New Mexico, Taos that is. This one is in the nature of a field trip, however, a search for the artifact. We look for a small metal sculpture, dull finish, all in all about the size of a brick. I know it's in a house out here, because I've seen it, sitting on a window ledge, behind it—what else? —the mountains. It's not a bad sculpture, derivative, obviously the work of a student, a tyro, but one who is talented. The reason that we've come out here, friends, is that it may well prove useful for you to see what may well be Bart Kahane's first successful piece of sculpture. Now we may leave Taos.

But why Bart Kahane? Or, who Bart Kahane? He is really unnecessary to this tale,* and might just as well sit on his ass somewhere in his Mercedes, enjoying life. I

---

*One wonders just who *is* necessary to it.

don't need a sculptor here, or a painter for that matter, it's just that the other day I got to thinking about old Bart, remembering him with a kind of fondness, that incredibly clear mind, scheme after scheme coming from it, and each scheme aimed at the achievement of success. Big-time success, I don't speak here of the kind of success my old friend Leo K. settled for—a little crumb off the table. Good old Bart. What was so enchanting about him was that he disguised this comptroller's brain behind a façade of la vie bohème. How many gobs of spit did Bart let fly upon how many rugs? How many times did he piss in the potted plants? Shit in a few bathtubs in his day too, old Bart. One remembers him throwing beer cans in friends' faces, etc. Punching his wife or trying to kick her in the belly when she was six months pregnant. One can forgive a man who does this, let us say, helplessly. It is incredible to see it all as a matter of choreography. Before he shifted to sculpture, when he was still involved in a kind of painting that might be termed real in some sense, i.e., there was at least a halfway commitment to the work, I remember him figuring how he would act at a particular party that night, or that week. The perfect outrage, etc. He was a Crazy Artist, in spades. The enfant terrible, the young genius. Plotted and planned, the strategy totally worked out when he was still in art school, the tactics candidly revealing the direction of the campaign, thrusting toward that house in Springs, that giant loft on Fourteenth Street, the best of booze and all the art-freak women he could handle. His wife, the charming hostess, entertaining the freeloaders on the Island all summer. A herald of that breed of artist with the sensibility of the Stakhanovite. Make plenty products good, feel nice, put on market for people who need, *da!* I am fascinated by them all with their paper suits and paper assholes, their faces have supported the hip slicks for at least five years. And Bart Kahane, many years a painter, saw it coming. Saw it all coming: saw *them* all coming, one should say. All the urban rubes in their ruffled evening shirts and lavender dinner jackets. Bart's feeling was, for every share they own, let there be a painting! One of his own, preferably, but this was too good to be true, and, in less than a month, there were many more people on the scene, so that now it is impossible to prove that Bart first saw the rubes advancing, plenty of dollars in their hands, a lust to speak real American words with real American painters, hang these real paintings with real oil on their real walls. Bart saw them all coming, through those lean years, living on Delancey Street, drinking ten-cent dark beer in a dump under his studio, saw it all on the way: a hip nouveau-riche, a class so modern that *they* call *themselves* parvenus. The idea is that one is to forgive them because of their candor. Bart saw that one might with safety even spit on certain selected floors here and there among these dazzlers and nippers. Whatever ultimately served the purpose, that he did. I can see him now, upon his arrival in New York, wearing a shirt and tie he had borrowed from a fellow painter three years before. I didn't know that then. The perfect friend for Bart is Dick Detective, and, of course, Dick was—and is—his friend. A perfect pairing, each seeking that position from which the other should be forced to eternally give, give, and give some more. That metal sculpture out in Taos is in the house that Anne Kaufman once lived in. She left it there when she moved to the Coast. It was a gift to Anne from Dick D., who had got it from Bart. Now, think about all that for a while and you'll have a rather arresting diagram. In the mind's eye, one sees that sculpture on the window ledge. The setting sun bathes it in a red glow, the same red glow that gives these mountains their fabled name, Sangre de Cristo. Out here one can find peace, so Harlan told Bunny. Why are people so shabby that even fictitious characters stand revealed as corrupt or damaged? Go ahead, tell me to fulfill my obligations by attacking the society that spawns such corrupt people and dismal art. I am attacking the society. While you make the revolution, I make

art. The Duty of an Artist Is to Make Art: The Second
Declaration of Manhattan.

But I want you to think of Bart. We'll build a stairway
to the stars with the young man.

Ultimate success. Or: Ultimate Success! Those are lovely
words, particularly to Americans, you can ask Truman
Capote if you don't believe me. Ask James Brown and
Gloria Steinem. Ask John Berryman and Nelson Rockefeller and Richard Nixon and Warren Burger. Ask Bart
Kahane. There are many ways of reaching the summit of
one's chosen field of endeavor. Law and order is one way;
on the other hand, if one is a mad-dog killer, the wanton
destruction of innocent, family-loving policemen, preferably with automatic weapons or sharp knives, is another.
If one is a policeman, the murder of niggers serves nicely.
I should say, to quote the police report, "subjects, three
Negro men." Ultimate success! In one's chosen field of
endeavor! You save string, and bottle caps, you save
something, pennies.

Found objects, that one saves.

Bart, it must be stated here, after the above false starts,
was a saver. Many people attribute his "ultimate success" to this fact. I, however, am not one of them. Bart's
success was dependent on a combination of circumstances, although I don't deny that the saving of things
was a contributing factor to his ultimate "success." It was
true, at least it will be true in these pages (since I own this
particular game), that Bart had the knack of hanging on
to things until he could find a use for them. Many times
he would create a use for things that, to the unskilled
observer, seemed utterly useless. Many people thought he
was a chintzy prick bastard fuck. He had that knack of
saving things for some mysterious "ultimate" use. That's
the way Bart said "ultimate." "Ultimate." When he lived
on Delancey Street he really wasn't too bad a guy.

But, really, there was nothing that wasn't saved, not
only things, but introductions, held cherished for years,

until they could be somehow used at the correct time to get to a party, or get away for a weekend. At the party there might be a buyer, or his dazed wife, resplendent in what she had been sold by someone she had been told about. Dazed and bored and tanned, that look of old leather from the sun, the blond hair, the bony chest, the alcoholic daughter. Why are the rich, as a class, so stupid? Bart at these parties was a beauty to watch, that perfect ability to fawn with dignity that the rich so love. Kissing ass with the grace of a dancer. Bart progressed rapidly at these parties, at the Southampton weekends, the Fourth of July out on Fire Island. At first, because he hated the rich for their stupidity and money, and was bitter because he knew that he was a good painter who had little hope of being recognized, he was a boor. Pissed in the tub, belched, felt up the married women, etc. Bad news. The rich tolerate that behavior only if you are already famous, i.e., Jackson Pollock might have got away with that, Marc Chagall might be able to do it in Leonard Lyons' house, and so on. But even the rich will not tolerate the unknown enfant terrible. You have to give the rich credit for the dignity of their enormous vulgarity. They will be shit on only by the best. Bart understood this presently, and was a model sycophant thereafter, until he had reached the status of up-and-coming important painter, at which point, etc., many a Givenchy-covered buttock was squeezed. Save, save, Bart even saved names, to use maybe years later. Fired them like rifles, or placed them deftly into conversations like rounds from a mortar. He was very good. In a tuxedo, his dark glasses, hair just shaggy enough, his Gitane hanging from the corner of his mouth, dashing fat cigarette, only the expert could tell that he was kissing ass. I must admit that Bart never stopped kissing ass. He had to sell, and so he had to kiss. He had to appear at the right parties, at the right times, all the time. When he had made it, he still had to show up, since he was only one of at least a hundred young artists dependent on hip collectors for their comfort. So

he was there, always there, sometimes elegantly late, as
if he was careless, sometimes drunk, as if he had almost
forgotten, etc. Sometimes with a neurotic girl he had
picked up in Max's, so as to establish his gigantic insou-
ciance, sometimes with a young homosexual poet whose
greatest influence was John Betjeman. But he was always
there, along with all the other painters, sculptors, and
environmental structuralists, and what have you, who
needed plenty of gasoline for their Jaguars plus the
wife's little MG out on the Island to run to the store.

A vulgar man, polished until he gleamed, as is the style
of this time. The polish is, of course, rich, and brings out
the subtle highlights. That also is the style of the time. I
have told you already that this is not a gallery of freaks.
This is a book about destruction. No tools to be found here
with which to build the new society. I would say that this
work is to be taken slowly, more like an antidote.

When Bart was in the navy—I seem to recall that he was
in the navy—he married. Very few people know this. As
a matter of fact, his present wife doesn't know that he
was married once before; she thinks he simply lived with
a girl. What is the point here? As if I care whether I allow
him marriage or not—there is a point, however. You must
know that Bart's first wife was Mexican, he married her
in Dago or some grim navy town like that. He married
her because he thought of her as being hot stuff—a hot
little Mex broad, soft lips, big mouth, wet pussy, hotcha!
Behind him all those desperate years of American midwestern boyhood. I should say, simply, American boyhood. Dear sweet Jesus, the quarts of semen shot off into
toilets and handkerchiefs, towels, bathtubs, the sisters,
teachers, nuns, salesgirls, etc., ravished in the imagination. And the giggling girls surrounding him, as it so
happened, in Terre Haute, though it could have been
anywhere; those girls who panted, fearfully stroking his
rod burning in his pants. A hot tamale! They got married.
They got divorced. Bart saved all that too. At perfect mo-

ments he let it be known that, in his youth (sometimes he showed you his tattoos), he was married to a Mexican girl. This was at a time in New York that for a Caucasian to be involved with someone who had some skin color other than Queens White was thought of by many to be exotic. I must admit that many didn't think of it in that way at all. Now that I consider it, in those years, the middle fifties, there were many in New York who didn't think of anything. One sees their ravaged faces in lost—well-lost—dreams.

But Bart knew just where and when to drop this information. He did it with a kind of forced hilarity, quiet, of course, and underneath a corner of bitterness showed. God, he grew up in those years, looking at him anyone can begin to understand Henry Ford, Charles Revson, J. Paul Getty, Bernard Baruch.* One begins to understand why there are people, outside of critics who are paid for it, who read Mark Van Doren, and why English professors can tell you all about Vladimir Nabokov but are ignorant of Ezra Pound. Bart was good, he made all the moves. Do you think that it's any slob who can learn what tie to wear just by looking around? Kissing ass with divine skill. Someday I'm going to read *The Real Life of Sebastian Knight,* and then Columbia had better watch its step.

Bart knew when to let fall, gently, spiced gingerly with bitterness, his story of Conchita.** How her father had taken her back to Monterrey, the threats of her two brothers, swarthy motherfuckers with drooping mustaches and big daggers. Are the mission bells still ringing there? The sun it is very hot beating down on the plaza, my son, and you are a perfect target there in your black suit of mourning. While Bart spoke, he did well with the drinks, did I mention that he was an alcoholic? I don't want to get involved with his alcoholism, it didn't trouble him too much, except for tearing his body apart. Periodically, he

*That's beloved Bernard Baruch, not the other one.
**A totally ridiculous name!—Zuzu Jefferson.

went on the wagon. He joined AA years later, that is, he joined AA when he remarried. I never liked his second wife, as a matter of fact, I'm not really interested in her name. I'm not interested in her character. As another matter of fact, she was always at home in Springs, doing something interesting out there. What a bore she is! Can you imagine being a novelist and having to make her up, make her—believable? I have a mildly interesting idea, though, for those readers—and they are, I understand, legion—who insist on a character they can "get ahold of." Let's say that Bart's wife is Lolita. I mean, she is the exact Lolita that Nabokov stitched together. O.K. Now you've got Bart's wife—there she is, already made, grown up, yes, as she is at the end of the book, with Humbert dead. And Bart has got this Lolita for a wife. Bart married Lolita in Judson Memorial Church. Afterward, Lincoln Gom, who showed Bart, gave them a little reception at his apartment. These people are lost from the start. And successful. One is nonplused by the idea of those who are lost and failures too. Later that year, Bart went to Rio de Janeiro for a Biennale. One soft night, bossa nova on the air, a dark-eyed girl in a small café smiled warmly at Bart, and he, suddenly realizing who she was, stretched out his hand—

The times that Bart had, playing with Little Iodine in the golden Midwest. Inevitable that he should ultimately marry Lolita. He told stories about growing up, the bluffs behind the house, overlooking the gleaming river, soft wind carrying the smell of thousands of acres of corn flung out to the west and north. In the sycamores the candlelight was gleaming. The old swimming hole, the county fair, the fantastic smell of his mother's pies cooling on the windowsill, as she picked snap beans in the kitchen garden. If you've heard one of these stories you've heard them all. They're like movies about boxing. Has there ever been a movie about boxing that didn't have crooks in it? Or stories about Midwestern childhoods that did not feature cooling pies? Yes, to the latter anyway: Edward Dahlberg's books on his childhood in Kansas City. (It strikes me as curious that Guy Lewis should come from Kansas City.) As a matter of fact, Bart Kahane probably came from Kansas City, that is, its environs, as well. Lou Henry once told me that April Detective came from Kansas City, which is totally ludicrous. However, I got a letter the other day from a friend of Sheila Henry's, and this informant told me that Sheila came from Kansas City, and not, as I have maintained throughout this history, from Brooklyn. There is something about this Kansas City that seems to fascinate my characters, so much so that they will lie to me. And to each other as well. I was in the airport in Kansas City once. They are correct: it is a magnificent city.*

Things that Bart Kahane maintained he liked. He did not like them.
  1. Cooling pies.
  2. Larry Rivers' painting.
  3. *The New York Review of Books.*
  4. Huckleberry pie.
  5. Yogurt.
  6. The Rolling Stones.
  7. The Beatles.
  8. Women.
  9. *The New Yorker.*
  10. Johnny Walker Red Label.**

Things that Bart Kahane maintained he disliked. He liked them.
  1. Yankee Doodles.
  2. John Wayne movies.
  3. Adolph Gottlieb's paintings.
  4. The novels of John D. MacDonald.

---

  * *Vide* remarks by Lou Henry and Vance Whitestone, among others: "God! A magnificent, truly magnificent city!"
  **A studied vulgarism.

5. Blood, Sweat and Tears.
6. Ketchup on fried eggs.
7. Franco-American spaghetti.
8. Blended whiskey and ginger ale.
9. *From the Terrace.*
10. Very large, noisy parties.

12 March 1952

Dear Conchita,

Boy, what fun we had last night. It was terificc. Me and the other guys you met took a bus to San Francisco and ate in Chinatown. What food. Terificc! But I was blue thinking about you and when you will be able to come on out here in the Valey to mary me and settle down. Boy I can't wait! All I do I guess is talk about you so much that the guys are kiding me a lot about it. I think of you all the time your dark eyes. Sometimes I think I'll go crazy thinking about you.

Well I can't think of much more to say. Guess I'll turn in since theres a lot work tomorow in the vine yards and the cow looks sick and ma needs help you know, cooling her pies and all. Sure wish you were here to help her cool them.

Say I forgot to tell you their was some swell John Wayne movie on in town last night. The girl in it reminded me of you with her dark skin and beutiful bosome.

I love you (xxxx),
Bart*

Got to know all the steps, the sardonic comment, the haughty look, vulgar wit, just right of course, the well-placed "fuck" or "shit"—Lolita with him at the right places, God knows where that ex-husband of hers went, but you know that Bart paid him off. Lolita was terrifically beautiful in clothes, she wore them with just the right flair. Got to know all the steps, old Bart. Imagine a sculptor—one who had been, of course, many years a painter—with the *literacy* he had, his all-encompassing

---

*The author has obviously made a mistake here. This must be some other Bart, or some other Conchita, or both. Mr. Whitestone feels that we should simply cut this letter out of the text.—Z.J.

curiosity, the magazines he read, the awareness of the new writers, film-makers. He had even seen Anton Harley's films. Interviews: "And so, Mr. Kahane, you *would* say that your basic interest at the moment is—less . . . sculptural . . . than it is—what shall I say?—environmental?" "Yes, man, that's fair enough. I mean, out where I live, you dig, on the Island, right? Well, I wake up, go outside for a smoke, there's this sand and this sun, the green, dig it? I mean, there it is, just waiting to be used. I mean, sculpture won't make it any more. You've got to get involved with these real things, make them part of the piece!" He was very good. Lolita did what she wanted, more or less, Bart had his studio on Fourteenth Street, came in when he wanted, stayed a week, ten days, worked with an ease and a surety that put bricklayers to shame. His prices were getting up there with Stella's and Noland's. His next show at the Gom will no doubt be noted, with photos of both a representative piece and Bart, in *Time*. Lincoln Gom's got a legman who earns his money.

I'm not interested, and neither should you be, in whether this man lay awake at night, or cried. What is interesting is that these things, if they occurred, did not in any sense change his life. He kept turning out those pieces, Jesus God! they were impeccably slick. The money kept pouring in, Bart cried or lay awake, or did something else totally out of character, who cares? Pretty soon he would get to the point at which he would think that what he was doing was valuable. Then he would say things like "God, it's a drag that Steve isn't making it . . . he's a *good* painter." I mean to say that he would act as if he thought there was some strange black magic at work that prevented Steve from selling pictures, and not that the market was closed to pictures by nameless painters. This is a strange time to be an artist.* I read a review the other day in which some flashing mind played the role of Professor of Morals and Ethics because it finally

---

*That is, if they ever find out that you really *are* an artist, watch out.

occurred to him, after all these years, that Genet means what he says about the beauty of Evil. This poor soul all this time thought that Genet was an act on television, some really weird comic who sneaked on the "Tonight" show. I'm cutting my throat here, destroying whatever chance this book has to get a "favorable review." If there's one thing that I need, at this stage of my career, it's a "favorable" review. I don't mean to denigrate all critics, God, no, not all of them . . . I mean, reviewers, not all of them, some of them are good, really good. They pay attention, and say "oneiric." They pose you questions of good and evil, and answer them. They "come to the conclusion" that Pound, after all, is more an influence and teacher and guiding light than he is a poet. That's what they say in these "reviews." (Don't tell me that this is a digression, this whole book is a digression: from the novel. I'll write a novel next. Title will be *Day Left When Eye: Suck Off My Pans* by Guy Lewis.) He has always been an interesting "experimentalist" however. He doesn't have the unifying power of a Frost, however, or a Berryman.* As a matter of fact, Pound's entire career, the tragedy of his career, might be said to consist of an obsessive need to create bogeymen in order to be able to dispel them, a need to create straw men so that he can knock them over. In other words, he's very strange and literary.

I see that this section is totally inexplicable, in every way. I have a suspicion that this chapter is totally inexplicable. I know what I meant to say, but the phone has been ringing all morning, some old friend of mine, in from Taos, bringing me news of Nature. Here's a poem he wrote some time ago, when he was living in Maine. This pioneer loves nature.

> Light my pipe—
>   drink tea,
> It's too bitter.
>   Got to get that old stump

---

*It is clear that in his anger the author is knocking over straw men.

Out of the ground after lunch
                              (rabbit and kidney beans)
Hell—I'd rather read.
                      Drink some more tea
And think about reading, light
                              my pipe, light
The stove,
            Oh—God. Homemade applejack
Is good, too strong,
                      Light my pipe, hell—
Out of matches!
                Thirty miles to town.

Anyway, he's been calling me, so I haven't been able to make this chapter coherent. The one fact that I really wanted you to know is that Bart has been having an affair with April. Sometimes he lay awake at night and cried about it. He felt like such a louse! (A *louse!*)

To be taken slowly, as an antidote. This book is full of ingredients, a specific brew, concocted to ward off the poisons that abound. Bart Kahane is an ingredient, he's difficult to get hold of, because I can see his face. Who can forget his hilarious excesses? Trying to set his Christmas tree on fire. Attempted drowning of a fellow artist off the beach at Sea View, Fire Island. I can see his face. Spitting on the floor, punching his wife. A really bad movie, that's what he was, whenever he was around, his "years of apprenticeship." Now that I think of it, he was a bore because he wanted to be famous at twenty-five, and it wasn't until he was thirty-two that he was famous. Not famous the way Mickey Mantle is famous, of course. Famous the way that Stanley Kunitz is famous. Not quite famous. It's difficult to explain what I mean, since the New York art world is a wilderness of hierarchy. He had made it, let's say that, at thirty-two. Lolita was in Springs, or who knows where? Worked on occasion with a little theater group, very hip and irreverent, the director a Genius Fag. A Genius Fag! Bart began his affair with April Detective, feeling bad, really *bad,* about Dick. I mean that he did *feel bad,* but he still plugged April. The pleasure of infidelity lies in feeling bad about it. It may be helpful here to note that Bart did not feel bad about Lolita, just about Dick. As far as he was concerned, Lolita's past had very effectively cut her off from any compassion at all. The way she fucked that really *civilized* Humbert around! Well, she could go fuck *herself* from now on.*

I don't care about these developments, except insofar as April has finally given Dick the works, which is a great pleasure, as far as I'm concerned. It's even more of a pleasure that she should be bedding down with Bart. This way, Lolita can go along, fairly well out of harm's way, and Bart can feel as if life has meaning for him. Bart is—Bart is really—I don't know how to put this. Bart is totally delighted that his really terrible sculptures are hailed and sell. His "environmental" work is coming into its own. A large "show" will take place in Woodstock in the summer, Bart and nine poets in white robes, in a gravel pit flooded with strobe lights, will present you with something new. I understand that one of the poets will be Clayton Eshleman, who will set you Free, as he sets himself Free. But what I'm getting at is that Bart currently puts on an act for those he knows very well. He gets drunk, and after spitting on the floor, or on his friends, and firing some beer cans around, maybe trying to piss on Lolita, if she's around, or on April, if she's around, he confesses that he's sold out, oh, God, he's sold out and lost his gift, oh, God, etc. This is true. What is not true is that Bart cares about it. He is a disgusting bastard because he thinks that he should put on this "lost artist" routine. Meanwhile, you see his smiling, mustachioed face in front of one of his plastic-and-spackle pieces, jumping out at you from *Vogue* or *Harper's Bazaar.* There's a black model in a white "little-nothing undie," her body contorted around the piece, legs spread, manag-

---

*It was only occasionally that Lolita did this. Most of the time it was Lincoln Gom who serviced her. She called him—of course—"Linc."

ing somehow to perform fellatio on a protruding chunk of white plastic. When Bart sees this photo—Lolita, let's say, throws the magazine at him, accusing him of laying the model—he laughs in what he knows is a curt and bitter way, and says: "First I have to work with these cunts, now I'm supposed to be fuckin' them!" He looks at the photo. "Wouldn't *mind* puttin' it to this spade chick, though." He looks up at Lolita, who is about to faint from the boredom of hearing this variation on a theme, laughs long and bitterly, "But maybe they'd figure I was taking it out in trade and not pay me—then where would you get your clothes?" Lolita, at this, does faint. Bart gets drunk, pisses in his pants, or shits on the lawn, or masturbates and comes all over the magazine—something disgusting that nobody you know would ever do. (There's been quite enough of that unpleasantness in life *and* literature.) Then he starts to moan and curse himself for "selling out." At this moment, Paul Cézanne, disguised as a deus ex machina, enters the scene, and kicks Bart Kahane's ass. Bart leaves the room, sobbing and begging for mercy. Lolita revives and allows* Cézanne to bugger her. Ah, the degenerate French!

May 17, 1967

Dear Bart,

I think it's clear, after the other night, that we ought to keep away from each other. I really don't want to hurt Dick. You probably know that he's put up with my indiscretions on more than one occasion. I'm sure, as well, that his respect and friendship for you would affect him very deeply should he find out about us. And there is, of course, Lolita to be considered. I think that there is definitely a "magic" between us, but we must consider Dick and Lolita. I really think that another meeting is out of the question, although I do want to be (oh, God, how corny this is!) good friends.

Your dear friend, with much care,
April

*The word should be "invites" if I know my Lolita.

The reader will note that this letter is very much like one sent about a year earlier, from Sheila to Dick Detective. It would seem, on the evidence, that Sheila and April somehow conspired in this device. Which means, of course, that Sheila not only knew that April was having an affair with Bart; it also means that April knew that Sheila had had an affair with Dick . . . I mean she knew for certain. Of course, this isn't necessarily so. Sheila might have helped April compose the letter to Bart, without ever revealing that she had once written a letter much like it herself. Again, she may have forgotten the tone and mood of the letter she had written Dick, and suggested this letter to April without remembering the style of her own. Perhaps it was a coincidence. Whatever it was it has happened behind my back, that is, these characters rush about among these letters and syllables doing, apparently, as they like. Retreating further and further into the pages, so that my book has become a street guide to some destroyed city. But what about the letter's impact on Bart? What shall we make him do, the poor bastard? He writes a letter back to April, a measured tone, voice quiet but intensely furious, does she think that he can be brushed off like this? Does she think that he is "some poor hack who can't get a woman?" And so on. The prose is not particularly good, but for Bart it's fine.

What is curious about this letter (which I have had the opportunity to compose and destroy) is that it is totally unlike the letter that Bart wrote to Conchita in 1952, the one that Mr. Whitestone wants to cut out of this book as being apocryphal. I'm afraid that Whitestone is correct and yet, at the same time, the letter might well be an example of Bart's rather sophomoric humor at the time. Perhaps there are code words in the letter that only he and Conchita understood the meaning of, and so on. One mustn't forget that Bart, at the time, was in the navy, and aberrations are quite common among men in the armed forces. What makes the possibility of, let us say, tension even greater with Bart is that he, for some reason that the military can explain, was stationed at El Toro Marine Air Base in California. Not a good place for a deepwater sailor* to be, not at *all!* But: the letter to Conchita, that yokel style, etc.

One sometimes wonders whether there was a Conchita or not. Bart lied, cheated, stole, begged, borrowed, and so on. Some of the things he has said check out and some do not. He has tattoos, which certainly prove something. And one of the tattoos, on the right forearm, seems to bear out his claim that he served in the U.S. Navy. The design is an anchor, through a wreath with ribbons. On the anchor are lettered the words, *U.S.S. Horace Rosette,* which, according to Bart, is the name of the destroyer he served on in the icy waters off North Korea. All right. I'll tell you the truth. I doubt very much the existence of a destroyer named the "Horace Rosette." As a matter of fact, those who have known Bart for years all testify to the fact that he served on a minesweeper in the North Atlantic, the *U.S.S. McClark.* I'm perfectly willing to accept this as a fact. Then why should he bother to have himself tattooed with the name of a destroyer which does not, and did not, exist? The suspicion is growing on me that this chapter may well have been intended to deal with somebody else entirely. I may be confusing three or four people in this attempt to "bring" Bart "to life" for you. But somebody will emerge and I think that we all ought to let him. What I suspect is that the moment Bart's identity is established, however tenuously, this chapter will be over. Let's hope so.

It was a clearly defined talent that he had. All so useless. But the talent was enough so that with application and attention it could yield the kind of work that gallery owners are delighted to show. Useless, and without beauty, decorations for the rich and the aspirant rich. One sees a room: Mrs. Roger Whytte-Blorenge, Larry Rivers, vari-

*Let's assume the truth of this for the moment.

ous girls in differing degrees of Anglo-Saxon guilt, others, Jewish girls, looking very Anglo-Saxon and extremely guilty over that, Ted Berrigan is there, Ron Padgett, etc. On the wall, a crushed tin and sprayed excelsior collage by Bart. You've got that, now simply extend this to a sense of its being the end of the artifact, i.e., its destination. Then you see Bart shaping the pieces this way. His conversation became that knowledgeable cant of the semi-imbecile that passes for art-talk. "Yeh, the piece, yeh, uh-huh—*like* a VW, a little . . . but I can't get the real thing, I mean, you dig, the VW is probably the most *perfect* . . ." And so on. Yet this imbecile was capable of smashing lives, forward, forward, on his trek to the Modern, etc.

Why did he marry Lolita? A moment's thought might give you the answer, which seems to me to be obvious. That thrill, it was that thrill of getting what he had at one time thought of as "damaged goods." He got that out of some movie, it seems clear. Damaged goods, fucked, buggered, sucked, and come into by a cultivated, educated, superior, European (that was most important) freak. And by others as well . . . who can forget Lo's career? Damaged goods. Bart actually panted with desire for a few months, then she became a drag on him. Vice versa. There was many a lonely night in Springs, Lo and her Four Roses and ginger. Thinking of HH, Jesus, even thinking of Schiller. It wasn't so bad. She'd have another drink, go back to her magazine: *New York.* It was sometimes a little hard for her to understand it, but she'd read what seemed most interesting. Bart was a good provider. Yes. Bought her *New York, The New Yorker, Esquire, Glamour, Harper's Bazaar, Vogue, Commentary, Partisan Review, Crawdaddy, The New York Review of Books,* and other leading journals of comment and opinion.

She started buying the *Paris Review* herself because some really charming young man sold her a sweatshirt that was really cute, just as he was, cute. She thought that it was all some sort of a joke, this nice young man with his Antioch-Bard-Berkeley voice, selling her a sweat-shirt. She stopped laughing when he committed several unnatural acts with her behind the sand dunes.* And one can understand her surprise when a few months later, she came across a copy of *The World* and there was one of the cleverest things she had ever seen: and by this young man. It was a kind of prose poem, or "prose" poem, that was all about the way a certain dog seemed almost human in his facilities or faculties. It was a kind of thrill to know that this young man wasn't just another beach bum, but a real writer. There were poems by a number of remarkable poets—somebody at a terrific party said—in that issue, too, a good issue for a young writer to publish in: men like George Stardust, Donald Hallbuck, Brett Carp—oh, on and on. A whole section on poets of the Midwest. It was really something to read those poets. From the Midwest. Lolita was impressed, the Midwest seemed great to her, as she remembered it, full of hazy streamers of romanticism, but it seemed so powerful. It was beautiful to see that poets who lived there wrote such, well, hip poems. They looked very hip to her, and Lisa Maru, who gave those great parties, thought so. How great it was to see that *The Paris Review* published a lot of the same people: it proved how hip *it* was. "It proves how hip it is," she told Bart. He said that she was right, they were right there on top of the scene.

Does it annoy you that these two people can be so stupid and yet so successful? Are they stupid? Perhaps I take my readers for granted. There is a certain kind of artisan today whose task it is to amuse the rich. Bart started out as a very different kind of man, and then, at a point in his life, found himself becoming interested in wanting to be the other kind of man. There is nothing tragic in this. Had he continued as he started, he would have been a mediocre painter, and a slightly better sculptor. As it turned out, he became a remarkably successful and

---

*What sand dunes? Where has the author taken us?

wealthy decorator, who pleased people, gave critics something to write about, and so on. There is nothing tragic in this, it's simply another manifestation of the destruction that this book is scratching the surface of. You think that we are not living in such a time? Or that the artist alone has escaped? One begins to think that the only escape is to have one's work totally ignored. I myself would embrace this position were it not essentially precious.

Bart is an unreal bore, and Lolita, hopefully, is more unreal than he, being a borrowing of another writer's unreal bore. It is perfectly all right that they should have made it. What is more irritating is to meet real people in the street, at parties, in bars, etc., who have made it the same way. That's not so funny, at all. I mean they are *real.* One can't purify oneself of them through the ruthless selection of art. There they are. I asked one the other day, as a joke, if he had seen Bart Kahane's recent work, and he said "No." That's all, "no." It was disturbing in that it made me feel that perhaps this isn't a work of fiction—however consciously shaped—after all.

It just struck me that Bart begins to look like a Hollywood movie version of a Hollywood director: something fat and prosperous about him, the dark cheroots, sunglasses, his Burberry thrown over his shoulders. Would Humbert Humbert have liked him? One doubts it. He would have found him rather vulgar, as he tended to find everybody. Yet what is fascinating is the thought of Humbert, had he never met Lo, amusedly chatting about the intricate pleasures of *Pale Fire.* You see, if you push hard enough, and shift these people into different terrain, there are more jerks than anyone imagines. I like it that Lolita passed from a subtle fool to an entrepreneur, with a nice, young fellow in between, to rest her. One can imagine his eyes widening, etc., as she put her finger up his anus. Thus do dreams come true and crumble every day in America.

But Bart never asked her anything. He hadn't read the

book, and wouldn't. Give him that anyway. He had an idea, at least, of class. It's not important, but Bart married Lolita on the same night that Dick Detective told the airline stewardess he was having an affair with that he was married. I mention this because it was the first time that Dick had ever told any of his lovers that he was married: it was a new phase for him—mature gentleman. Sensitive, a trifle guilty, etc. He was very good at it. One would guess that he was very good at it; on the other hand, telling an airline stewardess this does not exactly require the finesse and grace that such a confession would require were it tendered to, say, Jane Austen. It's not at all strange that April and Bart should find each other. Star-crossed marriages. Not that Bart and Dick weren't old friends. The sculpture that Dick had given to Anne Kaufman had been given to Dick and April on their marriage. The metal for the sculpture had been bought out of a loan given to Bart by Lou Henry, at a time when Lou was "losing himself in art," while Sheila, it so happened, was, at the same time, having an affair with Dick D. Lou somehow always felt the sculpture to be partly his, since it was the money that he had loaned, etc. When Dick gave it to Anne, Lou was enraged. "That rat bastard!" he said to Sheila. Sheila didn't hear him, as far as I can tell. In any event, she didn't reply. Lou even called Bart up, and told him about it, what the rat son of a bitch had done. Bart didn't care one way or the other: such sculpture seemed totally uninteresting and irrelevant to him now. Besides, he wanted to get this lunk off the phone because he was waiting for a call from a "young lady" whom Dick was trying to brush. (He picked up the phrase "young lady" from Dick: it was a euphemism for "mistress," "cunt," "lover," etc.)

It is certainly true that I don't want, at this stage of the book, to begin linking things together, and showing you where so-and-so did something, and who said what. Read *The Good Soldier* for the brilliance of interplay. This book is an antidote. Bart is going to go blind anyway. I have spoken.

Why is the pussy willow Bart's favorite plant?
Did Bart like Dick Detective's blurb on the Gom Gallery brochure?
Point out a failure of tone in *Lolita*.
Do you think that Dick Schiller would have liked Bart?
Is Lolita the most highly developed character in this book? Why is that?
Vulgarly speaking, was Bart a good fuck?
Do you think it rather melodramatic that the author should make Bart blind?
What contemporary artists might as well be blind?
Did Bart go blind before or after his Gom show?
What ship did Bart actually serve on in the navy?
Discuss the name "Harry Bore." Does it in any way remind you of Dick Powell?
Following is a short list of names. Study them and try to determine the author's intent in setting them down.

John Ashbery
Vladimir Nabokov
Norman Mailer
Kenneth Koch
Bruce Jay Friedman
Kenneth Noland
Mark Van Doren
Richard Lippold

Bart thought that Scott Fitzgerald's best story was "Absolution." Was he right?
The Perfect Fiction is not a study of Nabokov's novels. What is it?
"The Rolling Stones are shit, you hear, shit!"—Bart to Lolita, January 31, 1966. Discuss this attitude of Bart's. Do you think that such an attitude might be harmful to his position in the community? Why?
"See you in the funny papers" was Bart's favorite—albeit

affected—parting remark. The implications of this remark are profoundly aesthetic.

April 3, 1968

Dear Lolita,
Well. I dont know what kind of shit you think you are
puling, runing out on me just because I went blind. What
a bich you are. Your some real bich. Are you having a nise
time in Calif. with that fagott Bif Page? Boy you really are
a freak al right. Shiller was right when he got buged with
you like you told me. Your a plane freak no shit.
Ha ha I bett you lauhghed when I went blind. You never
loved me a bit you bich. Your an art freak to. All you care
about is partys and new clothes. I dont give a fuck you
runing out on me becase I love you but just to stay here for
a wile til I get rid of the studio and such. Then belive me
I dont give a fuck where you go or with who you go.
Well I hope you are having a good time with Bif The
Fag. You probably both have a lot of lauhghs over me with
my cane and all you cuple of freaks. And by the way dont
worry about muney, I mean dont even think about muney
because you are not geting any. Well. See you in the funy
papers,

Bart*

12 May 1968

My dear April,
How can I say what I feel? Here I am, blind. An artist,
blind!! It is the final irony, a-ha! ha! ha! Ah, God, I could
wrench the earth out of its orbit in my great rage! That my
life should come to this is unbearable.
Certainly, what we had together can't be taken from me,
nor, hopefully, can it be taken from you. Lolita doesn't
care a whit about me, she's gone, as you probably know,
to Big Sur with Page . . . God! If there's one young man I
can't stand it's Page.

*It's clear that the early letter to Conchita closely resembles this one
in style, spelling, syntax, etc. I tend to think that if this letter above was
written by Bart—which fact seems incontrovertible—then the letter to
Conchita was also written by Bart. Apparently, at certain times in Bart's
life, he resorts to such semiliterate correspondence—perhaps as a way
of concealing his true feelings. Whatever, my feeling now is that both
letters should stay in the manuscript.—V.W.

But enough of my unbearable torments!

How *are* you? Tell me all about yourself. Is life with Dick still that horrible round it's always been? How is old Dick? Somehow, I miss him, even though the last time we saw each other it was absolutely ugly. I think of you all the time, here under the trees, the sound of the wind in the grasses—those grasses that I cannot *see!* The pounding of the surf that is forever *invisible* to me! God! God! What has my great sin been that I should be condemned to a life of Eternal Night?

I think of your charms, constantly, and, yes, I must admit it, I abuse myself. It's hard, not being able to see my own proud manhood. But, somehow, strangely, I see your magnificent body even more clearly in my mind's eye. The blind, as you know, have amazing powers of concentration. You've probably heard that the other senses become sharper in this Endless Stygian Darkness of Ours. It seems to be true! At least as far as I'm concerned, it's true.

That seems to be enough for now. Strange, how tired I get lately with little or no effort. And not fifty yet! Write me, my dear, write me, if you will. A note from you would do more to ease this burden than anything I can think of, outside of a full retrospective at the Modern. I know, here in this Black Pit, that you are the one, and will always be the one. Why have you been so cruel to me? Or is it I that have been cruel to you? It's more likely Dick who's been cruel to both of us—he never understood you. I love you, and dream that you love me—that is, if you *can* love a Blind Man. With much love, from my mood indigo,

Bart

Supposing, then, that this is not fiction? Does anyone feel bad about Bart's blindness? Hardly. There has been no sense of sympathy whatsoever for this character. One neither hates him nor loves him. There is, in fact, no feeling for him in any way. Now. Take a brilliant day in early fall, the weather is perfect, golden, heavy sounds of bees, and wind soft in reeds. Some coast, a beach, the Atlantic absolutely glistening. On the beach, a figure, it is certainly Bart. Dark against the glitter of the white sand. The surf falling heavily, but gently, on the shore. It is certainly Bart. Rich and famous—almost. A little too much greed to be absolutely famous. You could always hear him panting—discreetly, to be sure—from five yards away when it was a question of selling, or showing, or a rich collector coming to the studio. The story is told that he once asked Lolita to give a potential buyer a "blow job" in order to get rid of a very large stainless steel and Styrofoam piece, "Gin City." I don't know if he sold it or not, as if it matters. There are portions of Bart's life so viscous that in them he moves, as well as do those involved with him, as an underwater figure. This particular day was like that. I see the scene: Bart, preparing drinks in the small studio pantry, taking his time, the collector, his pants wide open, bunched and lumpy around his thighs, his shirttails in the way, Lolita addressing his stiff penis with her cinnamon tongue. Maybe a tutti-frutti tongue or a vanilla-fudge tongue would be more exact. The quality of movement is slow and refined, even the collector has a patina of dignity, notwithstanding the fact of his deshabille, his awkward posture, and the fixed rapacity of his visage. I'd like to tell you who he is, but I really can't. The slowness, the thick-textured movement create the lie here. It is a scene of barter, yet it looks like sexual freedom. Perhaps it is Bart's quality to invest the marketplace with the look of the temple.

He was not really famous. There was too imperfect an attempt to hide the greed. Always that panting. He might have ordered everything correctly had I not ordained it that he go blind. There he is, perhaps standing, but more likely sitting. It appears from a distance that he is facing the sea, far out on the horizon a dazzling speck of sail, perfect white. Moving, it should be noted, with that same heavy and somnambulist quality that is Bart's at certain times. Bear with me, this chapter is almost finished.

Some miles away down the beach, a young woman, whom I will make Lolita, is giving what might be an old man a "blow job" behind some dunes. I don't really know if he's an old man at all, all I can see is her mouth and his penis. It is ironic that Lolita does not know of Bart's proximity nor he of hers. Just as well. He thinks that she's

in California with Biff Page. She was in California for a
while, I can testify to that. I should say that Guy Lewis
told me that he saw her there, he didn't say where. "In
California," I think he said. Guy was drunk and discussing *Benito Cereno,* as well the reader might guess.

In any event, Lolita was, at this moment, not in California, and not with Biff. That is, I don't think she was
with Biff. It seems unlikely that Lolita would travel 3,000
miles with Biff and then "suck him off" behind some
sand dunes, particularly since Biff is a homosexual. Far
down the beach, the lonely figure of Bart Kahane, many
years a painter, in the sun and wind. He is moving,
slightly. Down the beach, the penis is shooting semen
into Lo's mouth. It has been a real "blow job." That is, it
was a "perverse" act, since it was, in no way, an act of
"foreplay." Lolita, though, is like that. Now I see the man
that she's with! It's incredible! It's good old Dick, Dick
Schiller! I'm going to divorce her and Bart, so that maybe
she and Dick can make a go of it again. Since they split
up, he's started to drag race. I understand that he has
some small following and responds well to "blow jobs."
He and Lo are walking down toward the surf now, hand
in hand, a lithe and quite attractive young couple.

Bart, moving gently, somehow—rocking—is he moving
his arm? A casual sort of gesture of the arm . . . it's not
believable, but it would seem that Bart is—painting. Definitely. He's painting! He has a small easel set up, he's
using watercolors, doing a traditional seascape, he's
painting! Which, of course, means that somehow, somewhere, at some time, a miraculous cure has been
effected, and that Bart can see again. He can see again!
As far as I'm concerned, this remarkable development
perfectly fits in with the entire life of this intolerable
lout.

8
Amethyst Neon

So we get near the end of the book, and nothing resolved. But then, only segments have been given you of these few people. They are in no way representative of anything, necessarily. Such the perfections of fiction, as well as that honed cruelty it possesses which makes it useless. Everything it teaches is useless insofar as structuring your life: you can't prop up anything with fiction. It, in fact, teaches you *just* that. That in order to attempt to employ its specific wisdom is a sign of madness. Can you see some shattered man trying to heal his life by reading *Tender Is the Night*? In the back files of the *Ladies' Home Journal* there may, at least, be found the names of various physicians who will get you to the grave with a minimum of anguish—so they say. There is more profit in an hour's talk with Billy Graham than in a reading of Joyce. Graham might conceivably make you sick, so that you might move, go somewhere to get well. But Joyce just sends you out into the street, where the world goes on, solid as a bus. If you met Joyce and said "Help me," he'd hand you a copy of *Finnegans Wake*. You could both cry. Why is it that this should be? It is because fiction is real. When you writhe for Christopher Tietjens or the Consul, you writhe for real things that do not live, that do

not represent anything anywhere, that have no counterparts in life. It is insupportable to be so enslaved by the
writer. Many people hate it, so they will read only
"nonfiction"; they'll not be tricked! If I say that Dick Detective is a man with the qualities of the green tissue on
which I am now typing, and only those qualities, what
then? I make him up. What a pleasure, my pleasure, it is
true. He will teach you utter failure if you try to use his
chapter as a handbook for living.

It is this fact, that fiction is an invention of the voice,
that tends to make writers' lives a shambles. To be a
grown man and to deal with a Dick Detective! To make
him up, and then to be compelled to deal with him. It is
as a painter in his weblike aberration: first he puts down
this blue shape, then this green shape, and the painting
has him trapped. To deal with Dick Detective! To have
the desire to give him such a name. And out there in the
world, that you had better be convinced is a million light
years away from this green tissue, they want him to be
somebody they once knew in an office on Madison Avenue. I can see the elevator starter's face now, the banks
of artificial flowers and shrubbery in their low, green
boxes. At Xmastime, a young woman playing sugary or-
gan carols in the bank next door drove me to rage many
times. A girl, lumpy face and pug nose, but with a lithe,
strong body and luscious bottom, skates in the window
facing Madison Avenue. She goes through her boring
acrobatics and dance routines, graceless. She is on a
sheet of real ice. Incredible. Outside, messengers, the
wretched of the earth, the people Robert Kennedy felt
bad for, gape at her in their total ignorance, and wait for
her leotard to tear at the crotch, their feet freezing in
their Thom McAn shoes.

In the lobby, lighting a Players, is a man, impeccably
dressed, who looks exactly like Dick Detective. He ad-
justs his jacket in that meticulous, I-love-Bach way that
is Dick's and Dick's alone—or so we thought for a moment. For this man is not Dick D.—Dick is here, in these

pages, and has already done a few things, as you will, I trust, remember. Whoever this man is, I have no idea. Had it been Dick, he would have offered you a Players, and made a little joke. He never smoked Players. This man, in the lobby, has violet eyes, so he couldn't possibly be Dick. If you knew Dick, you would *know* it. Thank God that he hasn't come to life.

The first thing you should know about Dick is that he is given this impossible name in order that the reader may ascertain certain things about his character.* Or, in all events, one certain thing. Basically, he was a gatherer of information. He was a purveyor of partial information, distorted information, false information, and speculation—robed as information—designed to elicit information from his listener. He was a social detective, indeed. His essential task in life was so to arrange it that he could have something on everybody; I don't mean so that he could use such things for personal gain, but so that he could be certain that what *he* knew about someone, what *he* had stored up, contained a minuscule fact that nobody else knew. Then, at certain times, and in certain situations, he would release this information to someone else: one might say it was "wrenched" out of him. This activity, this divulging of facts about marriages, divorces, love affairs, abortions, bad exhibitions, abandoned manuscripts, alcoholism, etc., took the place of thinking for Dick, as writing takes the place of thinking for the poet and novelist. (Those readers who think that I derogate the latter by this remark know nothing of letters.) Dick also wrote. It amazes me to think of him, sitting at his glisteningly clean desk, typing those inept conglomerates of words. He types them and he looks at them. He reads them aloud. It is not credible that he cannot see that what he has done is rotten. His poems come out of him, concrete turds. He sits at his desk and looks at the poem, this literary gesture so fashionable

* *Vide* my beloved *Tristram Shandy.*

that it makes the work of Larry Rivers seem like a communication, from heaven, of Baudelaire's. Absolute advertising. "Tired? Square? Bored? Buy Dick D." April is on the phone, inviting somebody to dinner sometime, Bartók is on the stereo. In the smoke from his English Oval Dick's eyes flash. Of course, amethyst neon.

I like to think of him walking toward an assignation on the Upper East Side with an airline stewardess or assistant editor, his heart is beating, beating ever faster, thump. His cheerleader blonde awaits him in her elephant pants, the martini glasses chilling in the refrigerator. His heart is pounding, yet his face is serious, he is taking in his own feelings, nothing is lost on Dick. You must know that he is a consumer. Not a collector, a consumer. At the moment, he is consuming his feelings. He is pleased with the profound stirrings he feels in his "heart." This is a liaison he is party to, a *liaison*. No drunken fumbling at an office party, nor a little feel while dancing with the host's wife (unless the host happened to be Lou Henry—a different situation, as the reader will admit), but a liaison. Under his arm Dick has a bottle of champagne. He thinks of it, and calls it "wine." That came from some movie, the soft light and warmth that moved over him when he realized that "wine" was, on certain occasions, and if one were the correct type of person of course, "champagne." He would go in, Karen would be standing there, all the blue skies and manure of Iowa in her smile, teeth the white of bleached bones on some scrub hill, he'd say, "I thought I'd bring some 'wine.'" He said it now, under his breath so that he wouldn't disturb the contemplation of the agitation in his dark blood: "wine." The blood stirred a little more. Dick often confused, as now, sexual anticipation and activity with all other emotional profundities. It was a kind of shiny anchor to which his life was chained. To fuck is to feel: deeply. To find something out about someone that same day—complete triumph. "Wine," he said. What a pain in the ass he is.

Karen was waiting, April was out of town for a week or two with a friend, he would have to find someone in a bar tomorrow so that he could suggest the madness of desire he had to battle against. "And how's your sister?" he'd say, perhaps, hinting that he knew something about an abortion. His interlocutor would be helpless, disarmed, before the charm and delicate concern of the Dick. Why not? "And how is April?" the friend would say. Dick would mention some Man Thing, ha ha, a long time between drinks, you really miss them when they go, I'm really at loose ends, oh, you know the shit he'd say, disappearing behind his screens of amethyst, turning to the bar to order two more Grasshoppers.

Perhaps I should have made Dick blind, instead of Bart. Yet, thinking of that, I know that somehow he'd gather more information that way. Tapping with his white cane, or walking slowly with a cow of a dog, people might tell him anything. Dick filing it away. "Well, something happened to Lolita Kahane when she went to Rio that makes Bart's actions perfectly comprehensible." The still air, sound of a fan, this blind man before you. Bad enough, that scene, with Dick seeing as well as he does now. Blind, it is too much to face. Lolita? Bart? Dick didn't really want to say, no, no, please don't ask me. He selected a peach for you, proffered it gracefully. His interlocutor would open the conversation up completely after Dick had given his peach. A sour peach. Dick, taking it all in, waiting for the one thing he didn't know. So, he had something on Bart, finally, some little thing that made him feel Bart's superior. These were complicated games that Dick played at. At times, he would try to trick himself before he realized that he was he. I give you an example: one day, walking to the apartment of Sheila's old friend from Brooklyn, Luba Checks, who taught school in Oyster Bay and gave the best head that Dick had

ever experienced, he carried, as was usual in that particular phase of his man-about-town activity, a bottle of
"wine." He said to himself, as he turned into her block,
"I hope Luba likes this Pernod." You explain it. I feel that
Dick often lied to people because he had originally told
the lie to himself. But why he did this, I don't know. Let's
leave him for the moment—in that lovely phrase of the
novel—let's leave him alone with his thoughts as he
walks toward his paramour's apartment. Karen Aileron,
freezing winds and snow flurries blowing through her
head, smiles joyously at the huge slab of dead steer she
is about to prepare: she can almost hear it lowing and it
sharpens a sliver of memory. Ah, she thinks, there's the
bell!* Hope Dick's brought some "wine." She really
thought that.

Some years ago, before Dick and April were both so fashionable, things were not the same. It seems strange to
realize that they are those perfect products of towns like
Schenectady. Even today, underneath the Brooks Bros.
raincoats and casually knotted Henri Bendel scarves, the
astute observer can detect the middle-class nervousness
about ultimate comfort. That is to say, people like this
can go through any discomfort so long as they are convinced that in the end they'll win. Someday, the Detectives will move to Vermont, where they will entertain
weekend guests and talk about children, which they will
not have, and the "Coming Revolution": no sense of irony
or of the absurd will be noticeable in them as Dick prepares Black Russians and April lays the table. One imagines them searching for this sophisticated old
farmhouse, "properties" they tend to call the places they
see. God, nothing special about them at all. They bumped
into Art—God save them from it. I liked Dick better when
he was overweight from his hamburgers, malteds, and
French fries, his gross face bright with acne. Now, he

*It may not have been Dick, since we left him still walking toward her
apartment.

stuffs pike and makes salmon in aspic. Those first poems coming from his Olivetti, one could cry at the lack of intensity he brought to the art. Precious. April, all eyes, as now, but the face is self-assured at present, she has every reason to hate Dick and to be bored with everything but the reasonable facsimile of her life to "success in Schenectady": hip Schenectady, that is. Besides, Vermont soon! Ah, the woods, the crisp air, winter weekends with snowmen and sledding, Halloween among the birches, etc. Dick will surely keep a notebook, no? I can see them with some good friends in front of the fireplace, talking of the curious failure of Guy Lewis's art. If one looks through the window the right way, one sees a coven of witches in the flickering light. They drink a lot of gin, April delicately smokes hashish in a little jeweled pipe Dick gave her for their eleventh anniversary. In her youth she heard Harry James in person, suddenly, she was married to Dick, this dark kid from Sunnyside* who had heard Count Basie. What a swell "thing" he had, etc. But I am being needlessly cruel. Why do young people of the middle class marry at all? Get them out of my sight! Let them join the air force and live in trailer camps outside of San Antonio. They spend their lives stewing in their own boiling excrement, boring you to death with their goals.

Dick and April were married. They were married, and being Catholics, I'll have them married in Our Lady of the Bleeding Eyes R.C. Church in Mechanicville, in August. I can smell the thin odor of the parking lot behind that baking, sun-blasted church, see the white hats of the women of the family, the men sweating in the white sunlight, ha ha, they say, the heat of the cars and the horns blowing. April is sweating in her white Playtex panty girdle, longing for the cool of the motel room, then tomorrow; off to Asbury Park, sun and surf and desperate fucking. In the future, fresh Vermont! You don't have to

*There must be some mistake.

believe that just a dozen years ago, Dick Detective, raconteur, coterie poet, friend of Bart Kahane and Anton Harley, consumer of paintings, took his bride to Asbury Park,
but he did. Total vulgarity. Is it any wonder that Americans lose heart so early and replace it with that grinning
hope that makes one nauseous? The reception, dear
Christ, dear Lady of the Bleeding Eyes, one warm manhattan apiece, dances, drunken uncles, the ladies endeavor to catch the bride's bouquet, the men her garter.
The bar is opened in sporadic bursts of from fifteen to
twenty minutes a few times, guests wander outside
where the heat and the mosquitoes totally wreck them.
Then soon, the night is upon them—ah sweet rutting of
youth! I won't tell you of the sexual adventures of the
evening. April and Dick thought them "beautiful." So be
it. Dick wrote a lot of bad poems about this honeymoon,
in his developing manner, i.e., the subject of the poem
takes the place of the speaker, and furthermore, it lies.
His poems say: "wine." Got that? They are poems with
less energy than is manifested in the work of Tom Clark.*

There were plenty of things to do, Dick, going to school,
or whatever you want him to do, April, going to "business." That's what she called it, and it pinpoints her up-
bringing. If you don't know what I mean, you are
insensitive to the nuances of the American middle class.
I don't, to this day, know what Dick does for a living. I
believe he used to be a shipping clerk, or he worked in a
bookstore. Just trying to stay alive. Let's allow him to
possess April under the tree one Xmas Eve, youthfully
spontaneous, her dress up, his pants down, pumping to
the joyous rhythms of "Adeste Fideles": sweet Catholic
carol! I seem to see a pair of Clarks desert boots on Dick,
things have begun to change in just these few years. Let
him go on and on, gathering information, seeing, that's
the word, seeing his Miss Eastern Airlines all he wants.
Let April see Bart all she wants. I don't even want to be

---

*"Tom Clark" is a real name, i.e., the man lives.

harsh about their white house in Vermont. April is afraid of insects, bats, horses, cats, dogs, and trees, but in Vermont, those things are different than they are in Schenectady, right? Dick will get two hundred acres, by Jesus! He doesn't know what an acre is, really, but he wants two hundred of them. But let them go, and prosper. Somebody recently told me that Anton Harley was buying a house in Vermont with the monies received from the sale of one of his Lower East Side tenements, so he'll be a good neighbor. He's going up there to reflect, write some poems, and take notes for a handbook on guerrilla warfare. The supermarkets have all been warned. That is, the supermarts have all been warned.

It must have been at least a year and a half after the honeymoon that April's buried Catholic lusts began to surface. She was more chic now, certainly, by virtue of living in New York and going to "business" every day, and her basically good face and excellent figure showed to more advantage than it had ever done in the appleknocker boroughs of her adolescence. Then, one day, her boss had his hand on her thigh, her breasts, her ass, in a minute or two she was in his office, his stiff penis out of his pants, God, the redness of his face! because he didn't expect it either, of course. She protested and made a small show of resistance about taking her panties down, and then occurred the classic scene, the girl bent over the desk—the *boss's* desk—his jouncing phallus as he positioned his pelvis behind her cool buttocks. Certainly, one of the wonders of American sex is that it so often finds itself the very model of the subterranean clichés of youth: I mean that April may have had a flash remembrance of a drawing of Blondie or Brenda Starr, flushed and perspiring, the huge prong of the boss plunged into the hairy sex, thighs quivering . . . the marvels of the pornographic comic books she had seen in the high school locker room and cafeteria. She recalled herself at the time, her face hot at the little pamphlets. There she was, Blondie, the boss putting it in, now! O Sweet Suffering Lady of the Bleeding Eyes!

And so, became for a time a raging whore, Dick carefully discovering the world of sophistication as April groped, fucked, and sucked, not only her bosses, but her co-workers, the stock clerks, and finally the mailboys. She blew the new mailboy on the fire stairs, her skirt up, masturbating herself, hoping that someone would suddenly appear and discover them. The excitement! Of course she was sick, of course. Catholic whores are the best whores, their actions have the dark polish of depravity because they feel that they *are* depraved, how sweet: luscious sin! "Free" women without guilt or neuroses or the childhood images of an epicene Jesus, Satan with a twelve-inch phallus raging through the blistering night, cannot achieve that sexual abandon: they are intent on "total satisfaction" and consider the best sex to be shameless. But April knew that much of the beauty of it was the fiery sense of shame she felt when the man who was to have her in the next moment pulled her skirt up around her waist, her panties down to her knees. It was immodest! I insist it was immodest and therefore she was dizzy with its loveliness.

It went on and on, probably some three years or so, April moving to another job and then another, parties, vacations, Dick didn't know and yet he did. With Dick she was a complete wife, when he wanted her he had her, she was a good partner in bed, yet it was all so tame to her. Dick didn't give her the feeling of being wondrously whorish, the wanton female. When she stood before him naked, his face was not at all that dazed mask of the mailboy, his fly bulging. Of course this is pornographic, who can help it? These people are suffering and will die, let them be pornographic! They may think it will save them. Dick didn't want to know, of course, this is an old story, it must be the story that some readers are involved in at this exact moment. Laugh about *that*. When your wife comes home tonight, from "the movies," ask her where she was. Then show her this section and see if she responds. Ask her if she's been with—the truth now— Dick Detective. He will fuck anybody, but prefers the falsely sophisticated. I showed Dick this part and he was amused that I should make up such a story about April, a girl who still makes her Easter Duty. One could make a Sadean joke about that, but let it pass. But I could tell that he was angry. He's too cool to be *really* angry, though. After a pause, he tried to find something out about a mutual friend in Los Angeles, a man who has been having marital difficulties, beautiful phrase. What did I know that he didn't know? It was a fantastic half hour, the end of which was that he would send this section back to me, with comment. When it came back in the mail, there was no comment at all. It was Dick's subtle way of tempting me to call him back so that he could find out something, perhaps, just a splinter of something, about our friend in L. A. A feint, then the jab. Never say die. That brain bubbling and simmering behind the flashing neon of his eyes. But believe me, I'm certain that this section worried him. If I don't have it exactly right, it's close enough to be uncomfortable. Beauty of fiction.

The study. The clean lines of the Scandinavian desk, blond wood and dull metal. Here sat the poet, Dick Detective. Here he composed his poems, most of which never saw print. They were read to friends, or printed, some of them—the jewels—in small, private editions decorated by painter friends of the poet. These were then given away to the discriminating and distributed to small bookstores with a literati clientele. Batting that steady .285 in the minors. The desk in the study. Outside was—something. Does it really matter? Dick's heart is in Vermont anyway. But let's say that it's Stuyvesant Park, very nice, this particular day is icy cold, the park at its best, a crystal in the winter sun, the light clear and dry on the patinaed statue of Pieter Stuyvesant. Dick looks at the statue, he has been sitting at his desk for an hour and a

half, waiting for the poem to arrive. He sips Medaglia
d'Oro from a heavy, cornflower blue mug, smokes another English Oval. The sun on the staff of the old Dutchman. Dick writes: corner of sun/glitters on the old/man.
He crosses it out after a minute. The study is quiet and
warm, April is out working, Dick enjoys the luxury of
free-lancing these days. An occasional proofreading job,
and so forth. Whatever. Who cares? I want him in this
study, this weekday morning. His desk is remarkable. A
stack of canary-yellow paper. An Olivetti. A deep blue
vase with three sharply pointed yellow pencils in it. An
ashtray, bone white. His coffee mug. His box of cigarettes. He can't get his poem started, and I won't do it for
him. Perhaps for anyone else, but not for the Dick. He
writes: on the still statue the still/sun. Crosses it out. The
minuscule concrete turds, seeking exit. Dick stops again
and looks at someone with a gift-wrapped package bend
into the bitter wind, heading for Beth Israel. He lights
another cigarette. There is a speck of dust on the desk and
Dick brushes it off, moving it closer and closer to the
edge, then into his waiting palm, then into the ashtray.
He is in his writing-in-the-morning clothes. Blue, west-
ern-style work shirt, crisp khakis, thick, white athletic
socks, faded blue sneakers. He is shaved, his little beard
beautifully trimmed, his sex drive at rest, for last night
a Girl Friday for Ad Exec had finally asked him over to
her apartment—her roommate gone home to Akron for a
week. She caressed his penis with her mouth "as if it had
been a ripe plum"—a phrase from an old pornographic
book I have waited twenty-five years to use. I am curious
about these oilcloth people. Who remembers oilcloth, the
plastic of the thirties? The way it held, magically, a film
of grease, its vague odor of some arcane brew, how it
cracked and peeled. These people are oilcloth, at best.
Dull glints and gleams. I had no idea that oilcloth Dick
and April lived in an apartment overlooking Stuyvesant
Park. I'm glad they do. The rest of the building is also
inhabited by oilcloth people, of that you can be sure. One
of them may read this handbook and hate it. I submit that

one may think of it as wise-guy prose. That has not been, I assure you, my intent. Imaginative qualities of actual things. One dances as one can: I give you my gifts. One may consider Dick, dancing in his ruined brain. He would like his poem to be Fred Astaire, it is often attired in white tie and tails, or a Paisley ascot and soft broadcloth shirt. But a moment's inspection will reveal the little moving machine to be Killer Joe Piro, in vulgar disguise.

Give it up, Dick! Be that advertising copywriter you will be so good as, without any strings to art, however specious. The long lunches, the Perfect Manhattans, the pâté, why not? The exquisite suits, soft shoes, April in her job, settled now, an occasional fling with some false artist like Bart Kahane. Understood, by the both of them, to be slightly shabby, these affairs, but tolerated, with only occasional flashes of anger. The lust the Dick felt for Sheila though, that was an annoyance to April, indeed. He would sit at home, watching television, his eyes bright and burning, she knew it was a girl, but why this strange behavior? It got so bad that he stopped his endless scribbling of figures concerning the price of acreage in Vermont, what he made, her takehome over the next five years, just sat. Why don't you go and get the bitch? she said to herself. She told some friend about it. He was certain it had to be Sheila, and so it was. It was Lou that Dick was worried about, until he discovered that Lou would have been grateful to have his wife in an affair with someone that he knew, and whose work he—"respected." An artist of Dick's standing in the hip community: perfection. And so, with Lou's knowledge, ah, discreetly, discreetly, they became lovers. When Dick felt himself enter Sheila, her head full of visions of people. like Mastroianni and Mailer, he almost sighed with relief. In Sheila. Relief.

Lou was drinking that famous night, wondering what they were doing, one feels a touch of pity for this cardboard figure. If he were there, he would masturbate in a

frenzy of voyeurism. Let us hope so. That's what *this* Lou
would have done anyway. A real Lou, i.e., like the friends
you may have, might have been sick, or angry. He played
the jukebox and tried to make himself cry. Hurrah for the
life of the po-et! With every drink, he felt more romanti-
cally doomed. He was, but not in the way he thought, that
is, his doom was more like tuberculosis, long painful
years of spitting up blood, phlegm, pus, and pieces of
lung. He sat, thinking, "I thought of Lorca, drunk last
night . . ." He always had trouble with his syntax. The
reader may guess that this would be the first line of a new
poem.

So the beginning of Dick's affair with Sheila. It was
interesting in that it began at a time when April's ex-
tramarital sex activity was tapering off, so that, in five
more years, it is perfectly possible that April will be
totally faithful and Dick a complete satyr. Then perhaps he'll leave the poem alone. Give it up, Dick! Embrace that Black Russian! That exquisite Brie! That English picnic hamper, glassware in candlelight! Be
happy! Be delighted! Write letters to friends in
Cape Cod! One can hope for an intricate delicacy of
life to impose itself on the Dick, luscious as the useless rounds of the rich. He will turn into a John O'Hara
invention, I want him walking around in that mist of
fiction, an elegant, mellow leather bag swinging from his
hand as he boards a train. Perhaps he's leaving this book,
but I doubt it, I have to tie up the loose ends. No more
"fun," that is, "having fun."* If you're interested in the
kind of bag Dick would carry, check it in O'Hara—he'll
tell you unerringly. O'Hara would have hated Dick—art,
clothes, and all. Let's walk out on him quietly for now,
while he lofts innocuous questions at some information-
carrying lout in a black Stetson, protégé of Bart Kahane's.
The Dick sips a Dubonnet rouge, rubs his tweedy thigh,
checks his watch so that he'll be sure to be just late

*A reviewer's phrase, often used when a book shows its scaffolding.
It is also sometimes used when a book does not show its scaffolding.

enough for his rendezvous with Buffie Whitestone. He almost tangos off into the night at his pleasure with himself, this coterie poet of delicate talents, this Latin from Manhattan.

It is such a devastating bore to talk about Dick's young manhood that I beg the reader to indulge me, and allow me to get off the hook in this one instance. The reason that the Dick turned out the way he did is because he discovered that his mother was a Communist whore. Also, he had one percent Negro blood. One can hear his schoolboy friends, "Dick is a nigger, Dick is a nigger." They fire rocks, orange peels, water-filled condoms at him. This is all filmed through blue gauze. Dissolve: Dick being "blown by a nigger wench." Revenge, bitterness, self-hatred. The picture goes on, you get the idea. It's the story of a Revolutionary Artist. In Hollywood, or wherever they make pictures, this equals Clifford Odets, or Ernesto Guevara. That's the way they like it on the Coast. I mean, the Coasts. Maybe Hitler, or Bart Kahane—all revolutionary artists. "Bring me my Olivetti," he gasps in the last scene.

I will say that Dick was born and raised a Catholic, as I was. That's an o and 2 count. More precise than baseball.* The rules, the players, are all there. Dick may become a priest at about age fifty. Do you see him—where else—in the confessional? Crucified Jesus, the smile on his face as he gets that info. Got something on all these sinners. There's also a certain rather handsome nun, Sister Rose Zeppole, who, one day, while stretching out her soft, white hand, accidentally touches his, let us say, crotch. At this point the description of a pornographic photo in *Ulysses*** comes to my mind. I advise you to check it.

* *Will* the author never write a complete declarative sentence? This sort of thing strikes me as an affectation of the worst kind.—V.W.
**A novel by James Joyce, whose best work must be ranked with Nabokov's.

Good luck! Good luck and Godspeed, beloved Padre Dick!

The idea of Dick becoming a priest in his late middle age —to employ a needlessly clotted phrase—pleases me. It would mean a number of things, not the least of which would be April's freedom from his silly talk. And many blondes in New York would be spared his sly smile forever after. But what is most intriguing about imagining this winner as a priest is the fact that such an occupation would make him a follower of Pope Joseph. Dick's perfect end, Aristotelian in concept. A soldier in the army of this falsely humble ass. One sees him biting nickels in his childhood. This man is a pop art king, his antics make Warhol stand revealed as the busher he is. He is greeting John Wayne and Sam Yorty, then he sails down a tropical river in Disneyland, blessing the plastic. Later, a chat with Rap Brown, the latter has even removed his beret. The man is a master! Now watch, for the first time, for the first time in history, he is throwing out the first ball on opening day: not a bad throw, Papa! Viva Papa! The Senators' catcher pops his glove to make His Holiness look good. Shift: a Coke with old Joe Namath, beloved hero, how nice the old wop speaks English. "Is ver' nise dringk. Yes, ver' nise, diz Coca-Coca, delissus!" "Ha ha, hey that's pretty good, your Popeness, pretty good." Next, another speech about peace, a little prayer for the Bulgarians, long may they wave. (Are the mission bells still ringing there?) To the car, the mobs in Queens on the way to the airport are having more fun than the day three cops shot a crippled black man making off with a box of Jane Parker cinnamon doughnuts. They're yelling through their Juicy Fruit breaths, "Papa Joe, Papa Joe!" Jew and Gentile together; that's what's so astounding about Queens—it turns everybody into parochial school alumni. He's finally at Kennedy, mysterious gestures with the fingers to make every heart leap high, RC's real and honorary love it. Now he's having his ring kissed, licked, and sucked by Miss Jackson Heights and Miss Kew Gardens. This is the sort of man who *should* be Dick's leader. All the buried shoddiness of the Dick's life made concrete in the rites of King Pop. Now see him urging Jesus on the citizens of Peking, who would prefer to look at their fake Timex watches: it's the red sweep-second hand that gets them.

Who knows, Dick may in time become an aide to the pop king. In the meantime, he is known as the "dandy priest." One of the boys. Ask Sister Rose. All this reminds me of Bishop Pike, for some reason. I once saw Bishop Pike, in Aspen, Colorado. It seemed like the right place to see him. I mean that the nature of Aspen, Colorado, is such that it turns out to be a place for Bishop Pike but not a place for me. The Dick would love it there, as good as Block Island or Martha's Vineyard.

What? What? This is uncanny! I just got a call from Dick. He's going to Aspen for two weeks this summer. A little surprise for April, who loves music, ever since she studied the accordion under Mario Cazzo in Schenectady. He's calling me to get some information about Aspen, etc. All I remember are those unbearable mountains. They're beautiful, I say, why not? You climb up, you climb down. In a blast of light, I realize that he'll never be a priest, not even outside these words. He's going on about some magazine. What do I know about the contributing editor, is he a fag? Good old Dick.

12 August 1981

Dear Sister Rose,

It has become painfully clear to me after the tragic and sinful occurrences of the past few weeks, concerning, as you will of course know, our own sacred persons, placed here on earth to know God, to love Him, and to prepare ourselves to be with Him forever in the Kingdom of Heaven; it has become painfully clear to me, I say, that God, in His divine wisdom, threw us together so as to test

our fidelity to the holy vows of chastity. It is just as clear
to me that we have failed in this test. I do not blame you,
my good Sister, for it is I who must be held culpable in this
matter.

There is really nothing left for me to do but to request
a transfer to one of our African missions, a remote spot
where I can devote the remainder of my poor and
wretched life to Our Lord, in the humble hope that He will
accept my labors as some small atonement for this grievous sin.

As for you, dear Sister, do not castigate yourself, do not
weep and give way to despair. As I have already said, it is
I who am most guilty in this, I, your shepherd, who, instead of leading you in the ways of the Lord, took advantage of the natural weakness of mortal flesh, and led you
to sin, dark sin. I ask you to forgive me. It has indeed
crossed my mind that you have had some prior "experience" in such activity, but I am sure that all that was in
the past, long before you took your final vows—I certainly
do not intend to cast any blame upon you because of the
restless blood of youth.

   1. How many times?
   2. With whom?
     a. Names?
     b. Addresses?
   3. Were you ever engaged?
   4. Married?

I most certainly forgive you, my child, and rest assured
that in the long years that stretch before me in the Crea-
tor's African vineyards, I will always remember, with a
particular pleasure, your beatific smile, your soft and innocent eyes, and your extraordinarily bushy pudendum.

Yours in Christ,
Rev. Richard Detective, S.J.

His tasseled, shined loafers, his impeccable slacks. The
heavy amethyst crystal ashtray. His English Ovals. Dick
is about to listen to Bach.

I give you this scene because of its precision engineering. Dick didn't listen to Bach—nor to any other music for
that matter—by accident. Oh, perhaps, once in a while,
he casually listened to the Supremes, or the Rolling
Stones—that wasn't to be helped. But listening to Bach

was an aesthetic experience. He sets the massive ashtray down on the coffee table. It is just so, next to the crisp sheet of yellow paper on which sit three lines of a new poem. Thin, sweet odor of hashish as Dick lights a gleaming brass water pipe.

Before Bach can come into the apartment, the floors must be waxed to mirrors, the glass over the Dick's drawings shining with Windex. Come in, Johann! Sit down right over there—watch April's statice, thanks.

Antique grandfather clock that doesn't work, the hands set at 8:20. Of course. Rich luster of the floor. The smell of hashish is stronger, Dick feels it. It is time.

The Art of Fugue begins, the high fidelity stereo system is working perfectly, I'd guess, because Dick's face is serene. He gazes at his paintings, his drawings, his sculptures, his bits, pieces, fragments, his books jacketed in Saran wrap, arranged alphabetically by author. *The Art of Fugue.* He carefully sets the water pipe down, lights a cigarette. He likes the look of that first gray ash against the amethyst glass. Amethyst his color, glow of amethyst neon. He sees his paintings with the intensity the hashish lends him. Those he has borrowed he feels he owns. They are his. Not his and April's, but his. There has been a rumor around for years that he and April will never split up, despite the bourgeois discomfort of their arrangement, because he would then have to give April some of the art he now enjoys. Consumes. These are dull and vulgar things to be speaking of in the middle of an aesthetic experience. Bach is sliding through the air. Dick is at peace. Look at his face.

Art is the undoing of many a hick. I think of those twangy painters slaughtered in the floods of coin the pop art machine produced. Only people like the Pope can engage pop art and survive. I remember having lunch with one of these painters once, in McSorley's. Something about painting the pickle on my plate, my ale, etc. My face was stiff with my polite smile. I can hear that flat Nebraska speech right now. Or take the New York

School. Joys of decadence. Wait till the folks in Terre Haute see this! How to put it? That New York becomes a chocolate bunny, and that they print their work, in teams. You see them together, nice young men and women, looking at that bunny. They are amusing, glib articulators of arrested development. Their noses are pointed toward the Iowa Writers' Workshop, or some other Workshop, some Seminar in Contemporary Poetry. Safe in hamburger heaven. Back home again in Indiana. Were it not for the smallest of twists, these people—Dick as well—might have been exact equivalents of those caught in the dark amber of Winesburg. At Horace Rosette's one night, drunk, I saw the face of a Central Illinois carhop surface briefly in the visage of the most fashionable whore there. I tell you it was spooky—that delicate complexion, slate-gray eyes fixed on the red convertible turning in under the neon glow.

My paintings! Dick says. My drawings! He caresses the swell of his crotch. My crotch! He is at peace, high, consuming Bach, thinking of a phrase he can drop later on in Max's Kansas City. It's too good to be true, but I'm damned if he doesn't put his amethyst sunglasses on.

He has them on. This color his peculiar property. That delicate shade shows most subtly and glamorously as it crackles through the neon tubing over the cocktail lounges of his youth. *Chez Freddy; Club Tux; Tip-Top.* Inside, there is "DANCE," "EAT," and "COCKTAILS" as advertised. Dick recalls with a pinch of nostalgia the strange look of human flesh under the amethyst neon. Yes, I said nostalgia. The man is an ad. He gets up to make a Bloody Mary, moving carefully through the music Bach devised for him, for him.

Let us assume that at a certain point in their marriage, at about the time that Dick and April had become aware of their provincialism and had taken the first steps to correct it, Dick left. I like the cadence of that sentence— it hath a dying fall. He left, in order to be alone, and to think about the novel he wanted to write. Dick wanted to write a novel because he felt that a lot of things had happened to him in his life. Well, there's no need to go into all the boring days and nights of Dick at his novel— he took notes, he wrote Chapter One, he filled pages with descriptions of characters' noses and mouths, he sat, stunned at the difficulty of getting his people across the street, or settled comfortably in armchairs. It took him a page and a half to get his protagonist to mix himself a martini. In short, he had a most terrible time, but decided to stick it out for a year. I don't know where he went, let's say to a crumbling beach house in Far Rockaway: it was no journey to Tibet. He called April, he wrote her letters, etc. But they had agreed that they would not see each other during the creative period Dick had set aside for himself. So he might as well have been in Tibet, right? Wrong. Far Rockaway is inimitable. Of course he failed at this novel—that is, he did not "fail," he didn't write it. One might think that this inability to compose would have settled Dick's literary aspirations forever, right? Wrong. Only death can cure the hip dilettante.

A really blistering, cruel day in July. Dick is on the porch of the house, drinking a can of beer, facing in the direction of the sea. Now, a remarkable thing happens. In the mail, there is a small manila envelope with April's return address on it. Inside, two cardboard stiffeners, a note from April, and six photographs. The note reads:

July 11, 1962
My dear Dick,
  Here are some pictures of me that I thought you might like. I hope they make you think of me, as I am thinking of you. With all my love,

April

The photographs are in color and are of April in various states of undress, in suggestive, not to say erotic poses. They were clearly taken in their apartment in New York. The underwear that she models is stage underwear:

waist cinchers, corsets, G-strings, black net opera hose, transparent panties and bras. Her face is fixed in that stylized look of pain that has become a synonym, in cheesecake photos, for sexual madness. In the clutch, April is her old Schenectady self—pure corn. The Dick looks, he is beside himself with hatred for her, but encroaching on this feeling is the undeniable one of lust. He goes inside the house, and, laying the pictures out carefully on the lumpy couch (the couch must be lumpy if it is anything), he masturbates into a handkerchief. Impeccable Dick. The sweat streams down his face, his shirt is stuck to his back. Well, of course, the question that tortures him concerns the photographer—what old friend? Who went up to the apartment, camera around his neck, April waiting for him, undressing, changing costumes, posing? The laughter that disguised the desire coming over both of them, April's contorted face, luscious Catholic whore. Dick can almost hear that laughter, as they say in novels. He did nothing about this, nothing at all: April knew her man. To go back to Manhattan, to write an outraged letter, to appear coolly amused on the phone— none of these things presented themselves to Dick as possibilities that would appear sophisticated. What he did was to break out in boils, which, along with the vicious heat wave, kept him in the house, drinking beer through the long, humid days, looking at the photos for hours on end, trying to see in her eyes the man who stood before her, squinting through his viewer. Capture the moment forever.

The reader will understand that this is told here not to derogate April, nor to make him feel sorry for Dick. "I don't want your pity!" I will have Dick say. I want to suggest that the most suave man, the woman of unbelievable chic, may have in their lives somewhere the most putrescent garbage, safely hidden. Humiliated. They were both humiliated. If you don't believe that April was as humiliated as Dick, I do. You must believe me, for I have made up these characters, and there are a lot of things I haven't told you about them. April wanted Dick, she wanted to remind him of his past cuckoldings, she wanted to own him and be happy in the world of art. For she believed in Dick as an artist, and, for that matter, still does. Incredible! I don't know what happened when Dick finally got back to New York, but he and April are still together.

If, one evening, while Dick is expertly pouring a pousse-café, or opening Blue Points, you mention these photographs to him, I implore you to watch his face as he laughs about "wild oats." And watch April's flush—her faint homage to her Catholic girlhood. If he fails to float the liqueurs properly, you'll know you've scored. Well, taken all in all, he deserves it.

I've never seen these photographs, but I know, now, after all these years, the man who took them. He actually walked off these pages one night, although I hadn't even seen him. Apparently, he had been puking in the bathroom on the night that Leo Kaufman met Ellen. He walked off these pages and began, "Excuse me, you don't know me, but . . ." The curious thing about all this is that he's never seen the photos either. We sat and wondered who might possibly have developed them. Dick has spent years trying, unsuccessfully, to find out the identity of the photographer. He has never considered the possibility that the photographer was not also the developer. April has volunteered no information at all, and Dick will not ask her. Instead, he beds every woman he can to prove to himself that the photographs do not matter. But it troubles him, for, you see, it means that somebody, somewhere, has something on him. Intolerable. It is harsh to realize that now we all have something on him.

October 22, 1966

My dear Buffie,

Well, I don't want to be cruel or long-winded, so let me simply say that it's been fun, I mean, lots of fun. I know how *that* must sound too! I don't think I've ever met a girl with the verve and humor and sweetness that you have, and I've spent the last two weeks out here on the Cape looking at the sea and the gulls, listening to their lonely cries, feeling desperately sad, and desperately confused, and thinking of you. My dear.

Well, let me say that in this numbing agony that I have gone through I've even thought of killing myself. I know that sounds melodramatic, and I know that at this point you must be thinking—and I can see your lovely face, puzzled—that I've gone mad. Perhaps I have. But I think that perhaps I've done the sanest thing I've ever done in my life. I told you once, Buffie darling, that we should stay away from each other, and I remember how we both laughed at the triteness of that phrase. Trite or not, Buffie darling, *we should have*. For I have lied to you, lied terribly—oh, not in any overt way, but in a way that is even worse. That is, I lied by not telling you the whole truth. And that truth is, my dear—please don't despise my weakness—that I am married.

I don't know what else to say, except that it is impossible for me to divorce my wife. She has been through the hell of an artist's life with me, she has suffered the poem with me, suffered as I toiled at the inception of a novel. She has even given up the joys and rewards of having children so that her strength could be all for me. I have betrayed her, but here, on this desolate autumnal beach, I have come to the bitter conclusion that I cannot betray her by leaving her. God, God!

I cannot go on, I cannot in any way justify myself to you. All I ask is that you believe that I loved you, and that I love you now. Loathe me, curse me, but never for a moment doubt that. If we had only met—but again, the clichés are too painful to utter. Good-bye, my darling, my sweet, my truly irreplaceable Buffie.

> With my heart,
> Dick

After receiving this letter, Buffie left, some days later, for Taos, to forget. I said Taos, yes, goddammit, Taos!

Since I have the power to give it to them, there is no sense in depriving the Detectives of their house in Vermont. So, in Dick's middle forties, April's young thirties, they get their sophisticated house. Right out of Robert Frost, the

old well, the barn, the stone fence, the cemetery with the
Revolutionary dead—the birches, the pond, I give them
Vermont. I don't know where. It doesn't matter where, I
assure you that their basic aura would affect any natural
setting. You may imagine how they look at this time—
Dick's hair almost all gone, his mustache and little beard
salt and pepper. That distinguished look of the manufactured man. April is—what is April? April is svelte, she is
certainly svelte. She is well dressed. She still has that
hick edge to her speech that assures the listener that she
has not finished her education at any exclusive school for
girls. April is the well-trained and well-groomed wife of
a coterie artist whose work is appreciated by the select
few. The voice of someone who has married the manu-
facturer of Venetian blinds, or the corrugated-box
maker, or the taxi-fleet owner. A regular guy, good people. Lyrical! That lyrical nasality slipping and sliding
through exclamations of "Marvelous!" and "Oh, Jesus!"
One crawls to a spot next to the old fireplace to have a
drink or two and get away from this country fun.

I don't have to tell you what they "do" in the country.
They "go" to the country. The old birches! The old cemetery! Well, fuck the cemetery. There they are, in the sunlight, in the moonlight, the green grass grows all around,
all around, listen to the wind in the oaks, or the elms, or
whatever they are. What are those trees, Dick, dear? It is
a lovely movie, river in the distance, a mile or two down
a gentling slope of birches and pines or whatever, sunny
glades where the bee hums. The river glints blue-silver.
Dick is in the shade, reading Wallace Stevens, drinking
an Orange Blossom. He thinks he has affinities with Stevens because he holds a responsible, well-paying job.
There are a lot of writers who feel this way: they hold
responsible, well-paying jobs. But they can't write. That's
a shame. He reads Stevens and looks down toward the
river—I don't know what river! I've got you in Vermont
and I've never even seen Vermont. Ask Anton Harley who
lives just over the mountain. He rides these hills and

meadows, etc., on his motorcycle, a true adventurer. In
the afternoons, he takes target practice out back. ("Out
back" is a rural phrase.) Ask him. He'll tell you what
river, what creek it flows out of, where to place a mortar
on the hill to hit an armored vehicle coming up the road.
Che in the mountains, his wallet safely buttoned into his
fatigues, his pack crammed with cold chicken, tomatoes,
and Anjou pears, Gauloises and an old briar, a small oil-
skin bag with his special tobacco blend. He comes to see
Dick and April once in a while, looking at April, his genitals stir as she bends over her roses or whatever flower
you want her to bend over; her peonies, her hydrangeas
—what do I know of these things? She is a remarkable
sight in the garden, dressed in a floppy white straw hat,
black leotards over black hose, a thin gold chain around
her hips, pointed black boots on her feet. Working in the
garden. Give her some white flowers to work among,
lovely image. Mrs. Detective in her Vermont retreat favors comfort and chic when working in her garden. She
snags a stocking on a Kahane polished bronze phallus,
says, "Oh, Christ!" Dick looks up from his black leather
notebook. It is curious that he looks at her as if seeing her
for the first time.* In the notebook he is sketching out the
plot for a novel he is going to start soon. The title is *Black-
jack*. Dick, as you see, is incorrigible. The novel will be
about all the things that have happened to him in his life.
And here comes Anton on his bike, a carrot in his mouth.
Is it strange or not to see the three of them in this sylvan
setting? I don't know what to do, the scene mercifully
fades before my eyes.*

Winter. The Detectives decide to give what they decide to
call a "snow party." There is plenty of snow in Vermont.
People who go to Vermont in the winter always tell you:
"You should see the snow in *Vermont!*" You fall into your
beer, fending them off. It will be a weekend snow party,

*I am indebted for this phrase to the 9,000-odd writers who have used
it before me.

with just a few people, among whom are Bart and Anton, Jo Lewis, who is now Jo Buckie-Moeller, and Ted Buckie-Moeller, her second husband, and other congenial entrepreneurs who love the arts. The invitations were sent out right after the holidays, elegant white cards on which Dick's simple line drawing of a snowman smoking a marijuana cigarette is reproduced. "You are invited to attend a Snow Party at our house on January 14, 15, 16. Bring warm clothes and big appetites. There will be cocktails and a snowball fight and cocktails. Please come! R.S.V.P. Dick and April." I'm not making this up.

A Snow Party! The river is frozen, the snow is deep, the house is warm and cozy as the guests begin arriving that Friday afternoon. April is in black again—against the snow. Dick rakish in a bright red stocking cap, his Abercrombie boots gleam against the wide, waxed boards of the living room. The guests cluster together, they chat, they drink. It would appear that Jo Buckie-Moeller has turned into an alcoholic and is dropping a lot of gin down as Ted talks with Dick about what? About the snow? About Robinson Jeffers? The living room is glowing in the soft lights, flames shift in the huge fireplace. They eat hors d'oeuvres, tiny egg rolls, a lobster salad, fried shrimp in a "marvelous" sauce, pâté, truffles, caviar, deviled eggs, mellow cheeses, dips, pickles, a salad of radishes and cucumbers with a dry wine dressing. Dinner is a cold buffet, salmon in aspic with a cucumber sauce. April and Dick serve, mix drinks, and more snow is falling.

Later, they are all outside, singing, swaying under the heavy flakes, Jo falls down and has to be carried to bed by her husband. Anton comes back in the house quietly and finishes the salmon, washing it down with a bottle of Chablis. Bart peers lecherously at a young reporter for the *Village Voice* who is gallantly working at her bored face. The snow is still falling as they all retire.

The next day, they build a snowman eight feet tall, the scene looks like a Winter Festival, disgusting. They drink coffee with brandy from thermos bottles, and Bart makes a snow sculpture. They drink hot toddies. Jo falls down and has to be pulled from a drift before she suffocates. As the afternoon wears on, there is a big snowball fight, the "guys against the chicks." Long purple shadows falling across the snow, as they will. The night is a little chaotic, Dick and Ted both try their luck with the *Voice* reporter, Jo falls on the floor, her skirt immodestly high, and April embarrassedly kicks her. And so on. Somebody is hurriedly masturbated in the pantry, somebody else finds Bart's jockey shorts on the snowman's head the next morning. These people are alive. I mean that's what they do, they live. April waits for Dick to come to bed but he sits up all night with Anton, chatting about the fascists in the town some miles away. "My beard bugs them," he says, the radical. I see his balding head, framed by the *ojo de Dios* that Buffie Whitestone sent him three years ago from New Mexico.

Sunday: the football game. They sit in front of the televison set and watch the Jets, the men deep in arcane football talk, observing the linemen. All cognoscenti watch the linemen, don't think these winners don't know that. The women are polite, Jo is in bed, sipping vodka and apple cider, the reporter clings to the arm of Ted, he's not a bad lay, the hell with his wife, the lush bitch. How nice that they live so close to one another in New York. Purple shadows again, of course, as the game draws to a conclusion. The clock ran out and a team won. Let's get these people out of here.

That evening, the fantastic silence, branches cracking in the cold. The sunset, frigid and subtle, essence of winter. The dark trees stretch down the slope toward the shining black ice of the river in shadow. The colors of the sky are rose, blue, pale yellow, and violet—almost amethyst. Let me say that it is amethyst. A small perfection. Dick and April stand outside the house, happy in the quiet. Civilized. April strokes her husband's thigh, Dick holds April about the waist. Delicate amethyst in the sky, growing slowly indigo. They stand again, after supper, the brilliant ice-cream moon of North America comes up luminous. A portrait of the poet and his wife: you and I and moonlight in Vermont. Dick thinks this, then he sings the line and laughs. April laughs. They are in Vermont! Vermont! They are in the moonlight in Vermont!

where the dead walked
       and the living were made of cardboard.
                              —Ezra Pound